OPEN YOUR MIND...

Mason Merrick was right there. I could feel him there before he ever said a word. A soft thump reverberated against the door, and I could imagine Mason's palms right up against mine on the other side. Breathlessly, I stared at my hands, slowly splaying my fingers as I knelt on the ground.

What do you want from me? I wondered.

"I'm going to back off, okay? Give you a chance to settle...I don't want you to worry. I'll come back tomorrow," Mason said. His voice was low and level. He knew I was close enough to hear, and his words were strangely intimate, divided and huddled though we were.

"You're going to have to open your mind, Roxanne," he finally said, and then he struck the door hard as he stood up.

I flinched, my heart pounding. But there wasn't anything more, nothing besides the sound of footsteps fading. I didn't understand what the hell had just happened. I didn't have a clue what Mason Merrick was trying to pull off or what his motives could possibly be. Now he'd left me alone, as I'd asked him to, and it was a solitary confinement with which I was all too familiar.

Open my mind, he'd said.

I'd be a liar if I denied that part of me was glad he was coming back.

Other *Love Spell* books by Liz Maverick:

SHARDS OF CRIMSON (Anthology)
CRIMSON ROGUE
CRIMSON CITY
THE SHADOW RUNNERS

LIZ MAVERICK

WIRED

LOVE SPELL

NEW YORK CITY

For JP

LOVE SPELL®

July 2007

Published by

Dorchester Publishing Co., Inc.
200 Madison Avenue
New York, NY 10016

ISBN-10: 0-505-52724-3
ISBN-13: 978-0-505-52724-0

Printed in the United States of America.

ACKNOWLEDGMENTS

Thanks goes to the fabulous Marianne Mancusi, second half of www.rebelsofromance.com and partner-in-crime.

WIRED

PROLOGUE

It's graduation day. I've got a million things to do, none of which includes going to the actual ceremony. I look over at the shrink-wrapped square enshrining the cap and gown that I've abandoned on a side table. I'm completely aware of the fact that I'm graduating, and I don't need to sweat in a black robe for four hours in the California sun to prove it. Besides, what's the point if no one's there to watch?

"So, I guess this is it," I say.

Kitty twists the lollipop in her mouth, getting blue sugar syrup all over her fingers. A goldfish swims in the plastic bag she's clutching in her other hand. "Yeah. You're really not going?"

"Well, you're not going."

"The ticket was, like, a billion times cheaper if I left today."

I shrug. "And this interview's more important."

"That tech company? You are such a geek!"

I laugh. "I like the toys."

Kitty's eyes narrow. "You know you scheduled it on graduation day on purpose."

"Did not," I lie. "They asked me to."

"Bullshit."

"I'm serious." I laugh. "I'm just glad to be done. Things are going to start happening for me—for both of us. We've got the whole world ahead."

"They never even answered the invite, did they?" Kitty says quietly, biting the last bits of blue off the stick. "I'm sorry."

I try to play it off like I don't care that my family decided a long time ago to stop being my family. "I only sent it as a courtesy."

She pulls the lollipop stick from her mouth and it comes out clean. She crams the used stick in her cargo pocket. "Well, I guess this is it."

"I guess so," I say, frowning hard and trying not to cry.

"You're really not going to graduation?" she asks.

"Nah."

"Me, neither."

"I know. You've got a plane to catch."

We stand there repeating ourselves because we don't want to accept that everything's about to change.

Kitty lunges forward for a hug, the bagged goldfish swinging wildly in her grip, water dripping off her wrist down my neck. As fast as she lunges forward, she pulls back. "We hate good-byes," she says. She thrusts the plastic bag at me. "I tried to get Mrs. Bimmel to take him, but she said her cats might eat him. You'll remember he needs to be fed?"

I take the bag with a sigh. "I'll remember. He'll be here when you get back."

"I don't know," Kitty says skeptically. "He's pretty old."

I hold up the bag and we watch the goldfish together. Then we look at each other.

"Well," Kitty says, "I know you won't try to kill him on purpose."

We laugh to keep things from getting teary, but, of course, they get teary anyway. Kitty picks up her final suitcase and opens the front door. At the last second she looks over her shoulder at me. I echo her words before we fall apart: "We hate good-byes."

Kitty's black pigtails bob as she goes out in the hall and starts lugging her suitcase down the stairs. She stops and turns and calls up to me, "This is going to be great. You know? And just think, no waiting for the bathroom. It's all yours. So . . . you're okay, yeah?"

"Of course!" I chirp. I sound like I'm trying too hard.

"Good. Just remember, Roxanne, it can't always be about tomorrow. Sometimes it's about right fucking now." Kitty heads down, waving her hand behind her in farewell.

I shut the door and stand there for a moment, listening to the clomp of Kitty's combat boots on the stairs becoming less clompy with every step until there's nothing left. Sirens blare outside. I hold the goldfish bag up to eye level. "It'll be fine," I say, then look around for something to put him in.

The phone rings.

The doorbell rings.

I look between the phone and the door . . .

. . . and I pick one.

ONE

We had everything before us; we had nothing before us. I'd read that once, but I couldn't help thinking it had to be one or the other. Alone in the middle of the street staring into darkness, I wondered which was worse, and forced myself to keep walking.

I was on the way to the 7-Eleven. It was two o'clock in the morning. I was almost positive there wouldn't be anyone in there but me, so I could just go straight in and buy something and then I'd turn around and come straight back. What could possibly happen?

Nothing. Absolutely nothing was going to happen, so there was absolutely no point in panicking.

I'm not going to panic . . . not going to panic . . . not going . . .

I tried staring at my feet as I walked, tried to focus on anything at all that wouldn't freak me the hell out. The heels of my shoes struck the pavement with the sound of a confidence the rest of me just didn't feel.

Which was silly, because when I got there, there would be one person I knew, someone familiar.

Naveed. So, that would be fine. Although if I thought about it too much, I'd have to consider just how pathetic it was to count the manager at the local convenience store as one of my better friends. That was the last thing I wanted to think about: the state of my world. What had become of my so-called life since graduation.

I needed to focus on the positive, not on the negative. This was all about rebuilding, clean-slating, making dull things shiny. That's why I was here. At two o'clock in the goddamn morning on my way to the 7-Eleven. Two blocks down and two blocks over, a five-minute walk.

Granted, a lot of crime could take place in five minutes, but I liked to think that my neighborhood was far enough north of the really sketchy part of town to avoid that stuff, even if the 7-Eleven itself was really the line of demarcation. We had lots of quaint Victorian facades, only some of which were still crumbling, and we had fairly nice neighbors, most of whom tried to grow gardens. We were still close enough to the bay to hear the comforting low of foghorns at night, even if we couldn't see the water. We had hills near enough to climb and look over to see a grand city view, even if we weren't living in it. In short, my neighborhood wasn't the worst and it wasn't the best. We had lots of things I could think of to make myself feel like I wasn't being a complete idiot by coming out here like this.

I made a point of walking in the middle of the street, but it wasn't like I was loitering; all I wanted was to get to my destination, get my stuff, and get home. My head down, I jammed my hands deeper into my hoodie pockets and powered through the crisp air, moving from dark to light and back again as I passed beneath illumination from the occasional street lamp.

At the halfway point between my house and the convenience store, the panic I was trying so hard to keep at bay started to win. Once more I stopped in the middle of the street and tried to work it out in that same logical, rational manner.

What are you doing, Roxanne?

I'm going to the 7-Eleven. People go to the 7-Eleven all the time and absolutely nothing happens to them. Chances are that absolutely nothing is going to happen to me, which means there is absolutely no point in panicking. Keep walking.

The first step was always the hardest, for I'd discovered that once you got going, it was all a lot easier—in a relative sense, anyway. So I forced myself to move forward, trying hard to believe everything I was telling myself, because if I let myself panic, everything I feared would become a self-fulfilling prophecy.

I made it another half a block, then slowed to a halt and turned to look behind me toward home. A discarded *S.F. Chronicle* fluttered and slid across a shard of light striking the pavement. I turned toward my destination. The pale glow of the 7-Eleven was only a block away, a gas station beyond. It was so close. But so was home.

And as I stood there, staring at the glow, a figure emerged from the shadows and stepped into the street.

Give me a break. This would certainly have been

the moment to laugh if one was in the mood to do so, and I could feel my body begin to react—in a bad way, with all the symptoms of fear, coming together one by one. I shouldn't have thought about self-fulfilling prophecies.

I didn't make any sudden moves; I simply raised my foot to take a step, landed with the swivel of an about-face, and started walking home at exactly the same pace.

But suddenly, some distance in front of me, there was the figure of a second man, rising up from a crouch in the middle of the street, as if he'd been waiting for some time.

"She's mine, Leo!"

I whipped around and looked behind me at the guy who'd shouted.

"I think not, Mason," a British accent shouted back. "She's mine."

I whipped around to look at the guy who'd answered, and a funny little wheezing sound started coming out of my mouth. *I'm going to die.*

I pulled at the messenger bag strapped across my chest and started scrabbling for my phone, which was, as always in times of dire need, somewhere very far and very deep inside. While I was wheezing and frantically feeling out the corners of the bag, the two men started moving in on me, not more than a block away each, and hunched over a bit as if they were stalking me.

In my mind I screamed at the top of my lungs; in reality I suspect the noise was nothing more than a futile squeak. Arms out, taking tentative, sideways steps as they moved in on me, the men had gone completely silent with a kind of predatory focus that chilled me to the bone.

I dropped to my knees on the street, upending my bag. The contents spilled everywhere: tissues, Band-Aids, sunglasses, money, keys, an expired driver's license, and a few other bits of general crap that had no real purpose but to make me feel more normal. Last was my cell phone, which reacted to my sudden lack of motor control by flying out of my grasp and rattling off across the pavement.

I looked wildly from one end of the street to the other, at the men. They looked the way animals look in that split second before attacking. Sure enough, the men left their marks, sprinting full-bore toward me.

The pavement vibrated from the pounding of their feet. Terror clutched at my throat. I couldn't get air into my lungs. The curb seemed to spin around me as if it had been built in a circle. Dizzy and gasping, I focused on my cell phone.

The pavement shook harder, and I cringed downward, anticipating a fist or a boot in my face at any moment. I still couldn't breathe, and I could barely move. All I could do to prevent a complete surrender was stay focused on the phone. I inched toward it on my hands and knees, leaving a trail of personal belongings in my wake.

If nothing else, go down fighting. But I knew those old words and that belief were as hollow as the mantras I'd repeated over and over and over on the way here, and I gave in. Curling my head down into my knees, I rolled onto my side in the street. Even to save myself, I couldn't work past my panic and the fear. I felt so weak. So, so weak. I hated that feeling more than anything in the world. But I couldn't do anything about it.

The endgame came in a flurry of fisticuffs, arms and bodies and men shouting and muscle against muscle. I cringed again, waiting for pain. Silver streaked through the air, and out of the corner of my eye I watched a gun flip end over end until it smashed down hard on the pavement some distance away.

I sensed the presence above me before he even opened his mouth. The British-accented voice yelled, "I've got her!" Then two arms slid under my armpits, and I was wrenched up from the street. "I've got her," was repeated, the voice growling and angry.

How strange. The emphasis was all funny. The emphasis was on the *I've*, though I had no idea why in a moment of such terror I would even notice.

I waited for the end, but my captor merely crushed me against his suit, my face pressed into his chest. "Sorry, Mason," he said. "You lose. A bit out of shape, aren't you?"

"I tripped on a goddamn Big Gulp cup," the second man said sullenly.

My captor started backing away, and I was dragged along like a rag doll. The toes of my sneakers scraped across the pavement as I hung limply in his hold, my eyes squeezed shut. "This is where it ends," he said.

I didn't know how a person might prepare herself to die, and when a gunshot rang out in the next second, I thought I might never have time to figure it out. I fell away from the man holding me, landing hard on the pavement. But I wasn't the one who'd been hit. The most polite curse I'd ever heard flew from the lips of my English captor, who gripped the top of his arm with the opposite hand. I watched in a kind of trance as razor-sharp lines of red appeared between his fingers.

"This is where it begins," the American voice said, distinctly triumphant.

The two men looked at each other. A beat of silence passed between them. Then, with matching battle cries, the two charged each other again like horseless knights in some kind of 7-Eleven-sponsored urban joust; my former captor, the British guy in the suit, versus the other guy wearing a simple T-shirt and jeans. They were smashing their fists into each other again and grappling like a couple of high school wrestlers all because . . .

Because . . .

Let me get this straight. Are they fighting over who gets to mug me? There was no time to process that question. Hoping to God I wouldn't get shot, I lifted myself to my knees. Shutting out the sound of the struggle and testosterone-fueled grunting, I continued crawling hand over hand, knee over knee, down the middle of the street toward home, shaking so hard I could barely propel myself forward. It felt like I was moving slower than was even humanly possible. The likelihood of escape—

"L. Roxanne Zaborovsky!"

I stopped crawling. Only my closest friends knew about the L. It wasn't even on my driver's license.

"It's me! Mason Me—" The announcement was lost in a kind of gargle. The speaker had probably just been hit in the face.

Frozen in midcrawl, I finally looked over my shoulder. It all happened really fast from there. The

T-shirted guy was struggling in a choke hold, the suited man behind him. The darkness had leached to a smoky gray, making it easier to see their faces. One I didn't recognize at all. The other man, in the T-shirt and jeans . . . I could hardly believe it. Mason Merrick?

Mason Merrick.

His eyes met mine, and in the next second he'd made some fancy move and turned the tables. Suddenly it was Mason sitting on his adversary's chest, punching the guy in the face. He actually took a moment to look over at me in the heat of the struggle and yelled, "Get in the car!"

The car?

I'd crawled up next to Mason's car. It seemed long odds on a typical bumper-to-bumper San Francisco curbside, but I'd somehow crawled up next to it. I recognized the Mustang immediately; it was the one he used to wash and wax outside my house ad nauseam.

I reached for the door handle, my fingers trembling so badly I could barely work them, and opened the door. Launching myself inside, I banged my shin hard on the stick shift. I locked the door, pulled my feet up on the seat, wrapped my arms around my knees, and stared down at the keys in the ignition, which were faintly tinkling against one another while I did my best to will myself home to my room. I never should have come out tonight. I knew it. Self-fulfilling prophecies have always been my downfall.

When I looked out the window, Mason was still on top of his adversary but had one arm out searching blindly for the gun. It was just beyond his reach. He had to sacrifice his hold, but he got what he wanted by arching his back in a desperate grab.

The Brit freed himself, but he didn't get far. Mason swung the weapon around, pointed it onto the Brit's face, and yelled, "Advantage."

Favoring his bloody arm, the Brit slowly got to his feet. I thought he was going to lunge forward, but the two men both went slack, simultaneously turning away from each other to check . . . their cell phones? They just as quickly and just as calmly put them away again, and picked up the intensity of their conflict as if it had never waned in the first place.

The heat inside the car spiked. I automatically reached out to turn down the temperature, but the car wasn't running and the heating system wasn't on. Outside, the air had thrown off a chill that prickled my skin. Inside the car it was sweltering, hotter than seemed reasonable, logical.

I pressed my body back against the seat, my skin crawling as claustrophobia set in. Sweat slipped down my burning face onto my sweatshirt. I grabbed for the window handle, but the mechanism was stiff and my fingers too damp to get a grip.

Out the window again, I saw Mason was in the other man's face, gesturing in my direction, taunting, flailing his gun around. The other man was in some pain. He finally put his good hand on his hip, swore violently at the ground, and surrendered.

It was almost too easy, I thought, and any relief I might have felt at Mason's victory was tempered by the oddness of the circumstances and my discomfort over Mason having shot the guy, even if it seemed in self-defense. At least I felt like I could now take a chance on leaving the safety of the car. I was suffocating. I thought I might be sick from it all. My sweaty fingers finally bested the handle and I pushed the door open.

I basically fell out of the car, and for a moment I just lay on my back in the filthy street, staring up at the stars with my arms splayed above my head like a corpse, and breathing in huge gulps of cold air. It seemed to me that the sky should have been light gray by now, but it looked pitch-black again.

"Pack it in, Leo," I heard Mason say. "No straight line here, buddy. You'll have to go around."

I turned my head and saw the man called Leo shake his head and walk away. His good hand clasped his bloody arm.

Mason quietly watched him go, then stuffed his gun in the waistband at the back of his jeans and looked at me. I scrambled to my feet, swaying backward against the car as the blood rushed to my head.

"Hey, Rox," he said. He grabbed my messenger bag and started stuffing my belongings into it.

I was grateful for a few extra moments to compose myself. The last thing I wanted was for Mason Merrick to see me completely fall apart in front of him. By the time he reached my side I was as close to normal as I was going to get. Assuming normal was speechless and gaping.

If you'd asked me back when my first college roommate, Louise, broke up with Mason Merrick whether or not I'd ever see the guy with the two last names again in my lifetime, I'd have said the chance was nil. Then again, the last time I saw him he was wearing nothing but boxer shorts and eating my sugar cereal, and I'd have given even lower odds at the chance of finding myself in a situation with him involving weaponry beyond a cereal spoon. In the span of one short night, both unlikely events had come to pass.

Thing is, I don't believe in coincidences.

TWO

Mason handed over my bag and, as if nothing unusual had happened, asked, "You okay?"

I stared at him for a moment, then blurted, "Am I *okay*? No!"

"How do you feel?"

Totally disoriented. "Not well. If you need something more specific, I'm somewhere between a heart attack and a nervous breakdown."

"That guy's not going to hurt you again. Not while I'm around."

I didn't know where to go with that. I was a mess. Actually, I was beyond even the concept of a mess, mentally and physically. I looked down. My palms were scraped up; the knees of my sweats were shredded and absolutely filthy.

Mason looked over his shoulder, turned back, and casually picked up where he'd left off, as if we'd bumped into each other at a party. "It's been a long time, Rox. It's good to see you again," he said with an odd hitch in his voice.

"Stay away from me." Clutching my bag against my chest, I turned and started booking it.

"Hey! That's it? I just saved your ass!"

I glanced back at him and picked up my pace.

"Hey!"

I was so getting out of there.

"Roxy, stop!"

I realized immediately that even if I could have run faster, he would have caught me. I stopped short under a street lamp—if anything else happened, this would make it easier for someone to witness from one of the apartments. Mason closed the distance between us as if it were nothing. As he came up to me, in the glare of the light the brutality of the fistfight really registered; those were raw cuts and bruises on his face, a real swelling over his eye. Somehow, I'd expected him to look fine. That he wasn't fine made what had just happened all the more frightening, all the more real.

"Can I give you a ride home?" he asked.

"No."

"I'll walk you home then."

"*No.*"

Mason fell into step next to me. "You're probably wondering what all this is about. Me showing up like this . . ."

I stopped abruptly and turned on him. "I don't believe in coincidences."

He managed a tight smile. "I don't either."

I started walking again. He stayed right with me. "Are you stalking me, Mason?" I half-joked.

"Who said that to you?"

"What?" His response was not what I'd expected.

"Did somebody tell you I was stalking you?" I looked over at him and he wasn't smiling. "That's really not funny. Kaysar likes to use that one."

My stomach plunged. What the hell was going on? "Kaysar?"

"The man I was fighting. Leonardo Kaysar. He's very dangerous—no, listen to me. *Listen* to me."

I was already walking again.

"Leonardo Kaysar is trying to . . . get to you, and I'm trying to stop him."

" 'Get to me.' Uh-huh." I was still walking.

"I've been following your situation for a long time, and things have finally come to a head."

I put on the brakes. "Following my situation, or following me? How did either of you know I was going to be at the 7-Eleven tonight?"

"He's a dangerous man, Rox," Mason repeated, blatantly skirting the question. "A very dangerous man."

"Mason."

"Yes?"

"You're freaking me out. If there's some kind of bet involved, tell me what it is and I'll help you win. If there's some kind of joke, tell me what it is and I'll help you make them laugh without the joke having to be on me. But stop this. For old times' sake, okay? You have to stop this. It's very, very scary."

I'd backed up to allow for a nice, big amount of room between myself and Mason, and if he so much as put a pinkie into my personal space, I was going to go berserker all over his ass. Well, that's what I liked to think I was capable of, anyway.

Mason didn't move.

I turned and tried to pick up my pace again, but exhaustion hit me hard. Mason followed me home in silence. I considered pretending another place was mine, but he'd lived here for a couple of years, so he already knew the address.

It was a two-story condo in a complex with a bunch of other condos. The place was given to me by my parents as compensation for marrying into new families and never contacting me again, and I'd lived there forever. And while there were walkways and stairs in the complex that I was certain I knew better than Mason, he'd already made it apparent I wouldn't be able to outrun him.

At the top of the steps up to my place, I froze. The dumbest thing I could possibly do would be to open my door and give him an opportunity to overpower me. Once we were both inside, I would have no escape. I had to get rid of him.

"I know what you're thinking," he said.

I raised an eyebrow. I didn't know what to think. How could he possibly know?

Mason hesitated, as if he were testing words on his tongue before saying them out loud. "Look, this is very complicated. The most important thing for you to understand right now is that you're in trouble. You have something Kaysar wants."

"What does he want?"

"Your future."

I didn't say anything. He didn't say anything. The phrase just hung in the air waiting for a laugh. Neither of us laughed. Mason stood there, his head tilted, waiting for his dramatic proclamation to impress me in some way.

My chest tightened. "You jerk! This *is* a joke, isn't it? It's a *joke*." The only thing worse than being attacked for real was being attacked and the butt of somebody's joke.

Mason looked at me impatiently. "Kind of an elaborate gag, don't you think?"

"You and your *colossally stupid* practical jokes. This one is really out of line. You're trying to humiliate me or scare me, and either way it's a nasty thing. I don't know why you'd do this to me after all these years." Choking with the effort of holding back tears, I was barely coherent when I spit, "Good-bye, Mason."

"Rough splice," he said.

After a moment of incomprehension I looked with complete disgust at the cut on his forehead and replied, "You'll live."

"Hey, you liked those jokes. I mean, you pretended you didn't but that was part of our thing. You know. We had a . . . a thing. It was funny, those jokes and gags and stuff. You thought it was funny."

"There was no 'thing,' and I don't remember whether it was funny or not. What I'm saying is, it's not funny *now*."

"Oh, there was a thing," Mason said suggestively.

"It was just you looking for attention."

"Maybe it was me looking for attention from *you*," he tossed out.

I didn't know what to say. All I knew was that there was nothing funny about any of this now, and I wanted him out of here. I widened my eyes and said, "Oh, shit. I dropped my wallet."

He turned and looked down the stairway, then

took a couple of steps away, exactly as I'd hoped, at which point I ran over, jammed the key into my door, launched myself inside my place, and slammed it shut.

A second later his shoulder hit the door with a dull smack. "Give me a break!" he shouted through the wood, in between pounding it with his fist. "What kind of joke involves two guys beating the crap out of each other like that, over a girl one of them doesn't know and the other one hasn't spoken to in over four years?"

A really bad one. He was right. It didn't make much sense. I waited for something more from him. Something to justify the real punches and real bruises and very real men grabbing at me and trying to prevent me from running away.

"Roxanne," Mason said, the effort to remain calm obvious in his voice. "It's not some game we're playing here. It's *not* a joke."

Stop saying that. If it's not a joke or a game . . . what is it?

My knees gave out and I slid to the floor, holding my breath while I carefully leaned in and pressed my ear against the door. I huddled in a ball of quivering flesh and bone while Mason called my name a couple more times until someone across the way opened a door and told him to shut the hell up. Mason swore and mumbled something, and the door vibrated as if he'd stepped closer.

I held still. Something metal scraped against the wood. Some kind of tool? His gun? Or maybe nothing more than a zipper.

"You're going to have to open this door at some point, Rox," he said quietly. "You know you want to."

I did want to. Part of me, at least. Mason had always lived a big, bold life, whether he was simply giving himself the run of my apartment or making big, blowsy plans for himself and my roommate Louise. When I wasn't busy envying her for it, I guess I was busy admiring him. He was too thick to see it—or at least I hoped he was. Otherwise, I'd be as mortified now as I was terrified. The thing was, it didn't really surprise me that he was running around town in some kind of lethal skirmish with an Englishman ripped out of one of the spy novels I loved to read; what surprised me was that I was suddenly running around with him.

A soft thump reverberated against the door, and I could imagine Mason's palms right up against mine on the other side. Breathlessly, I stared at my hands, slowly splaying my fingers as I knelt on the ground.

What do you want from me? I wondered.

"I'm going to back off, okay? Give you a chance to settle. Leo's gotta go deal with that arm and . . . stuff . . . so I don't want you to worry. I'll come back tomorrow," Mason said. His voice was low and level. He knew I was right there. He knew I was close enough to hear, and his words were strangely intimate, divided and huddled though we were.

"You're going to have to open your mind, Roxanne," he finally said, and then he struck the door hard as he stood up.

I flinched, my heart pounding. But there wasn't anything more, nothing besides the sound of footsteps fading. I stumbled to my feet and fled upstairs, barricading myself in my bedroom with a chair that I knew couldn't possibly do any good.

No, I didn't understand what the hell had just happened. I didn't have a clue what Mason Merrick was trying to pull off or what his motives could possibly be; I'd cut him off at every pass. Now he'd left me alone, as I'd asked him to, and it was a solitary confinement with which I was all too familiar.

Open my mind, open the door, he'd said. I'd be a liar if I denied that part of me was glad he was coming back.

THREE

I remember flipping through the phonebook for the nonemergency police line and getting a busy signal. I remember hanging up and not bothering to try again. I remember getting under the covers with my clothes on and wrapping myself in the enormous down comforter spilling over the sides of my bed.

I would have expected that night to be a sleepless one, but it wasn't. I slept deeply, easily, and when I awoke the next morning, I had the weirdest desire to do that *seize the day* thing everyone's always talking about.

I shed last night's clothes all over the hall where I'd left my tennis shoes, and headed for the room I used as my office to check my schedule. The room was pitch-black, with no windows to provide any light from the outside world. I ran my palm over the inside wall and flipped the switch, but the single bulb made a pretty sorry difference.

I turned my computer on and scanned the office while waiting for the machine to boot up. Bookshelves full of paperbacks lined the walls. Boxes teetered in stacks piled all around. A hot plate and an electric teakettle sat atop a minirefrigerator tucked in the corner next to a chaise longue that commandeered the lion's share of the room.

I barely had space to walk around. The clutter, the towers of boxes, the dimness, the smallness of the room seemed to curl around me like a cocoon—not a bad thing, although oddly unfamiliar. I scanned the titles on the bookshelves and picked up one of the dog-eared novels. Clancy. I put it down and eyed some of the others. Fleming. Brown. A set of TV tie-ins for *Alias*. All of them I remembered reading. So this was definitely my collection. But . . .

In some way that I couldn't quite put my finger on, I was a stranger in my own home. In my own skin. All I could think was that the prior night had affected me on a much deeper level than I'd first imagined.

The whirring and clicking from my computer's booting hard drive eased up. I opened my calendar and, still standing in yesterday's bra and underwear, I scanned it. The entire month was blank save for two entries. A couple weeks ago I'd turned in a project. Today I was apparently supposed to go to the agency to discuss getting a new one. The rest of the dates were squares of plain gray before today and plain white after.

We had everything before us; we had nothing before us.

My hands hovered over the keyboard. I stared down at them as though they were part of someone else's body. Then I ran for the shower.

I don't know why I moved so fast. I don't know what I expected would happen. Absolutely nothing happened. I showered. I got out. I headed for the closet still drying myself off. I slung the wet towel over the doorknob. Nothing happened.

I pulled a clean pair of underwear and a bra from the top dresser drawer, even managed to laugh at myself a little. Until I opened the closet. It was filled with black. I pushed the hangers around. There must have been ten pairs of black jeans and twice that many black T-shirts of all shapes and necklines. There were a couple pairs of black sweats piled unceremoniously on the top shelf and one pretty cute jacket—all in black. Other than a single dress that was mostly black with some red satin detailing, there were absolutely no Saturday-night clothes—unless one included the incongruous presence of a barely-there pink negligée in that category. Assuming Saturday night went well, of course. No skirts and no other dresses. I looked down at the floor. I saw a second pair of black Converse Los exactly like the ones I'd pulled off in the hall, a pair of black flip-flops, a pair of black slippers, and a single shoe box with an illustration of ridiculously high heels on the side.

Slipping into a random selection of the black clothes, I stared down at the box. I didn't know what to worry about more: the fact that I had no memory of having a taste for such a limited palette or that I had no memory of a desire to wear shoes so tall they had the potential to put me in traction.

I flipped the lid off the box with my toe and immediately lurched backward, coming down funny on one of the slippers. My legs slipped out from under me and I hit the ground. I sat there propped up with my elbows behind me and just stared. Two admittedly attractive black satin high heels nestled in the box, alongside a handful of bullets and a gun.

Huh?

I don't own a gun. I've never owned a gun. I don't even know anybody who owns a gun.

Actually, the truth was that I couldn't even think of too many people I knew at all, which I suppose would reduce the number of guns likely to be owned.

There was something kind of dirty about the idea of a gun in my closet, something dirty and dangerous and scary about not knowing why it was there or how it got there. Mason? But I hadn't let him inside. Not that he was really the type who waited to be asked, but if he had put this here, when would he have had time to do it . . . and why the hell would he?

I sat up and pulled the shoe box toward me, turning it around to look at the size. *My shoe size, all right. My shoes.*

My gun?

I looked over my shoulder as if I were being really naughty and didn't want to get caught and then picked up the gun, weighing it in one hand. With the other, I plucked a couple of bullets from their tissue-paper nest. The equipment was surprisingly heavy, and there was no question in my mind that all of it was real. Very carefully, I put the gun and ammunition away, fit the lid back on the box, stood up, backed out of the closet, and closed the door.

Denial. It's an important emotional stage often overlooked in favor of the others involved in traumatic situations, such as anger and acceptance. But I focused on denial as I shook my damp hair out, grabbed the jacket off the hanger and the messenger bag off the chair next to my bed, and headed for the bathroom to put on a quick face.

But I couldn't find my makeup bag. It wasn't next to the sink.

I pulled open the top drawer under the sink and gawked at the contents. It was packed with unopened boxes of makeup, the cellophane not even sliced open. I closed the drawer very carefully, very quietly, as if doing so would contribute in some way to the maintenance of my fraying sanity. I hesitated for a moment, then opened the second drawer. More boxes of face powder, tubes of lipstick, mascara, containers of eyeshadow. All sealed, unopened, unused.

I pulled the third drawer open without any ceremony. Skin care. At least I was organized, even if I couldn't remember having spent the hundreds and hundreds of dollars it would have cost to buy all of this.

Almost defiantly, I opened the top drawer again, grabbed a mascara and a lip gloss, and ripped open the packages. I stuffed the lip gloss into my pocket, applied the mascara, and gave up on the rest in favor of breakfast.

Still working hard on denial, I wandered down to the kitchen. I looked around and breathed a sigh of relief. There was nothing I didn't recognize, though I still had the feeling I'd had upstairs—like I was having culture shock after a long stint overseas. Maybe it was me who was the foreigner.

I opened the fridge and scanned the sparse shelves. Eggs, milk, juice, carrots. Well, what else did a person really need? My hand froze on the milk carton; I remembered that I'd been on the way to the 7-Eleven when things started to get strange. I must have needed something.

In the chaos of the prior night, I'd never actually made it to the store and, accordingly, never purchased what I'd set out to buy in the first place. Which shouldn't have mattered, really, given the circumstances, except that when I tried to think about last night, there were . . . holes. Holes in my memory. What was I craving so badly at two a.m. that just couldn't wait? I stared into the emptiness of the fridge and tried to focus, but it was the strangest sensation, this mental hole.

A magnet slipped off the door and pinged on the ground, followed by a shower of menus. With a sigh, I crouched down and started picking them back up. Sweeping my hand under the edge of the refrigerator, I pulled out a plastic packet of twigs or something. I used to find the same kind of stuff all the time, various bits of Kitty's New Age paraphernalia, flotsam and jetsam from her latest woo-woo obsession. I hated finding the stuff. It reminded me that we hadn't spoken since the day she left for Europe. I guess I was embarrassed about not making anything of the big plans I'd once confided to her. Though I hadn't tried to get back in touch, it nonetheless bothered me intensely that she hadn't either. I tossed the packet on the kitchen counter and finished collecting the fallen menus.

Holding a handful of flyers in my hand, I focused on the already packed metal surface of the refrigerator. The sheer number of take-out menus plastering the doors was staggering, with five pizza delivery services alone.

I don't remember these.

I took the milk out and stuck it on the counter. I pulled a box of cereal from the cabinet, then poured a healthy serving into a bowl. I ate my breakfast contemplating the wall of menus on the refrigerator door.

These holes—maybe they weren't a blankness so much as a blackout. Like, if the electricity went back on, I'd be able to see, and I'd remember what recipe ingredient was missing from an early morning cooking project, or what candy bar commercial had played just before I absolutely had to get myself to a 7-Eleven at two a.m. What was it I'd absolutely had to have?

For that matter, what was it really that Mason and that Leonardo Kaysar guy had to have? After all, I was still here. I was eating breakfast in my apartment with neither of them holding a gun to my head.

My future, Mason had said.

But then, Mason was full of crap. He'd always been full of crap. Not that that made him any less appealing on the basest of levels, of course, but it was something to keep in mind if he really did come back around.

Mason Merrick. Good God. That guy could charm the granny undies off a girl who'd taken a virginity pledge the prior night. He'd certainly charmed my old roommate's off on a regular basis. I remembered that well—how they'd put the stereo on 10 and I wouldn't see them for the rest of the night.

In the mornings, while I was sitting at the table nursing the thickest, oiliest, strongest cup of coffee I could force out of an ancient Mr. Coffee machine, Mason would often wander out of her bedroom scratching his balls. He'd honor me with a rhetorical grunt, yawning and stretching so that the snake tattoo around his biceps writhed, his hair sticking out all over the place and his cock practically falling out of his boxers; then we'd ignore each other for approximately fifteen minutes while he fixed himself a bowl of cereal and commandeered my morning paper. It was always a bowl of *my* cereal, although neither of us ever referenced that fact. I suppose it was a fair trade.

During this portion of the ritual, I'd pretended to be engrossed in my reading while I wondered for the millionth time what on earth he and my roommate saw in each other. Finally, I'd get up and pour the remaining coffee into a battered Starbucks travel mug, and as I passed Mason at the table I'd sneak a peek at the slit in his boxers, hoping to see a little action. When I got past him, he'd look up from my morning paper and nod an almost imperceptible farewell as I packed up my stuff.

There was usually a smirk in his expression, and at first I'd wondered if he realized I was ogling him unapologetically every single one of these mornings, but I soon figured out that it was more likely about the rubber cockroach he'd planted in the bathroom or the bra he'd stuck in the freezer. Who was I kidding? I didn't know why I refused to admit it the prior night, but Mason was right; I guess we did have a thing with the jokes and the pranks and the silly toys showing up in my book bag. Judging from the shenanigans of last night, he'd apparently moved on to more elaborate schemes.

Anyway, after the smirk-nod, Mason would go

back to my paper, slopping milk and cereal all over the sports section, and about ten minutes later I'd leave for class feeling caffeinated and pleasantly sexed up, which was, in my opinion, a great way to start the day. I'd forget all about him until the next morning. This ritual went on for months.

Then one morning I sat there in the kitchen and Mason didn't come out of my roommate's bedroom. Three days passed and he still wasn't around. Finally, I was doing the laundry and discovered a pair of his boxers, the green ones with the pink-and-orange fruit slices—I remember this because they were my second-favorite pair of his—and I kind of realized as I stood there with a wad of Mason Merrick's underwear that he probably wasn't coming back.

I asked my roommate about it the next time we crossed paths, because it seemed like a big deal after all that time. She just matter-of-factly said they were over. I got the feeling I was more upset about it than she was. At the end of the year, she moved out, Kitty moved in, and Mason Merrick became a distant memory.

That was, until last night.

I took a last bite of cereal, tipped the bowl and sucked down the remaining milk, then dumped the dishes in the sink. Denial is the best friend of the easily frightened, so after running upstairs to brush my teeth, I grabbed my stuff and headed out the door as if everything were completely normal.

I took the bus to Market Street and hopped off at the end of the block. The agency was located between one of those big-and-tall suit shops and a picture-frame store. I was sure the agency could have afforded a much better location, but I guess they either liked the rent or the anonymity, or both.

The building looked deceptively small from the front but extended quite a way back into a long, narrow building. Dodging a pile of take-out food spilling from a dropped foam box, I pushed through the door and went to the reception desk. The phone was ringing off the hook, but the desk clerk was nice enough to put the callers on hold for me.

"I'm Roxanne Zaborovsky. I'm here to pick up a new project," I said.

The clerk looked at me blankly, then grabbed a pencil. "What did you say your name was?"

"Roxanne Zaborovsky. Z-A-B-O—"

"Got it. I wasn't sure if that one letter was an A or an O. You've worked with us before?"

"Many times." The minute I said it, I realized I had no idea if it was true. I looked over my shoulder to scan the waiting area, my eyes threading through the people: the jeans, the T-shirts, steaming Starbucks travel mugs, the—

"Excuse me! I asked if you were in the computer."

I looked at the clerk helplessly.

"What's your clearance? Public, private . . . ?"

I stared at her for a moment, then muttered, "Both," not quite knowing how I knew it to be true, even though I knew it was. I was remembering bits and pieces, though nothing completely fit. What was going on with my brain?

The clerk punched at the keyboard and frowned. "Who were you here to see?"

"Uh . . ." I had no idea. Who did I usually see?

A guy waiting behind me sighed deeply, the kind of sigh meant to indicate his displeasure with me and my apparent inability to process information on a timely basis.

"Do you have an appointment?" the receptionist asked, clearly losing her patience.

I blinked. "I think so," I said kind of lamely. "It was on my calendar."

"Do you normally get your assignments via e-mail?"

"Oh. I . . ." Maybe the notation on my calendar was a reminder to send an e-mail, or maybe to call someone on the phone.

The clerk shrugged. "Just go ahead and have a seat. I'll see if someone's available or if anything's been left for you."

I'd been working for this agency since junior year in college; I remembered that. I'd done more projects for them than I cared to admit, even lame ones they could have handed off to someone less experienced. This woman was acting like she'd never heard of me, even though they used to recognize my name immediately when I called them on the phone—didn't they?

"Are you . . . new here?" I asked.

She looked surprised. "I've been here for years," she said, picking up the phone and turning away from me.

I went to the waiting area and found a spot against the wall. Chairs were still available, but somehow I didn't feel like slipping into any of them. Nobody was specifically crowding me, but I felt totally overwhelmed by all of these people, by this company that didn't even remember one of its longest-standing employees. I wrenched myself away and headed for the bathroom, stumbling with sudden dizziness as I went down a hall and barreled through the swinging door.

Inside, I ran a damp paper towel across my forehead. I'd felt exactly this same way in Mason's car. Overheated. Dizzy. Plus, there was an odd sense of displacement.

Something's wrong with you.

My face looked so pale, my reddish brown hair and brown eyes were practically black in contrast. I ran my fingers over lips that flatlined into a surprisingly grim expression. Suddenly self-conscious about the way I'd shown up here, I raked my unkempt hair into something closer to a deliberate hairstyle. Then I reached into my bag, pulled out the lip gloss and reshellacked my lips. There was nothing I could do about the bags under my wide, wondering eyes.

Nice job, I thought. *All that concealer in your bathroom, and you brought nothing with you.*

I grabbed for a second paper towel, but instead rapped my knuckles hard against the metal canister as the lights went out and I completely missed the sheet. I stood for a second in the dark, knuckles smarting, my arm still outstretched, water dripping down the sides of my face.

"Hello?" I said loudly. "I'm still in here." I don't know what I was thinking; no one had entered and no one had left. Very slowly, I retracted my arm and turned in the direction of the door. Nothing. I spun toward the bathroom stalls. Silence.

I backed away from the mirror, grabbed my stuff, and blasted out of the bathroom into the hall. I didn't care what anybody thought of me.

No matter, because there wasn't anybody there. The hallways were dark, the hubbub of office workers running around now silenced.

I looked behind me for an emergency exit, but I couldn't see a thing, and I hadn't paid attention to the building's layout when I'd had the chance. Turning back in the direction of the reception area, I swallowed hard and said, "Mason?" into the gloom.

No answer.

The only exit I knew of, the only one I could get to in the dark anyway, was straight ahead. Feeling my way along the wall, I moved off in the direction from which I'd come.

My hand hit a doorknob. I tried to open the door but it was locked. So was the next. And the next. No one was working. No one was here. The only light was at the far end of the hall, where the reception area was boxed in by glass windows. The sound of my breathing seemed incredibly loud. I swallowed hard and tried to stay as quiet as possible as I crept toward the light.

When I looked behind me, I still couldn't see a thing. In that direction there might as well have been a black curtain an inch in front of my face.

I swiped at my eyes with my forearm, for some reason afraid to let the droplets of sweat beading on my face fall to the floor. I don't know why I assumed something bad was ahead of me, or behind, but what about the things I'd experienced recently could really be described as good?

You've got to get out of here.

Too late for that. I froze with my hand flat on the wall and stared at the figure of a man sitting casually in the reception area. He was facing me. And if he could see into the thick black I was standing in, he was also watching me.

Mason would have called out. Mason would have said something. This wasn't Mason's body language, either. I stood there, breathing as shallowly as possible, squinting at the outline of the man's body. One leg was crossed over his opposite knee. He held a cigarette in his hand, in an aristocratic curl of his fingers. He sat there, his face hidden in shadow while the rest of him bloomed in pale gold light.

Definitely not Mason. I barely managed to swallow.

The man stood up. He remained silent for a few moments, just smoking. He exhaled a thin ribbon of gray, and the spicy smoke wafted down the distance between us, curling around my body like a rope sent out to reel me in.

"Leonardo Kaysar," he finally said. Then he bowed.

Nice suit. Tie. White cuffs. Cuff links. British accent. No question. "Leonardo Kaysar," I repeated in a whisper.

Then I braced myself for the danger Mason had foretold.

FOUR

A wave of claustrophobic angst swept over me as I huddled against the wall in the darkness staring at Leonardo. "You've got the wrong girl," I blurted.

He took a drag, looking at me from under lazy lids. "I don't think so," he said.

I gauged the distance between him, me, and the door, recognizing that it would be impossible to get out before he'd tackled me to the floor.

"What do you want from me?" I asked, all bravado.

He shrugged. "Your work."

"What work? Describe it and I'll see if I can think of anything I've done that would fit. There's nothing I've worked on worth my life."

"I can't describe it in any way that would be meaningful to you, I'm afraid."

"Why not?"

"Because you haven't written it yet."

I was taken aback. "I don't consider myself particularly slow, but I don't even begin to fathom whatever it is you're talking about. If I haven't written it yet, then it doesn't exist."

Leonardo smiled politely. "I completely agree. It doesn't exist. Yet."

Really, the only thing to do was laugh hysterically and hope this joker would follow suit. Unfortunately, my hideous horse laugh was met by only an arched eyebrow and complete silence. The guy was serious. As serious as Mason had been when he'd said that odd thing about it being my future Leonardo wanted.

Leonardo Kaysar shrugged, flicking the stub of his cigarette onto the floor. He walked toward me; I stepped back.

"Brilliant," I said. "So, how about I leave now . . . and you give me a ring sometime later after I've written . . . it."

He continued moving in on me. I continued moving backward.

"I prefer to take a proactive approach to things," he said. "Especially when I'm working opposite Mason Merrick."

"You've worked together before?"

"Not together," he replied, his voice suddenly clipped and his face shutting out all emotion. "Against. We've met on several other cases."

"Other cases? Am I a case?" I asked, the last word getting a bit drowned out by the fear clogging my throat.

"Mason spends most of his time trying to thwart me. I run off ahead; he follows."

But that didn't answer the question I'd just asked. I watched him curiously, but he gave me nothing more to work with. "What's the point of running when you don't know what you're chasing?" I asked.

He reached out to me and instinctively I turned to bolt, but I was no match. He moved so fast I didn't have time to take a breath. One hand around my waist, he pulled me back, holding me fast against the length of his body.

I pulled fruitlessly at the fingers he'd hooked into one shoulder like metal teeth. Leonardo Kaysar was the quintessential iron fist in a velvet glove. While the fist scared me to death, the velvet ignited my skin. I swallowed hard; he touched my trembling hand and curled his fingers around mine.

The intimacy sent a shiver up my spine. I gasped. Just a tiny sound, but one that exposed my strange attraction to him. Obviously this was nothing more than a carefully crafted seduction; if I was really his and Mason's "case," Leonardo had undoubtedly researched me. Me, and my weaknesses.

I stood paralyzed as his lips brushed my ear.

"The point of running when you don't know what you're chasing," he said, "is to be at the destination before everybody else when you finally figure it out."

He tipped my face back. "Roxanne," he murmured, and it seemed as if the wheels in his brain were turning, trying to figure out what to do with the moment.

Everything in me screamed danger. I tried to pull away, suddenly frantic to escape. "You're hurting me!"

"Stop struggling and it won't hurt a bit."

I stilled, and though he was as good as his word and didn't pull or force, he still held me close.

"If I haven't written what you're looking for, why am I important to either of you?" I asked.

"You're on the wire," he said simply. "You were next in line. And it's finally come down to you. You're the new Major."

What?

"I have no idea what you're saying," I said, managing to feel a lot of dread nonetheless. "I'm the new Major? Meaning what?"

"Meaning that what you wrote . . . you simply haven't written yet. Mason will try to prevent you from writing it—or if you do, to prevent you from letting me have it."

"You've got the wrong girl. I don't work on anything that could possibly be of interest to you. I do things like set up databases or create web templates for boring corporations. That sort of thing. And that's it. This is just an employment agency for freelance geeks."

"I *don't* have the wrong girl," Leonardo purred.

I blinked, confused and panting. "You do," I croaked. "People like me work freelance so we get to pick our own hours and take as many or as few jobs as we like. It's totally low-key. What I'm doing, what I have done or am likely to do, won't come close to changing the world. I mean, it's not like I work for a weapons company or something."

"How can you be sure what you do?" he whispered. "This isn't so bad, is it, Roxanne? You've been dying for a little excitement in your world. Dying for it and fearing it all at once. You don't have to be afraid anymore."

I turned my head away, drawn against my will. My

skin burned everywhere. I swallowed, trying to close myself off from the implication that his spy act somehow aroused me. "You and Mason. What makes you think I'll give either of you want you want?"

He eased up and let me slip away. I slowly turned around, making an effort to look like I still had all my shit together.

He chuckled softly. "I appreciate your moxie. Really, I do. I find it very appealing. A very American characteristic, moxie."

"You like my moxie, do you? Well, then how about this—tell me what the fuck is going on here or you're not getting a goddamn thing from me." Of course, even as I said my piece, I was completely terrified. The fact that this man turned me on hardly made him less dangerous. Maybe more so.

Way to go, Rox. I closed my eyes and waited for him to get violent. He took handfuls of my jacket and pulled me tightly against him. Then, in a voice dripping with contempt, he said: "Did Mason explain anything to you?"

"No. And let me guess; you won't either."

"Of course I will," he said. "Since the time of the altercation, you've been experiencing quite a lot of confusion, jumbles, mismatched memories, and blind spots."

Yes. I found myself shuddering. I nodded. *Oh, God, please tell me there's a reasonable explanation.*

"What it is, is entirely natural and to be expected. Until this . . . situation is resolved, you will, indeed, experience memories that seem out of place or that don't match up with your expectations or current understanding. You will also find yourself in places you don't expect, or perhaps you will think you remember something that happened long ago but doesn't seem possible with what you now know to be true. My advice to you is to just try to accept—accept, and simply let things happen."

"You mean keep an open mind?" I asked sarcastically, recalling Mason's seemingly cryptic words.

"Precisely. Everything will smooth out eventually. Regardless of how confusing things seem."

I waited for more information. There wasn't any.

"That's it?" My voice sank to a faint tremble. "This . . . all this is crazy. I mean, you don't think this all sounds crazy and impossible? And you haven't explained anything!"

"I can see how you might think recent events are crazy. But everything that happens is entirely possible. And entirely true."

I found myself suspicious, even if—or maybe because—he was acting so helpful. "Mason didn't try to stuff any crap down my throat," I said, taking a step sideways. "Maybe he didn't tell me this because *this* isn't a reasonable explanation."

Leo shrugged. "Mason does two things. He either says nothing or he lies. Be careful what information you accept from him. And remember: There are two sides to every story. At least."

"And your side is . . . ?" I asked.

"The truth. Doesn't it make you wonder that Mason has been keeping tabs on you for a matter of years?"

"Some people would call it flattering," I hedged. It *did* bother me.

"Some people would call that stalking."

Stalking. Mason warned me this guy would go there. But what if Mason knew that because it was true?

"How could he be stalking me if I haven't seen him in all this time?" I asked, unaccountably angered by my fears.

"What makes you think he hasn't seen *you*?"

"Look, the way I understand it, you tried to mug me and Mason saved me."

"I wasn't attempting to mug you," Leonardo said, clearly annoyed.

"Then what were you attempting?"

He opened his mouth, apparently thought better of his first answer, and ended up saying, "It was more an issue of . . . possession."

My skin suddenly crawled. I guess the look on my face showed it.

"If I wanted to hurt you, I would have done so by now," he said. "I don't even plan to do anything here."

"It doesn't add up. You fight over me, grab me . . . then you find yourself in the perfect position to take me with you and you're just going to walk away? Not that I would go anywhere with you," I added abruptly.

"It's not to my advantage," he admitted. "I don't have a move at the moment." Leonardo adjusted his suit jacket, shaking out several wrinkles. "So I must manufacture one. After which, I'll be back."

I moved forward this time and grabbed his sleeve, suddenly afraid that if he left I'd never get another chance at answers."Where is everybody . . . everything?" I waved my hand around at the empty agency.

"Did this happen because you 'made a move'? Is that what this was?"

I followed his curious look to where I clutched his sleeve. He seemed surprised that I'd dare to touch him. Then he looked up at me, saying with a polite smile, "It was a small adjustment to counteract a rather anemic beginning on Mr. Merrick's part."

"That says nothing and you know it."

He stared into my eyes in response. His were very green. He stepped closer and exhaled a soft breath, and the release of air was strangely seductive against my cheek.

"Ah . . . um . . ."

He unhooked my hand and took it in his, bending down to kiss the back. *This doesn't happen in real life. Men like this don't happen in real life.* When his lips left my skin and he looked into my eyes, I felt like the most important, fascinating person in the world. That it felt so good made me want to cringe.

I found my voice, just barely. "I don't know people like you," I gasped.

"Do you want to?"

It was a strange question to ask, and I honestly didn't know the answer. Would it be odd if I said yes? My brain might be totally scrambled here, but it wasn't so scrambled that I couldn't see and admit the truth about myself. I had no life. I had no friends. I had no family. I just had work, which lately I'd even had trouble remembering. And it had had trouble remembering me. On the face of things, Leonardo Kaysar represented the kind of something—the kind of someone—I'd fantasized about after falling asleep in the early morning in front of movies chronicling lives I'd never lead and adventures I'd never have.

"Mason was right when he said you were a dangerous man."

"Yes, he was," Leonardo said with a smile. His hand fell away. "I'm dangerous to *him*."

"Why do you guys hate each other so much?" I asked.

He turned away, then back to me. "My father was a great man," he said incongruously. "He was intelligent and successful and all of that, but he also lived for his family."

I swallowed hard, realizing that as much as Kaysar knew about my inner life, it shouldn't surprise me that he knew my personal history. Did he know what I would give for a father who sounded like his?

"Mason took the meaning out of life for him and never showed an ounce of remorse," Leonardo continued. "When you most desperately need loyalty from him, that will be the moment you will know without a doubt that all you have from Mason Merrick is betrayal. He would kill you if he had to, to get what he wants."

My jaw dropped. "You're crazy. He would never *kill* me. You're not really saying that, right?" I asked, feeling oddly caught between laughing and crying. These were simply words, a suggestion. I didn't know why they should affect me like they did. "He just walked me home. He's had a million chances to—"

Leonardo gave a casual shrug. "At the moment, it's not advantageous for him. But make no mistake, what he is doing now is ingratiating himself, making you trust him so that you will stay near him."

I narrowed my eyes. Maybe Leonardo really *did* know about my history, as he seemed to know about my tendency to live life through a TV screen or the pages of a book. But distrust filled me. "Maybe that's more like what *you're* trying to do."

Kaysar didn't seem the least bit concerned by my accusation, and I was getting closer and closer to completely losing my shit.

"Why are you telling me this?" I finally asked. "Why are you here if you don't want to hurt me or take me with you or whatever?"

A look of irritation crossed his face. "To have a moment for us before Mason completely poisons you against me. It's bad enough that he knew you before. He has the advantage of planting whatever story he so chooses, which gives me the disadvantage of trying to prove to you otherwise."

"You haven't proven a thing to me yet," I said. "Neither of you has."

Leonardo ran his fingers lightly across my cheek. "Mason's true colors will do it all for me, and then you will know that I have not been lying to you, that I want to work with you, not against you."

His cell phone must have been on vibrate; his hands suddenly fell away from me and he took a step back to take the call. "Please excuse me, Roxanne." A few silent moments later, he slid the device back in his pocket, and I knew from his body language that he was leaving. With his eyes fixed on something behind me, he pulled a silver case from his breast pocket, retrieved a cigarette and absently tapped it on the lid.

Only now did I notice his hands were free of the cuts and welts one would expect to see, given the evidence of the fight left upon Mason's face. Leonardo seemed . . . healed. Odder than that, even, was the easy way he'd been moving his arm—as if he'd never taken a bullet. "How—?

The tip of the cigarette suddenly slid across the silver case and Leonardo dropped the smoke to the ground. He curled his fingers into a fist, as if he were trying to resist something. "What is he up to?" he murmured, his eyes narrowing. "Mason's working on something. So like him, these tentative fits and starts. His style is so rough. Bumping and jerking us around." He frowned and muttered something under his breath about not being sure what layer he was on.

"He's not even here," I remarked.

Leonardo murmured another gracious apology and checked his cell phone again. He seemed to be struggling with a decision, seemed aware of something to which I wasn't privy.

Then, without any warning, he pulled a gun from his waistband. I flinched, but he shook his head. "I want you to take this." Flipping the weapon around so that the barrel pointed away from me, he handed it over, following up with a fistful of bullets from his suit pocket. "And these." He poured the bullets into my free hand.

"I already have some," I said, in a voice that I hardly reco gnized as my own.

"Take them," he replied, strain evident in his

voice. "And do not hesitate to defend yourself. This is not a game."

He grimaced suddenly, and I thought I heard him say Mason's name under his breath like a curse.

"What?" I asked.

Leonardo either didn't hear me or didn't choose to answer. His gaze shifted beyond my right shoulder and he stepped back into shadow.

"Hey!" I tried to find his eyes in the dark, but to no avail, then slowly turned and looked over my shoulder. Nearly blinded by white light, my eyes took a moment to bring the fuzziness into focus. The buzz and blur of a busy office swirled once more around me. The receptionist was holding a manila envelope out. "Sorry for the confusion. It seems you normally do this by e-mail. But he said just to give you this."

I stared at her, just stared at her until she rustled the envelope under my nose. I managed to extend my arm and take it in spite of trembling fingers.

"Who's 'he'?"

"Dunno," the clerk said with a shrug. "Haven't seen him around before."

"Can you describe him? Was he wearing a suit? Or just casual?"

She looked taken aback. "Oh. I guess I really didn't notice. I was on the phone and someone dropped it on the desk."

"Thanks," I murmured. She blended back into her workday; I glanced around at the hall. Leonardo Kaysar was gone, but a black cigarette lay under a chair.

I went to open the envelope I'd been given, and

saw a jagged edge where someone had hurriedly run their finger to burst the seam. Had it been like that when the clerk handed it to me and I was just too distracted to notice? I looked inside. Nothing. I stuck my hand in and searched the corners with my fingers. Still nothing.

I wheeled around and practically mowed down the new person being helped by the receptionist. "It's gone," I blurted.

A crease wrinkled her forehead and she sighed. I held up the envelope to explain. "There's nothing in here."

She shook her head, pursing her lips in what I interpreted as an effort to keep herself from calling me an idiot. "I don't know anything about it," she repeated. "Sorry, but maybe they just forgot the papers."

"But it was thicker than this, wasn't it? When you handed it to me? And it was sealed?"

The man I'd interrupted crossed his arms over his chest, and both he and the clerk looked at me blankly. He wore a charcoal suit. I glanced around at the others standing in the reception area. The Starbucks travel mugs were still there, but the people holding them weren't wearing jeans and T-shirts. They were all wearing suits or skirts.

"I said the guy gave it to me to give to you. It was a sealed envelope, just like the others. And I handed it to you and that's all I know. Was there anything else?" the receptionist asked crisply. She was through with me.

"No," I whispered. "Thanks." The two went back to their discussion and I numbly folded the empty envelope and stuck it in my bag. I hadn't thought much about a new project itself at all; I'd just come to pick one up, feeling it was the most natural thing in the world to do. But in light of Leonardo Kaysar's words, I wish I'd looked things over in my apartment a little more, scanned my computer for any clues as to what I might be working on, and more than anything I sure wished I knew what had been in that envelope.

I pushed out onto the street and started walking, playing bits and pieces of Leonardo Kaysar's conversation back in my mind. I was halfway down the block when certain discrepancies occurred to me, like, I'd passed neither a big-and-tall store nor a frame shop. Slowly I pivoted and retraced my steps to face a now wall-windowed agency storefront, shivering as cool air swept over my damp skin. Beyond the glass I stared through the bustle of the agency down at a cigarette being stepped on and kicked along the floor of the waiting area by the oblivious. Crushed tobacco scattered into the crevices of the beige carpet, disappearing like so many grains of sand.

I glanced around me. Somehow, some way, I wasn't on the block on that route I'd walked many, many times. I was on the block in the middle of . . . who the hell knew where. I turned in a circle, taking in the buildings and street signs once more just to be sure. But I was sure. The block on which I'd entered the agency wasn't the block on which I'd exited. In short, the agency had apparently changed locations in the time I'd been inside. And somehow I knew I was close enough to home now to skip the bus and walk.

This is not a game. That one phrase was just about

the only thing Leonardo and Mason had agreed upon. Maybe what they really meant was that this wasn't a game for *me*. On some level, even if neither of them was willing to admit it, I would bet that this was most certainly a game for them. One they seemed to have been playing together for a long time.

Denial. Denial is denial only the first couple of times. After that, it's just a polite word for delusional. I turned away from the windowed agency and started walking.

The walk home from the agency took me a few blocks north of the 7-Eleven near my house. I thought about the contents of my refrigerator and those menus and what I must have craved last night. While it would have been just as easy to head straight home, I had the sense that something in the convenience store was a missing piece of this growing puzzle into which Mason and Leonardo had dropped me.

A prickle of dread fluttered over the surface of my skin as I opened the door, a contrast to the welcoming electronic chime as I stepped over the threshold. Naveed was restocking cigarettes behind the counter. He looked up at the sound and smiled at me. "Good day, Roxanne."

"Hey, Naveed. How's it going?"

"Excellent, excellent." He set the carton down on the counter and clasped his hands there, following me through the store with his eyes. I wandered up and down the aisles, looking for something to trigger a memory, or at least for something to catch my fancy.

I could sense Naveed still staring at me and tried a

discreet glance up to one of the round security mirrors. Not discreet enough for someone who was watching my every move.

"You are doing well," he said in a pep-talk voice. "*Very* well. Something has happened?"

I turned to him and studied his face for a moment, suddenly paranoid that everyone I knew, however obliquely, was somehow in on something I wasn't. But he seemed his usual mild, pleasant self.

"Oh, you heard," I said. "Yeah, I'm fine. But let me ask you something. Do you remember a guy dressed in a nice suit with a British accent coming in here recently? Someone who just maybe seemed a little out of place in the neighborhood?"

Naveed looked puzzled for a moment, then cocked his head. "No, I don't think so. No."

"Nobody actually weird?"

"Nobody except you," he blurted.

I laughed and he looked at me, horror flashing across his face for a split second, as if he felt he'd overstepped the bounds of acceptable etiquette between 7-Eleven proprietor and regular customer by telling a joke. I was quick to reassure him.

"Funny, Naveed. Very funny. Just wondering. Thanks," I added as I wandered over to look at the boxed doughnuts. I couldn't think of how to describe Leonardo more than "a guy with a British accent and a nice suit," not in a way that would be meaningful to Naveed. I doubted "a gorgeous male, mature in the debonair and worldly sense, impressive, sexy, and totally can-do in that MI5 sort of way," would do much for him. And Mason's all-American look, his jeans and T-shirt, wouldn't have stood out from the usual customers, so there was little point in even asking. If he hadn't been wearing a jacket I could have asked about the snake tattoo, but no go on that. Everything made the fact that I didn't even know what I would ask Naveed about them had he seen either one completely moot.

The oppressive sensation of being watched just wouldn't go away. I slowly stood and looked toward the counter. Naveed continued to eye me intently. He lifted his hand in a hesitant sort of wave.

"Is something wrong?" I asked.

He straightened, a look of mock innocence on his face. "No, no. I am just very happy to see you shopping here like this."

My hand paused over a box of powdered sugar minis. *Okaaaaay*. "Well . . . thanks, man. I'm very happy to be shopping here . . . like . . . this." And figuring that, after his overblown pleasantry, he might be expecting something more personal in return, I asked, "How's the family?"

He beckoned me forward, consumed by proud enthusiasm. I breathed a sigh of relief. This wasn't the behavior of a truly suspicious man.

"My daughter is getting so big," he said. "I am certain she is going to be a genius. I have a picture of her right here."

I passed on the doughnuts and picked up a bag of chips instead. At the counter, Naveed handed me a family photo: mom, dad, big brother, baby sister. "She's adorable," I said automatically. "You have a really nice family."

But as I handed the photo back, I started to get nervous. Like, I needed to leave immediately. I put the chips on the counter with a five-dollar bill.

Naveed started ringing me up, and it seemed to take forever. I had to force myself not to ask him to hurry, and I almost yelped out loud when he put his hand on my arm. He said, "If you are going to come often, maybe think about coming earlier. It is getting dark sooner now."

He took his hand away and I breathed a sigh of relief. I went to the door, turned back at the threshold, and forced myself to concentrate. "This is a really dumb question, but you don't happen to remember what I bought last time I was in here, do you?"

He looked surprised. "Of course. You came right to the counter and purchased some gum," he said, pointing to the impulse-buy section along the front of the counter.

Which tells me absolutely nothing. Nobody craves gum at two in the morning and actually acts on it. Chocolate, yes. Salty snacks, yes. Gum, no. I must have gone for something else.

I forced a smile for Naveed, then slipped through the door, ushered out by the chime, and was already pulling the package of chips open and eating compulsively as I headed for home.

As I reached the spot where Mason and Leonardo collided with me and each other at two o'clock yesterday morning, my nerves amped up even more. This was the beginning of a panic attack, not the hot sweats I'd been having lately. It was more like . . . a self-fulfilling-prophecy sort of panic. The kind that came directly from within. The kind I manufactured myself. It came on like the dark roar of the ocean, a mind-numbing thing that nearly swamped me.

My mind flashed with visions of thrown punches, of barricading myself in Mason's car, of standing on my doorstep as he foisted his ridiculous story on me, of opening my refrigerator door.

I staggered to the street lamp near where Mason's car had been parked and grabbed on to it to keep from falling, my head spinning, my sweaty hands sliding on the metal post. My bag of chips crunched under my shoes, ground into the pavement.

Something's so very, very off here.

I bee-lined home. There were people everywhere, going about their business. It was still early enough for the sidewalks to see the end of rush-hour pedestrian traffic. It should have been completely safe, but that didn't stop me from looking over my shoulder every five seconds. I picked up my pace to a brisk walk, then upped it to a jog. I was home in five minutes, but I was wheezing and gasping with my heart nearly pounding out of my chest.

If Mason's story that I was involved in something dangerous and Leo's story that Mason wasn't here to help me were true, I'd have to train myself to run a lot faster.

FIVE

I staggered up the stairs and dropped my bag at my front door, wincing as the heavy contents slammed down on the ground. The gun. The bullets. Still, for a moment it was all I could do to keep myself from falling over as I caught my breath.

I pulled the latest notice from the homeowners association off the door and let myself in. The house was pitch-black and deathly quiet. I half expected Leonardo Kaysar to pop up on my couch and Mason to be in the kitchen retrieving beers for all three of us. But the place was as empty as I'd left it. Too empty. I guess I liked it that way, though it was hard at moments like this to remember why.

I turned on a bunch of lights and stood in the middle of the living room, trying to decide exactly how weird I felt now and what if any of the strangeness Leonardo had described was really happening. Mind blanks? Jumbles? Confusion? Yes to all three.

I glanced at the notice in my hand and almost laughed. The homeowners association had decided to paint again. The doors and the molding this time, in blue. They'd done up a sample down the hall if I wanted to see what the finished look would be with the undoubtedly hideous color they'd picked. There was actually something comforting about the normalcy of this one small maintenance detail; regular life did go on. I patted my jeans pocket to make sure I still had my house keys, then opened the door to go check out the sample.

Stepping forward into the hall, I was engulfed in a blast of heat and lost my balance on the threshold. I went plunging downward into wide-open space as if I'd just stepped off a cliff. *Not so regular after all.*

Just as I'd experienced before, a series of frames unfurled in my mind. I watched my old roommate Kitty open a can of soup, saw myself sitting on the living room floor crying as I stared at the doorknob of my front door, gasped at Mason winking at me as we drove down the freeway in his car, rolled my eyes at the graduation cap and gown sitting on the side table still wrapped in plastic. . . .

I opened my mouth, but no sound came out as paved concrete rushed up to meet me. I mean, the hall floor. But it was pavement. And I was certain I would hit hard.

"Roxy?"

I came to, cradled in Mason Merrick's arms in the open doorway of my apartment, and immediately launched myself up and away, practically face-planting myself on the ground. "What the hell." It was all I could say for the next several moments. Just, "What the hell."

"You see something?" he asked.

"Absolutely not," I replied, trying to process the something I'd just seen. A hallucination? Food poisoning? Drugs? Mental illness? None of those possibilities was appealing, and certainly none of them was something I wanted to cop to, yet I'd have taken any reasonable explanation.

"You look like you just saw a ghost."

I gave him a look. "I was just thinking about me and Kitty on graduation day. I guess that since I haven't seen her since then, she would qualify."

"You miss her?"

I knew instantly from the too-innocent lilt of his voice that he was fishing. But for what? "Yeah, I miss her. She was my best friend."

"Because you lost touch. You haven't seen her in a long time. Not since graduation."

"Where are we going with this, Mason? What does Kitty have to do with anything?" *And what do you have to do with what I just saw?*

"Nothing," he said too quickly. "Just curious."

Leonardo's words of warning rang loud in my ears. Ignoring Mason's hand, I scrambled to my feet on my own. I grabbed the front of my T-shirt and pulled it away from my sweaty skin, flapping the fabric to let cooler air circulate. Swallowing against the burgeoning nausea, I ended up letting Mason lead me back inside my apartment.

"I'm fine," I said lamely, trying to get out of the chair he set me in.

He held me down by my shoulders. "Take a minute to let things settle."

I leaned back.

"So, where were you going?" he asked.

"It's really none of your concern."

"You just passed out on the floor. I have a right to be concerned."

I gave him a steely-eyed stare. "No," I said. "No, you don't." I closed my eyes and took deep breaths, opening one eye every once in a while to confirm that he was still there. He sat patiently, his body leaning forward, hands clasped together. Waiting.

God, I'd just let him walk right into my place. I didn't *really* believe Leonardo, did I? That Mason was capable of hurting me? And yet . . . *I should kick him out immediately.*

"You should let me stay with you until it's safe," he said before I could open my mouth.

I didn't want to bring up Leo's warning, so I just played it cool. "So you can eat my groceries and park on my couch? That's really not necessary."

"It's no problem," he said. "I don't eat as much as I used to, and it's not like we've never lived together. I'll take Louise's old room."

I rolled my eyes. "When I said it wasn't necessary, what I meant was, 'No.' I use the second bedroom for storage."

Already starting to make himself comfortable, Mason paused in the middle of taking off his jacket. "I'll take the couch. It's no big deal. You don't fully realize the danger you're in; I totally understand that. It's no problem at all." He dropped his jacket over the back of my couch and started giving my place the once-over. "Your reaction is completely normal. And I accept that it's going to take some time to ease you into things. . . ."

Ease me into things?

"Still, at the very least, err on the side of being overcautious and let me look out for your survival."

I shook my head. "Okay, we're done here. I need you to leave." I grabbed his jacket, ran to the door and held it out at arm's length. He didn't move, so I opened the door and tossed his jacket over the threshold. It landed in the hall with a dull thud. We both looked at it, then looked at each other. After a long pause, Mason rose, walked out, picked up his jacket, and put it on.

"You're going to change your mind at some point."

He started to walk off, then wheeled around and came back at me, fast. "You're really not going to let me move in with you?"

"No."

"No?"

I stared at him for a moment, tempted to sock him in the gut. How dared he return to my life, wrapped in danger and deceit and mystery? How dared he expect my trust?

"Roxanne—" I stood in front of the door and so he reached over my head and pushed it open again. I blocked him as he tried to bully his way inside.

"I said, no!" I hit his chest with the bottom of my fist, but he tried again.

I don't know what happened. I suddenly found myself pounding my fists against him, yelling as if he'd done something really terrible to me for which he should be sorry. Something *really* terrible.

"Okay! Stop, Roxy. Just stop!" He grabbed me by the wrists and pulled me against him. I knew he was just trying to close the distance between us so I couldn't hit him again, but his embrace was so what

I needed right then that I closed my eyes and melted into him. This felt right. I was confused and I was angry, but most of all I was horribly afraid. I needed Mason just then in a way far beyond how I'd wanted him in earlier times when it was just a dorky crush.

A wave of remorse hit me. I'd distrusted Mason? It felt so different to have his arms around me, rather than Leonardo's, and I was ashamed for falling even the least little bit for Leonardo's impressive seduction. Why would I believe a stranger?

"I'm sorry," Mason whispered into my ear. "I'm not coming in. I'm going away. Okay?" He let go of me, and my skin prickled at the loss of warmth. He walked backwards across the landing, then slowly down the stairs to the sidewalk, his hand out in front of him as if he were trying to tame a wildcat. "I'm not coming in."

I nodded. That would be for the best.

Turning, I went inside my apartment, slammed the door shut, and stood there shaking. *What is my problem?* I just wasn't myself. That's what people always say: "I'm just not myself today." That phrase had never before sounded quite the way it did now. *You've got to pull yourself together, Rox. Just pull yourself together. Try to find your balance.*

I took a moment to compose myself, then saw my messenger bag. I remembered what was inside. Gingerly I opened the bag and peeked in. The gun was still there, the bullets rolling around in the bottom along with the crumpled envelope.

I trudged upstairs, peeling my jacket off and draping it over the banister before heading into my bedroom. I opened my closet and kicked the lid off the shoe box, a gasp of shock slipping from my throat as I saw the box was full . . . of shoes. Just shoes.

I dumped out the box, shook it even. I sat down on the floor of the closet and dragged my bag over to me. Spilling the contents out, I picked up the gun. Same coloring, and though I couldn't say with technical certainty it was the same model, the fact was, I didn't have to. I just *knew* it was the same model. I knew this was the same gun and the same bullets.

Impossible.

Again they flashed through my mind, those images I'd seen as I stood on the threshold of my apartment. Some of the events I distinctly remembered; some I didn't recall at all. It was as if only some of these memories were from my past, and the others were . . .

I let the bullets slip through my fingers into the shoe box, then put the gun in beside the shoes and put the lid back on. For the second time in as many days, I stood up, backed away from the closet, and closed the door on what was happening to me.

After a moment, I began to think about what Leonardo and Mason wanted. It wasn't outside the realm of possibility that I'd written something I didn't remember, particularly given the Swiss-cheese state of my brain.

In all fairness, lots of jobs weren't memorable, some for the very reason Kaysar suggested: Freelancers were often subcontracted for only a piece of the pie. All you really needed were the parameters to write the one slice of code. Like the receptionist had verified, I did have high-security clearance. I could conceivably work for the government. In fact, I did have the vague memory of signing disclaimers promising not to discuss my projects with anyone.

But I didn't recall anything recent that these men would want. And if I had any outstanding jobs, someone would have called me about them, or the receptionist would have found a project associated with my name in the computer.

I sat for a moment, then had a brainstorm. Anything I'd already written would be backed up on some drive or another. Frankly, under the circumstances, if either myself, Leonardo, or Mason could identify what they were looking for, I'd hand it over in exchange for a simple promise that I'd be left the hell alone.

I snatched the manila envelope from my messenger bag and practically ran down the hall to my office, intending to figure out some sort of Web search that might give me some answers, but when I flung open the door, I was in for a shock. I should have known. If I wished I'd done a little more research before, I wished it double now. My computer was gone. A clean square on the desk represented the spot where the monitor had once sat. A bunch of disconnected wires hung limply over the side. The monitor was gone, as was the CPU. My computer, my life. In essence, my brain. I'd just been lobotomized.

There wasn't a disk in sight—no flash drives, no peripherals, no backup system, no nothing. Well, except for one speaker, left behind and tipped on its side. Otherwise, every piece of computing equipment was gone. The sense of violation was greater than the loss of property itself, and I felt the loss of property keenly.

I crumpled the envelope in my hand into a ball and slammed it down into the bottom of the empty garbage can, pressing the back of my other hand to my nose as I tried to hold back tears. How was I supposed to plug holes in my memory when the best source of memory a person could have was gone? Or was that the point?

With a pounding heart, I looked wildly around. Whoever the thief was, he had rifled through my papers. He'd done it neatly, but he'd still done it. I looked through what remained: the most generic bunch of paperwork I'd ever seen. It was the sort of stuff that might be in the props closet of a TV show. Scribbled notes regarding housework. Receipts for online purchases of groceries and sundry items. The most mundane and nontelling stuff imaginable. My life suddenly felt staged, and I was starting to feel like a bad actress who hadn't done enough research on her character before stupidly tackling the role.

The door to the closet was closed. Suddenly afraid that maybe someone was still here, I picked up the orphaned speaker and raised it over my head. I approached the closet, my heart still pounding, and flung the door open, shrieking as something came flying out at me.

Nothing. A pack of freebie Post-its with some lame floral design.

I wheeled around, speaker still at the ready, but clearly whoever had been here was gone. I put the speaker back in the center of my vastly empty desk and slumped into my fancy ergonometric task chair.

Pulling out my cell phone, I dialed the police to make a report about the break-in, but all I got was the all-circuits-busy recording. Again. It was as if all of my information and communication pipelines had been cut off or rerouted. I hung up and realized that I had absolutely no idea what to do.

The landline rang and I grabbed it on the first ring. "Hello?" I yelled into it more aggressively than I meant.

"Just checking up on you."

Mason. It was *Mason*. A level of rage I didn't even know I was capable of just about blindsided me. "What the hell did you do to me?"

On the other end, a pause. Then: "Didn't we just share a nice hug? Regretting it already?"

"Shut up. My stuff is gone. What did you do with it?"

"What are you talking about? What kind of stuff?" I expected him to laugh at me or admit that he'd taken it—just another of his practical jokes—but the shock in his voice said different.

"My computer stuff. All of my equipment. All meaningful paperwork. I've been robbed blind. And since I was just with Leonardo Kaysar, it couldn't have been him."

"Yes, it could." I had to hold the phone away from my ear as Mason swore a blue streak, referring to "that son of a bitch" who was going to be "shut down hard in the end."

"I'm coming back over," he growled.

"No, you're not!" I yelled. But Mason had already hung up.

Leonardo's words began racing through my mind again. Who could I trust? I tried to figure out whether my stuff had been missing before I'd opened the front door and fainted, but there was no way of knowing. What scared me most was the idea that maybe Mason had been inside my place when I'd come home. That would explain how he'd been there so quickly when I'd fainted. Of course, I couldn't be certain of the amount of time I'd been unconscious. I didn't know how quickly he'd arrived.

Within fifteen minutes, there was a banging on the door and a totally excessive amount of doorbell ringing. I stood for a moment, uncertain whether I should answer or not, unsure whether or not I was willing to trust Mason at all. Finally I flung the door open and burst out with, "What the hell is going on?"

"Why didn't you tell me you'd seen Leonardo today?" Mason grabbed my shoulders and looked me over like a horse at market. "Are you okay? Did he hurt you? I can't believe I was so stupid! I didn't think he'd . . . dammit, I should be here with you. You should let me stay. You don't want *anything* to do with Kaysar, do you understand me?"

If he was acting, he was good at it. I would have sworn in court that he thought Leonardo Kaysar had been to my condo and stolen my things. And that Kaysar was the most dangerous man alive. "He didn't hurt me. Nobody hurt me. My *stuff* is gone."

"Let me see."

I hesitated this time, not so quick to tell him no. I was feeling the same pull I'd felt earlier, the pull I'd felt in his arms. And yet, there was some saying about inviting the devil into your home, and since I didn't know for sure who the devil was yet, maybe I didn't want to take any chances.

"Roxanne, this is not the time. Please just let me in your apartment so you can show me what he took."

"There's nothing to show. It's all gone," I said robotically.

"Be specific."

"Like I said—computer, storage devices, disks, even the crap like boxes of old floppies. The whole shebang. Everything."

"All your projects were there? All the code you write?"

"Well, yeah. Everything." *I think.*

"Did you back it up?"

"Now that's just insulting. Of course I backed it up. But my external hard drive and flash drives and all that stuff is gone too."

He swore, then raised his hand absently to the side of his face and stroked the stubble. "Anything else? Anything that struck you as odd?"

"No. Well, not here. But when I went to the agency to get my next project, they gave me an empty envelope. I guess someone took the stuff out before they gave it to me, but I don't see how it could be Leonardo. He was talking to me at the time. I doubt he ever saw the envelope, much less took what was in it. How could he? But *you* could have seen what was in it. Maybe *you* took it."

Mason swore again. Then we stood there for what must have been several minutes while he alternately stared off into space and checked his cell phone. "I guess a fast-forward. But then . . . ," he muttered cryptically. "Then if he had it, it would all be over. Right."

The oddness of the sentence pulled everything back into focus. "What did you just say?"

"Just trying to put the pieces together." He let out a big breath of air.

I couldn't hide the tremor in my voice when I asked, "You said something. You said 'If he had it, it would all be over.' "

Mason sighed. "He thought maybe you'd written the code by now. He stole your computer to look for it, but if he'd found it, we would know because then he would have it and this would all be over. But it's not. And Leo's not going to stop trying until he gets what he wants."

My head was spinning. "Well, that's ridiculous. He knows I haven't written the code. He said so. Why would he suddenly think I have it now unless this is the future you said he wanted?" I said sarcastically. "Enough with this crap already. What's going on?"

"I don't want you to freak out, is the thing."

"It's a little late for that. Give me an explanation for what you claim Leo has done that I can make sense of."

He tugged at his earlobe, and then said, "You know at a club, when they scratch a record backwards and forwards but it's always continuing on to the end of the song?"

"Yeah?"

"Yeah. Think of it like that."

I stared at him in disbelief. It wasn't really an explanation. He was making fun of me. He had to be. But I had a weird feeling like I almost understood. If I opened my mind like he asked me to . . .

The gun was there; the gun wasn't there. The

agency was in one place; then it didn't exist in that spot. Backwards and forwards . . . *Ridiculous*. Ridiculous. *This is Mason Merrick, the same Mason Merrick you knew before. He says things like this. He does things like this. And like he said, you used to like it. Part of you still does, but what he's suggesting is just too much.*

"So, can I come in now?" Mason asked. "I'd like to see his handiwork." He gestured behind me to the inside of my house.

I didn't budge, though part of me wanted to despite everything. He couldn't have known how close I was to letting him in this time. But whether all of this was one of Mason's games or not, it was being played with real weapons, and that wasn't something I could just laugh away.

"Okay, fine," he said tightly, making it clear that it wasn't. "We'll just continue talking here in the doorway. Wouldn't want to sit down and make ourselves comfortable or anything while we talk."

"No. No, we wouldn't," I said, not giving an inch.

Our standoff lasted another few seconds; then Mason finally said, "Jesus, I should have known when you went all aggro on me earlier. He got to you and told you a bunch of lies about me."

I kept my mouth shut and thought about Leonardo's similar reference to Mason getting at me first and "poisoning" me.

"When did you see Leo?" he pressed.

"A few hours ago."

"Tell me everything he said."

"He explained that you two are at odds, trying to get this damn code you think I've written. Or that you think I'm *going* to write. In any event, the long and the short of it is that he's going to try to get it from me, and you're here to stop him."

"That's actually a really fair summary, all things considered," Mason said. "Where did he find you?"

"I was at the employment agency and he just suddenly . . . appeared." I raised an eyebrow. "Why are you doing this, Mason?" I asked quietly. Was it too much to be told the truth? "Why are you suddenly all over me when we haven't seen each other in years? We don't know each other anymore."

"We know each other," he argued. Then he admitted, "but I guess that when I think about it, maybe you never really got a chance to know me for who I truly am."

Oh, please. What a line. I tried to put him in his place: "How does 'oversexed hunk of meat' sound?"

He grinned. "It sounds like a compliment. I know you considered it an attractive quality at the time."

I totally blushed, and the hotter my cheeks got, the more embarrassed I became. "How could you possibly know, much less remember, what I thought about you?" Was I fishing? I didn't want to think about it.

Mason leaned against the wall and gave me the impression he was thinking carefully. "I remember you were . . . complicated. I remember a tense, seething mass of black sitting at the breakfast table eating Cap'n Crunch. I remember the way you looked at me like I was dogshit—when you weren't busy drooling over my ass."

His mouth widened into a full grin. "One morning I glanced over the top edge of the sports section at you, and it occurred to me that I might be with the wrong roommate. And I'd have bet a lot of money that you were thinking the same thing. But what sane guy is going to trade a simple girl in for a complicated one?"

It was true. All of it. He did remember. And while I didn't want to admit anything, something else in me didn't want to deny it, either. I liked the idea that he knew I'd once had a thing for him, just as I liked the idea that he liked it too. I liked this all-American Mason in a different way than I had been moved by Leonardo. In a powerful way. So I just stood there in the doorway with an invisible wall up, my arms folded across my chest like armor, trying to again appear like I couldn't stand anything about him.

"You want more?" he asked.

"No," I said in a disinterested tone. I immediately regretted it as he rolled his eyes.

"Is there anything else Leo said that you forgot to mention?"

I knew Mason would know more about what Kaysar was up to than I did, and that I should give him the details if I were to trust him, but I was still afraid. I didn't know how much I wanted to tell one about the other. Not yet. Maybe not ever.

"Right. I see how it is. So, you're not going to let me come in even to look around?"

"Not a chance in hell," I agreed.

After a long pause, Mason sighed. "Mark my words. At some point you'll be begging me to move in with you."

I gave him no reason to believe that point would come anytime soon.

Finally, he just nodded. Slipping a really cool device out from the side of his cell phone, he fit it over his index finger like a finger glove with a small stylus protrusion and tapped some information into the phone. Then he pulled an old-school reporter's notepad from his pocket and twisted part of the plastic device around to reveal a pen. He licked the nib and wrote something down, and for one mad second all I could do was concentrate on the licking.

He tore the sheet off the spiral and held it out to me. "My cell. Call me if anything more out of the ordinary happens. Even if you think it's nothing and you're just scared."

I felt myself melt a little further as the sweetness in him shone through. How could I listen to some stranger over a guy who lived in my apartment and joked with me and shared with me an unrequited crush for a couple of years? One who'd never so much as harmed a hair on my head all that time? I wanted so badly to believe him. To believe *in* him. But Leonardo . . .

My heart says yes, Mason, but there are a million ways to explain what you are doing here being so wonderful to me that don't involve you actually caring about me.

"I can't," I started to say. "I want to; I just—"

"I know. You will. It's okay. Leonardo's a clever man, and I know all of his tricks. But you will."

I had to fight the urge to collapse against him and hope he'd take me in his arms the way he'd done earlier.

"Wait for me to contact you. Keep the doors and windows locked, and don't let anybody else in." He chuckled and added, "That shouldn't be too hard for someone like you."

Someone like me? *Nice.* He just couldn't resist. I guess the bastard realized I didn't have too many men pounding on my door, begging to come in, begging to *move* in, for that matter. So much for sweet. But just because I never brought anybody home during college didn't mean I never brought anybody home now. So what if I couldn't think of one single recent date?

I watched Mason walk to his Mustang. He turned around and lifted his hand in salute. Then he got in the passenger side of his car. I could see some movement inside and wasn't sure what it was all about until I realized he was putting the seat back. I watched for a good fifteen minutes before I realized he wasn't going anywhere. In fact, he was digging in. He was either here to watch over me . . . or to watch me.

Don't buy into a stranger's words so quickly, I told myself. *You have a choice.* Mason and I had history; he was watching *over* me. He had to be.

I went to my phone and dialed the police station again, absently watching the tremors in my hand as the call tried to go through. All circuits were busy. They were always busy.

I tossed the phone on the counter and stood in my foyer for a while without thinking up anything helpful to my situation, pushing Mason out of my mind as best I could, though he was right across the street. About two seconds later, Mason called my phone from his car. While I went upstairs and strained to get a glimpse of him from the storage room window, he asked me again if there was anything else I wanted to tell him, then made me repeat a couple of times that I was okay. Other than that, it was a short call in which he begged me again to let him come in. I refused and he begged, and I refused and he begged, and then we hung up.

I called the agency and left a voice mail alerting them to my situation, then told them that I'd let them know when I was back up and running. Then I pretty much sat around in my office staring at my disconnected wires. At last I went into my room, lay on the bed, and stared at the ceiling, trying to tell myself I was meditating. When I tired of that, I watched some television. I tried to think of someone to call but really couldn't think of anyone I wanted to talk to. Well, actually, I really couldn't think of anybody *to* talk to, which was even worse.

You've been working too much, Rox. You need a life. You don't want to get to the end of your life and be sitting in the dark like this.

I lay on the bed with the door locked and the lights off, waiting for my computer equipment to spontaneously reappear. My mind was spinning with all that had happened.

Around midnight I ran down the hall to the storage room, wove myself through the maze of boxes, and plastered my face against the window. The angle gave me nothing more than the back slice of Mason's car for a view, but that was enough. I went back to my office and twirled in my task chair. Then I went and lay down on my bed again. Then I checked out the view from the window. To the office chair. To the bed. To the window.

SIX

Sleep did not come easily; my mind wouldn't stop grinding. It must have taken me a couple of hours to finally try to fall asleep, and even then I woke up fitful and uncomfortable in my own skin. So it took me a moment to figure out if the thumping sound I'd just heard was in my flat or just in my dreams.

A second thump later, I knew somebody was definitely in my flat—in real life—and for all I knew, they could have been inside my place for some time.

I inched toward the far end of the bed, still under the covers, then quietly slid to the floor, the silk of my pink negligee rustling against the sheets. My bedroom was pitch black, of course, what with the heavy shades on the windows. I couldn't turn the light on, as I didn't want the intruder to know I was up and alert. Keeping my eyes on the slice of light under the door, I crawled to the space between the far side of the bed and the wall.

The floor vibrated as someone climbed the stairs. He hit the landing and the floorboards out in the hall shifted and squealed. The gun. The gun was in the closet. I stood up, my movements made clumsier by adrenaline, and lurched against the wall. My shoulder bumped the framed picture there, sending it crashing down onto the nightstand. I stood in bare feet, breathing loud enough to wake the neighbors, and now there was no question the intruder knew where I was and that I was awake.

I had no idea how far the glass had scattered, so I leaped as far as I could—back on the bed—then scrambled over the end and walked toward the closet. Flapping my hand out into the darkness I found the closet door, pulled it open and shrank inside.

In the closet now. That was the first step. I closed the door and felt around on the floor until my hand hit the shoebox. I pushed the cover aside. Was this why Leonardo had given me a gun? Did he know a moment like this would come? Did he know this exact moment would come?

I was sitting on the floor of my closet when the door to my bedroom opened. It wasn't cut right, and the wood slid against the pile carpet with a hissing sound. The lights did not go on.

My right hand reached inside the shoebox. I wrapped my fingers around the gun. With my free hand, I combed through the tissue paper for bullets, but then I realized I knew nothing about loading a pistol. For that matter, the gun could already be loaded. No matter. The intruder wouldn't know either.

I sensed him near the closet door now. With both hands wrapped around the gun handle, I watched the wooden boards beneath me depress slightly. Someone was right there on the other side. Someone who wanted something.

Maybe I should strike first. Maybe I should kick the door out. I'm trapped in here. I should go for it. They won't expect it. Besides, I don't want to die in a negligee on the floor of my closet without a fight. You've got this in you. You know you do.

I oh-so-slowly stood up in the closet, staying hunched over in an effort to avoid the hangers. The only reference that popped into my head for a situation like this was an *A-Team* rerun. Not ideal, but good enough. Aping the character in the show, I bent my right knee up toward my waist and kicked the door open, screaming, "I've got a gun!"

The intruder stumbled backward but managed not to fall. He had a gun trained on me, but mine was on him. I could see, just barely, the stalemate, as it were. Scared out of my mind and struggling with the unfamiliarity of wielding a real—and possibly loaded—weapon, I looked nervously at my adversary.

Except . . . I squinted in the dark at his shape and it looked familiar. "I'm going to blow your fucking head off if you don't get out of my bedroom," I said.

"Holy shit."

It was Mason, all right. But he didn't put the gun down. "Put it down, Merrick."

"You put yours down."

"I don't think so."

Mason reached out and flipped on the closet light. I cringed at the sudden brightness.

"Is that what you normally wear to bed?" he asked.

I rolled my eyes. It wasn't, actually. For reasons I did not care to analyze, I'd put the pink thing on for the first time tonight.

"Hey, I remember this bed! Louise left her bed?"

"You and Louise," I muttered, not falling for his obvious ploy to distract me from my purpose. "It's *my* bed. All my furniture. You were sleeping in my bed."

His mouth melted into a slow smile.

I fought my body's reaction. "Oh, please. That's not what I meant."

"I bet you wondered why was I going out with Louise," he said.

"Let me guess. She was the first girl with large breasts to fall into your bed, and that's how she became your girlfriend."

"I admit that she had very large breasts, but that wasn't it. And she really wasn't my girlfriend."

"Quite possibly that makes it worse."

"You're sure uptight, aren't you?"

I'm holding a gun. My life has changed and I don't remember it all. Yeah, I'm a little uptight. "Don't call me that. I hate that."

"So, it's happened before?" He cocked his head and smiled.

"Why don't we change the subject?"

"What would you like to talk about?"

"How long you plan to stand there like an idiot while I point this gun at you."

"You don't want me to leave now, do you? This was just getting interesting."

"What are you talking about? This is not 'interesting.' You are not interesting to me. You're annoying. You're like a gnat. You broke into my—"

"I think you're a little jealous of Louise? Mmm? Admit it."

"You're out of your mind. Certifiably."

"You're not used to flirting."

"You're *flirting* with me? We're flirting? I guess I thought it would be better."

"So, you've thought about it," he crowed.

"Oh, shut up. How did you get in the house?"

"Funny coincidence. I woke up and saw that the front door was open, and I got worried. So I came inside and then I heard something smash, and then I was really worried." He eyed the gun in my hand and smiled. It was a friendly smile. In truth, it was a worried, caring smile. But it was also a liar's smile, since I'd double-checked all the locks before bed.

"Oh. The door was open? How silly of me. I must have left it unlatched." My arms were starting to get tired, and I actually did want to put the gun down. Not to mention I wasn't wearing anything underneath the nightie, and I wasn't sure how high the hem was riding in this position.

He looked at me curiously, then recovered. "How about on the count of three we both lower our guns?"

"You're kidding. Just put down your gun and then I'll put down mine."

"You don't trust me?"

"Obviously not."

The sunny charm went out of his look, but he lowered his arms and uncocked his gun. Just like that. I was so surprised that I just stood there with my gun still pointed at him. "I need you to trust me," he said. He put his gun down on the bed and lifted his arms to show me his empty hands.

I couldn't figure it out. He stood there frowning at me and looking like a hurt little boy.

He said, "You don't honestly believe that I broke into your house and came up here to kill you, do you? Is that what you're thinking?" The corner of his mouth quirked up; his voice held a note of disbelief.

I thought about it as my tired arms sagged. Did I believe that he broke into my house? Yes, I did. There was no way someone else had broken in. Not with him sitting out front.

But I couldn't believe that he'd come up here to kill me. Which meant I had no idea why he would bother breaking in at all, especially with my computer equipment gone. Of course, I'd probably have given him a similar reception if he had actually rung the doorbell.

"I'd like to look around," Mason said. "Like I should have done earlier." He sounded only a little smug.

"Nice attempt to cover your ass. It was you, and you know it. Back away from the bed and keep your hands out with your palms showing, just like you had them."

He cocked his head and humored me, but I could see a vein in his neck throb as he clenched his jaw. When he moved back far enough to please me—which was practically out the bedroom door—I grabbed his gun off the bed. "Stick 'em up," I said.

Mason laughed until I started toward him, double-fisting guns, the adrenaline pouring through me so fast my movements were getting jerky.

"Just don't . . . Whoa, hey, watch those triggers!"

"*You'd* better watch them. Now back out that

door and we're going to go downstairs and walk you out of my house."

"Roxanne, hold on one second. I really need my gun."

"Look, I'm tired. Just turn around and start walking." I jiggled the guns in his direction and his eyes widened for a second before he shrugged in an exhausted, resigned sort of way and did as I asked.

I walked him down to the front door and said, "You can come again tomorrow and I'll give you your gun back. Then we can talk."

"You don't understand what's happening here. I need—"

"Right now? You need it right now? It's—what—three in the morning? Are our lives in danger right now?"

"Possibly."

"I see. Well, I'm well armed and probably not going to be able to sleep again tonight, so I think I'll be okay. See you tomorrow." I pressed the guns against his chest and pushed him backward over the threshold with the muzzles, then shut the door in his face, locked it very carefully, and immediately went upstairs to the storage room to see if I could see anything.

I flinched back, irritated to find that Mason had anticipated my move. He had walked to the one angle where I could actually see him, caught me looking, and waved. I moved away from the window and went back into my bedroom, moving a chair to cover the broken glass in case I forgot when I woke up in the morning.

I must have been more tired than I thought, because I actually fell asleep pretty fast. Unfortunately it wasn't a long sleep, due to the sound of the doorbell ringing at five o'clock.

I woke up fast, alert, and pulled on a pair of sweats underneath the skirt of my lingerie. I picked up Mason's gun and went downstairs. The doorbell kept obnoxiously ringing, and I figured it had to be him. It was, in fact, Mason, with a surprising amount of stubble. I saw that as I opened the door and pointed his gun at his chest.

"Good morning," I said with a complete lack of enthusiasm. "It's five a.m."

"Five thirty. I'm hungry and I have to take a piss." He looked grumpy and uncomfortable, and without hesitation he reached out, moved the muzzle of his gun out of his direction, and pushed past me into the house.

I looked at the gun. My ability to scare Mason with it seemed to have disappeared with the dawn. That, or he had to go pretty badly. I shrugged and left his gun on the small table next to the door.

Mason joined me in the kitchen a few minutes later, opened the cupboard, and pulled out a box of cereal. He'd obviously slept less than I had. He looked like hell—which kind of suited him, of course.

I left him in the kitchen and went back upstairs. In the open doorway to my office, I just stood in shock. My stuff was back. All of it, from the looks of things. And it wasn't just scattered everywhere; it was as if someone had taken a picture prior to stealing everything and used that to put everything back in the proper place. Impossible.

I clasped my shaking hands together to still them and stepped out of my office and went to the top of the stairs. "Mason!" I called.

He appeared almost instantly at the bottom of the stairs, holding his cereal spoon in his fist like a dagger. "Jesus, Roxy. The sound of your voice . . . I thought something had happened to you."

"I need you to come upstairs and look at something."

He took the steps two at a time and followed me into the office, where I showed him what I'd found. "This was all gone," I said, gesturing to the equipment. "And now it's back exactly as it was before."

He nodded. "If the computer is back and they didn't find the code, what they will come for next is the person with the code. Here is where it starts getting interesting. I was getting tired of waiting."

"Are you . . . enjoying this?" I asked.

He looked a little guilty. "I like puzzles. I like the puzzle part."

I thought again about Leo calling Mason a liar, and my thoughts must have shown.

"Roxanne?" Mason said, moving the flat of his hand up and down in front of my apparently glassy eyes. "Stay with me here."

I expected him to follow up with some rant. He just muttered something I couldn't hear, then said, "Leonardo surely told you that I'm full of shit." He took me by the shoulders. "But you know me."

"Sort of," I agreed. I searched his eyes, but I didn't know what the hell I was supposed to be looking for. He'd spoken with an almost religious fervor. The sort of fervor that meant he was either totally convinced of his righteousness . . . or I was about to make a terrible mistake.

"We have context," he said.

"In the sense that you had sex with my old roommate." I shrugged. "Yeah, I guess we have context."

His right hand moved up and touched my cheek. "You *know* me," he repeated softly.

He kept saying that. I couldn't breathe. I couldn't concentrate on anything but the feel of his skin against mine, and that scared me to death—this impossible connection.

Take your hand off my face. Take your hand off my face. Take your hand off my face. I didn't want him to see inside me. I desperately didn't want him to see how I felt. I didn't want to know how *he* felt.

He took his hand off my face, and I know I must have been blushing bright red.

"I want you to move in," I blurted. "I don't feel safe." Then I made myself busy reorienting my equipment on my desk because I didn't want him to see the confusion on my face.

"My suitcase is in the car. I'll be right back."

SEVEN

When Mason decided to move in somewhere, he wasted no time making himself comfortable. It was positively vintage the way he sprawled himself all over the chaise longue in my office the same way he'd once commandeered the living room couch while dating Louise. It was maddening.

I spent one whole day investigating my computer for clues. Both then and today, he just walked into my office without knocking, complete with a Big Gulp and a book, and flopped right down. Like a husband or something.

Today, I complained. "You don't get to do that," I said. "You absolutely do not get to waltz into my place of work and commandeer my chaise like some . . . like some beer-swilling hog."

"I don't waltz," he replied. He didn't wait for me to answer before he pointed to the tiny refrigerator in the corner. "Say, do you have any beer?"

"No!"

"Too bad. I think you could use one."

I sat there, my hands frozen over the keyboard.

The office wasn't that big, what with all the boxes, and when I was on my computer it was strange to sense him behind me. Even more claustrophobic.

I would have liked to be able to tell myself that the small stick-on mirror protruding from the side of my monitor had always been there, that it was the product of my fear of someone looking over my shoulder while I was working, but it was clear there'd been no one in the house but me for some time—and the truth of the matter was that the newly appeared mirror pointed directly at the chaise where Mason was sitting. He seemed to realize that, because he would alternately try to be as annoying and effortlessly sexy as possible. There were a lot of yawn-and-stretch moves, which showed off a nice swath of six-pack, and if it got particularly stuffy in the office, there was no doubt in my mind that he'd actually take off his shirt.

I felt crowded by his presence. I felt . . . unreasonably aware of his presence. And yet, I didn't ask him to leave. The fact was, I wanted him there. I'd begun to accept him.

"Rox?"

I jumped.

He motioned to the computer with a tilt of his head. "Anything weird yet? Files missing, stuff moved around?"

"I'm almost ready to pack it in. If Leonardo took something, put something in, or altered something, then it's been totally masked. His engineers must be good." At first glance, everything was there. At second glance, everything was still there. I couldn't find any evidence that files had been moved or even read.

The only bread crumb I could find was that the last date and time of access had been reset to 00/00/00, 00:00:00. *That* was weird.

"So Leonardo didn't find anything he could use."

"Like some code, perhaps?" Mason hadn't revealed any more details of his mission.

He grimaced. "Like some code. But like I said, we'd have known about it by now if he had much to work with."

"How so?"

He looked at me over his book, cagey. "Oh. I just meant that he'd be kicking things into high gear if he could." And with that, he closed his eyes and stretched out, both legs propped up on the arm of the chaise.

Well, that had cleared up absolutely nothing.

"Mason?"

"Mmm?"

"You are so transparent. I don't think it's humanly possible to be more vague."

He didn't answer. Annoyed, I pulled up a search engine and typed the name I'd heard a million times but hadn't gotten an adequate explanation for:

> *Your search—"Leonardo Kaysar"—did not match any documents.*
>
> *Suggestions:*
>
> *Make sure all words are spelled correctly.*
> *Try different keywords.*
> *Try more general keywords.*

No documents. *No* documents? There was not one reference on the Internet to the man?

Most people were there somewhere. Okay, not necessarily most people. But a man like Leonardo? How could he possibly fly below the radar on the Web? That just wasn't a good sign.

Mason opened one eye and yawned.

"You're still here," I noted dryly. "Shouldn't you be out there somewhere trying to stop Leonardo from world domination or whatever he wants?"

"I'm waiting for some info from my office," he said absently, shaking the ice in his cup.

"Oh." I knew I wouldn't get any more from him.

Mason apparently had drunk all the way down to the really loud slurpy point of his Big Gulp. It was nearly impossible to concentrate, and why I didn't just throw him out would be fodder for thought for yet another sleepless night. So I couldn't work and I couldn't let on that all of my old feelings for him were seeping back into my system like . . . like . . . rusty water dripping from a faucet, constant and irritating.

Apparently today his choice between annoying and annoyingly sexy was the former. He slurped loudly again, knowing that I'd look. Which, of course, I did. I glanced behind me, ready to give him a piece of my mind, when my glance caught the cover of the book he was reading. The cover was . . . pink. Mason Merrick was reading a book with a pink cover? *Heh.*

I spun around in my chair and looked at him. "You're reading a chick book?"

He didn't look up. "I feel confident enough in my masculinity to answer in the affirmative without even the slightest hint of embarrassment."

I got up and walked over to him, twisting the paperback so I could see the cover. "You *are* reading a chick book," I repeated, snorting with laughter. It was just so incongruous.

He finally looked up at me over it. "Yes, he said. "I am." A beat passed, and he squinted at me. "Roxy, is that a smile? Are you smiling?"

I tamped whatever was happening with the corner of my mouth back into a straight line. "Does this happen often?" I pressed.

"No, you never smile. I'm beginning to wonder if you're coming down with something."

"Ha, ha. I was talking about the book," I said.

"Oh, this?" He gestured grandly with the paperback. "Absolutely. I feel it gives me the sort of insight into women you just can't get from personal experience."

I snorted again, imagining. "Mmm. That makes sense. Having wine constantly thrown in one's face can teach one only so much."

"You scoff, but consider this: Boil it down to its most simplistic components: Chick books are about relationships. What could be more beautiful, more"—he gripped at his chest, again entirely serious—"more meaningful than reading about two people destined to be together after a series of struggles?"

I leaned a little closer and set my internal calibration to double-plus sarcastic. "Hot damn, Merrick! That's not a tear welling in your eye, is it? Oh, my *God*, I'm getting so turned on!"

He dropped the book, leaped to his feet, and began backing me toward the desk in a feral sort of way. "Really?" he asked.

"I was kidding," I said hastily. And I had been.

Mason's reading a chick book had made me curious about the chick book, not about Mason. That's what I told myself. Except, this stalking business of his really was turning me on, which scared the hell out of me. I ducked under one of his grabby paws and beat a hasty retreat down the stairs, calling out, "Better read on, Merrick. Read on. 'Cause the grubby pages of that book are as close as you're going to get to a sex scene in this house."

"Relationships," he called out. "Feelings! Emotions! You should try them sometime, Roxy!"

I paused on the stairs, annoyed. I retorted, "I do have feelings, Merrick. I just don't like to waste resources." Then I tripped down the rest of the steps to the living room, wondering why I was giving him such a hard time.

Slumping on the couch, I found myself unsure what to do now that I'd made such a dramatic exit from my office. I heard a loud bang: Mason using the banister like a set of parallel bars to swing himself from the top of the stairs to the bottom. And then there he was suddenly in front of me, blocking me, moving in on me.

"Roxy." He leaned down and gave me that wide, All-American grin. "Are you flustered?"

I planted my palm in the middle of his chest and pushed him away, back out of my personal-space box, which would have been glowing red at the corners if it had been visible. There was no way I was going to wipe off the sweat on the back of my neck in front of him.

"I'm . . . don't . . . flustered," I babbled. *You moron, Roxanne.*

"Try forming a complete sentence."

I collected my wits. "Look, we might as well just say it. We've beaten around the bush before. We're experiencing physical attraction, commonly called a crush, but without the requisite hopes for an emotional attachment—at least on my part—that most often goes with such a condition. Not with your past and this present. And what that means . . ."

His grin got wider and wider.

"What that means," I repeated loudly, "is that in approximately two days I will be unable to stand the sight or smell or . . . or—"

"Taste?" he inserted hopefully.

"Unable to stand," I barreled on, "the . . . the mere existence of your presence, and in fact I will be *racking* my brain"—my voice just kept getting louder, and I couldn't help myself—"just *racking* it, trying to figure out how I could have ever felt *any* sort of attraction for you!"

"Well, at least you admit you're attracted to me now."

Shit. But I was up to it. Admitting it would end the unspoken—now spoken—nonsense between us.

"Okay, yes. And I was once before, what seems like decades ago. But if anything, that was just some kind of twisted puppy love. If I was as attracted to you as you seem to want to believe—erroneously attracted, I want to stress—then it was merely in the way that people are attracted to those hairless, scalpy dogs." I exhaled loudly, then unfortunately had to inhale a huge breath immediately because I seemed to be hyperventilating and knew he'd just scored on me . . . okay, more than just once. My resistance to his charms was ebbing. I actually felt light-headed and confused. Hell, I was emotional. I'd even go so far as to say aroused. Needy.

But Merrick wasn't showing any mercy. He went for the extra point. He marched right back into my personal space and stuck his index finger on my lips; I was breathing so hard I practically sucked it in. For God's sake, I could taste the salt. He leaned down, way too close, and said all low and rough, "Roxy, baby, if this is puppy love, then why do I feel like a wild dawg?"

And then he disappeared up the stairs, left me hanging, a bundle of mindless, senseless, tormented, and frustrated boneless limbs.

"Give it time," I warbled feebly, even though he was probably out of hearing. "You'll feel better soon."

I don't know if I was talking to me or him.

After waiting downstairs, reading magazines I'd already read many times, trying to let enough time pass that I could reasonably go back into my office, I squared my shoulders and marched up the stairs. A noise struck me before I was even halfway up: Mason snoring. I pushed open the office door and had a look.

His arms were tangled above his head, and God help me, but his T-shirt and sweater had sort of crept up so that a slice of toned skin sat there peering at me maliciously. I think I could have spent some significant time watching that swath were it not for a light on his cell phone that started blinking. He'd set it to mute, I guess. And it sat on the side table next to his keys.

I stared at the phone, wondering if he'd stuck any notes under my name and number. I stared a little closer and realized to my enormous delight that this wasn't so much a phone as it was a . . . gadget. Some sort of crazy, high-tech gadget. And it certainly wasn't my fault if he was dumb enough to leave it out and think I wouldn't start salivating or wanting to play with it.

I looked at Mason's face. The corner of his mouth twitched and he made a sleepy little snorting sound. Adorable, but I had more interesting things to focus on. Very carefully, I crept to the side table and held still for a moment to make sure he didn't wake up. He didn't, so I extended my arm slowly and picked the phone up and stepped away again, turning my back on Mason. I glanced over to see if he'd stirred, but he just lay there with his legs hanging over the side arm of the chaise.

So, I opened the device. It wasn't like any piece of technology I'd seen before. Not really. I mean, it had all of the usual bits and pieces one would expect in a handheld or whatever, but it expanded like a Swiss army knife into something much, much more. I cradled the clamshell design in my hands, staring down at the whisper-thin slices of green-gray opacity representing screens, a snap-out leaf that looked like a built-in microphone and detachable earbud system, and a whole deck of in and out plugs that weren't the usual sizes. Tiny controls on sliders popped up out of nowhere when my finger grazed over bumpy touch-screen fields of various shapes and colors. A red glow emanated from a small glass square: some sort of infrared or wireless technology that probably projected an input device or perhaps the content itself into thin air.

I'd never seen anything like this—because there

wasn't anything like it. Not even in what I'd read. The geek in me just about died from sheer happiness. He must have picked it up in Japan as a concept beta; it was too advanced. Frankly, it was an impossibility, but since I was holding it in my hand and could see for myself, the only thing that came even close to making sense was Japan. Or the military.

I tentatively pressed the pad of my index finger down on one of the screens. The screen saver flickered and the screen brightened. And even though I knew it was the lamest of the lame and lowest of the low, I continued snooping anyway—I wanted to see what kind of listing Mason had entered under my name.

It wasn't set up like a normal address book, but more like a radio bar with presets. The presets included ROX APT, ROX 7-ELEVEN, and ROX AGENCY. Kind of strange, but kind of exciting to find that not only did he have me as one of a limited number of presets on the top screen, but he had three of me. Though I couldn't imagine why he'd call Naveed at the 7-Eleven. Just on the off chance that I was making a doughnut run and could pick up?

"Give it to me, Rox."

I made a ridiculous sound, a kind of horrified squeal, as Mason took the device out of my hands.

"You want me looking in *your* computer?" he asked.

"No."

"All right, then." He was so quiet. It was a kind of controlled calm that bespoke more danger and intensity than all his yelling put together. His fingers flew over the device; I couldn't see what he was doing but the light went out.

"I apologize," I said. "It's just . . . it's unbelievable, that thing. All those—"

Mason didn't say a word. He frowned down at the device, his lips moving slightly as he read something off the screen that was serious enough to erase every ounce of the old, playful, flirty Mason from his being.

"Mason, I mean it. I'm really sorr—"

My words were arrested as he looked up at me. His face was totally blank, as if he hadn't the faintest idea what I was talking about. Like I was the farthest thing from his mind. He ran his hand over the back of his neck and looked at me impatiently. I pointed at the device and shrugged haplessly in a final apology.

He looked at my finger, then at the device. I think he might have cursed under his breath just before he looked back up at me. He blinked, and I could almost see the wheels in his brain stop and turn in reverse as he tried to find his place in the conversation. "Oh. Yeah. The smartie. The *reader.* Smartie is slang. But most of that stuff doesn't work," he said quickly. "It's just tricked out, is all." He stuffed it in his back jeans pocket and looked around, still disoriented, maybe from having just woken up.

"Mason."

He turned, startled by my vehemence, I guess. I was a little startled, too. "It's not just 'tricked out,' is it?"

"It's—"

"It's not just tricked out." I took a deep breath and forced myself to keep my cool.

"It's . . ."

I raised an eyebrow.

Mason stood in the middle of my office, his face a study in tension and strain, one hand compulsively curling and uncurling into a fist.

"It's not just tricked out . . . ," I repeated in a more encouraging tone.

"It's not . . . it's not just tricked out," he actually admitted.

My jaw dropped. We faced off. It seemed like half a day went by as we thought about how much we wanted to trust each other. That's what I was thinking, anyway.

Finally he nodded. "It's hard to know when the right time is. But you're right. I mean, there are things you're going to need to know, things you deserve to know. I can see . . ." He sighed heavily. "Maybe I waited too long."

I waited for Mason to really start explaining, afraid to say another word myself for fear I'd derail his decision to tell me the truth. He was going to tell me *the truth*.

"Just . . . don't be scared."

"Okay. Um, that's not ominous or anything," I said, throwing in a little laugh to try and keep things light.

"Yeah, sure," Mason said absently, chewing on his lower lip. Then he snapped his head up and looked me right into my eyes. "I mean, no. The thing is . . . it depends."

It depends? Fabulous.

EIGHT

I folded my hands on my lap and waited for the long-overdue explanation. Mason got up. He paced the room. He sat down next to me. He got up. He paced the room.

"Mason!"

"I know, I know." He looked around the office. "This is not the right space. I'm not feeling it. Let's go downstairs."

I gave him a look and he rolled his eyes and said, "Humor me. This isn't easy."

I followed him downstairs, and Mason pulled out a chair for me at the formal dining room table I never used. Then he pulled out a chair for himself. The whole thing was suddenly reminiscent of a boardroom meeting. Not to mention he was clearly stalling.

After another good five minutes, he finally opened his mouth. "It's a difficult thing, what I have to say. I really need you to keep an open mind. I need you to accept the possibility of the seemingly impossible. I've had to do this many times before, and I know from experience that it doesn't usually go down easy," he continued.

I waved impatiently. "Just say what you have to say. Just . . . lay it on me." He really had me on the edge of my seat now, so I was completely prepared to be underwhelmed. After all, I wasn't involved in any drug cartels, I hadn't been kidnapped, and to the best of my knowledge I hadn't broken any federal laws. There were lots of strange things going on, but it really felt like this explanation was going to be the real one.

Mason leaned in and forced me to meet his eyes. "Have you ever felt a strangeness in the world?"

"Oh, well—"

"A palpable discomfort?"

"I—"

"A sense of wrongness?"

"It's—"

"An inability to remember something you are certain you should know, something that you think must have been so obvious before? The sensation of something on the tip of your tongue but you can't spit it out? A really disturbing case of déjà vu?"

"Yes," I said.

"Don't answer so quickly. Think about it."

I did, and this time he didn't interrupt. "Yes. I can honestly say that I've experienced all of those things. And fairly recently, I might add. What's it about?" I wanted to get to the meat of the matter.

"That's realignment, Roxanne. That's the realignment of your reality."

I looked at him askance. "Um. I, don't remember you being the woo-woo type."

"It's not woo-woo. You see . . ." He took a deep

breath, a kind of here-it-goes look on his face, and said, "Fate can be altered. In casual terms, it's called wire crossing."

I pushed back an absurd little blip of dread. "I've never heard of it."

"That's because it hasn't entered the common language yet."

"Uh-huh. When does it enter the common language?"

"Later," he said, looking at me meaningfully.

Unfortunately, I didn't catch his meaning. "What do you mean by that?" I said. He just looked at me. He'd told me to open my mind and try to believe the impossible. "Later?" I repeated weakly.

"Later." He nodded and said, "In the future."

I pointed my index finger at him, too light-headed to formulate the question.

"I'm a wire crosser. My job is based in the future. This is usually where I get the drink of water."

I made no arguments. My mouth had gone completely dry, because either I'd let a lunatic into my house or what he was saying was true. He must be joking. "But we knew each other from before. In the past."

"That's true." He got up, and I heard the faucet turn on; he came back with a glass of water and put it down in front of me. I took a gulp.

"The thing about time is that it has no straight edges. It seeps through the cracks and binds things together again. It's a liquid thing, always moving. Seconds aren't like pennies, Roxanne. They can't be put in a jar to be spent at a later time. It's all about the now. It's always about now."

"That sounds like something Kitty used to say," I murmured.

The way his eyes held mine, it was almost trance-inducing. I felt calm—calmer right this moment than I had since he'd first reappeared.

"Okay, you're processing. Good. So . . . there's more." He kept looking at me like he was afraid I would freak out at any moment. "Each case can last years. One can even span a wire crosser's whole lifetime. I've been on your case since sophomore year of college."

"When you started dating Louise," I said.

Mason winced. "I couldn't date you," he said with a grin. "I can't even begin to say how that would have affected your case."

Which is maybe why you never really talked to me. And why nothing's happened between us now.

"Besides, you were different then," he added.

"Weren't you?"

"It's not really the same thing."

I sighed.

"Let me back up a little. I'm what you might call a restorer. I take on cases that involve restoring fate. Meaning, I work hard to lock in the original outcome of a given situation. Usually, we're called in to restore something only if someone has messed it up, which means that there's always an adversary wire crosser trying to stabilize his mess and there's one of us on the other side trying to right things again."

"Leonardo Kaysar is trying to mess something up and you're trying to stop him?" I clarified.

Mason nodded slowly, as if he feared I'd suddenly call bullshit. "The key players on a wire are called

Majors. Players who are affected or who could be used to finish a case are called Peripherals. Peripherals usually don't notice when anything happens. The reality splice is too small for them. But it's not so small for Majors, and the splice is not always very clean."

Bad splice, he'd said that first night. I'd assumed he was talking about the cut on his forehead.

"The closer things get down to the wire, the harder it is to make the splices clean."

Down to the wire. Wire crossers.

Mason peered at me as if I were a small child. "Are you okay with this so far?"

Um . . . no. "Go on." I was deathly afraid he'd stop talking, decide I couldn't handle the truth, or regret revealing things.

"You are a Major on a wire I've been following for years. You went on the hot list some time ago, but weren't red-lighted until . . . well, until recently."

"What's the hot list? What does red-lighted mean?"

He thought about it for a moment, then pulled out his smartie and navigated through the screens with his index finger. He held it up to me.

L. ROXANNE ZABOROVSKY. Next to a red light. In a list of other random names. Some had red lights; some were grayed out.

I stared at the L. "If it's not just tricked out, you've got to tell me more about how the tech works."

Mason managed a smile. "You like the shiny toys," he said.

I nodded, on the edge of my seat, "C'mon, c'mon."

"Okay. So, you need two major pieces of equipment. The smartie . . ." He held up his turbo-charged cell phone handheld device. "And a punch." He pulled a small silver object that I hadn't seen before out of his jacket pocket. It looked like a cross between an egg pricker and something a creepy dentist might get excited about.

"To cross a wire," Mason explained, "you work with a team to identify a sweet spot, then text in the move you want for execution and hope you hit it just right. But to move yourself between layers of time, you also need the punch. It injects a tiny amount of liquid nanotech into the body that will communicate with the smartie." He made a punching motion with the object.

"Ew," I said, flinching at the sight of the needle-head. "You had presets. How do they work?"

"Yeah. Fastest way to travel. Set the preset, punch, boom." He followed his words with three quick motions to illustrate, and I just about burst out laughing. It wasn't that I didn't believe him; it was that I did. And I had so many more questions for him, I didn't even know where to start.

"Leo made a move. He triggered your involvement as a Major in the case, and you went from hiatus—where you've been for years—to red-light status. There are people who keep track of these things. The minute he made that move, we both knew it."

"And you both tried to get to me first. But why? If I haven't done what it is you two are so interested in, why does it matter right now?"

"Once a Major gets established on a wire, whoever gets possession controls the game."

I just sighed. I was like a jump ball in a basketball match. Then I remembered the strange sense I'd had that the two men had been in the shadows in the street for some time, waiting for me. "Why did I go to the 7-Eleven in the first place? I can't even remember what I went to buy." Somehow it seemed important.

"I don't know," Mason said.

"But if you've been watching me for so long, wouldn't you have some idea what I was up to?"

"I wasn't there before you got there, Rox. I don't know what was on your mind. I wasn't around."

I wasn't sure I believed him.

"I was on the case trying to make my own move to negate his."

"Leo's? What is Leonardo Kaysar trying to do?"

"He's a very powerful man, Rox. He owns a major corporation. It's the modern-day incarnation of a business that has been in his family for centuries. He wants the code you've worked on for one of his projects. He wants to profit off you."

My head was swimming. I couldn't take in any more. "Prove this, Mason. You'll have to prove it. I just can't . . ."

"I know. It's okay." He went silent, weighing things, I guess. I would have given just about anything in that moment to see him angry or at least trading verbal zingers. It's the silence that always kills you.

Finally he looked up at me and said, "Okay, there's something we've really got to take care of. Believe me, if I've told you this much already, the rest is not that big of a leap. It's just . . ." He glanced at his reader, then looked up at me and went silent for so long I thought maybe all that pummeling from Leonardo was starting to kick in.

Finally he cocked his head and said, "There's a party. Would you . . . do you have a party dress?"

"A party?" I echoed in disbelief. One, he'd just given me the most insane explanation possible for my situation, and the shift in gears kind of threw me. Two . . .

"A party dress?" I blurted in horror. "You want to take me to a party?"

"After I check something out. It would be stupid to come all the way back to change."

"What are we doing first?"

"Do you remember when I said that Leo thought you'd written that code and that's why he stole your stuff? To look for it?"

"Yeah."

"Well, now he's trying something else. And we're going to try to slip a move in to stop him."

We stood there looking at each other. But if I wanted any answers, Mason was right about what he'd said a couple of days ago: I needed to open my mind.

"Okay," I said. "Party on." I headed upstairs, wondering if any clothing I owned was appropriate garb for matters of future and fate.

I still owned only one dress: the black-and-red number. And I still owned only one pair of dress shoes, which threw any potential nail-biting decision right out the window. I pulled the plastic off the dress and laid the garment on the bed. I pulled the shoes out of the shoe box, ignored the gun and bullets, and rummaged around in my bureau drawer for other appropriate accoutrements.

Holding up a black bra, garter belt, and stockings, I limited myself to five seconds to wonder if this combination was appropriate—or even me. The saleswoman's voice came into my head, a very distinct warning about the hazards of panty lines. Well, just like the lingerie I'd started wearing to bed, maybe this was a new me. I kind of liked it.

Getting dressed took about fifteen minutes, getting the rest of me arranged somewhat longer. Of course, I had enough makeup and hair products to fill an entire showcase of the Home Shopping Network, so it wasn't like I was wanting for anything. I just wished I knew how to use it all.

I paused at the top of the stairs. From my vantage point, I could see Mason pacing in and out of the living room. I pulled my foot back before my stiletto heel had time to strike the stair. Mason was muttering to himself, pulling at his collar, running his fingers through his hair. He looked like a nervous high school prom date. He looked like he was nervous . . . for me.

He turned and caught me watching. I immediately started down, gripping the banister for dear life. He moved to the bottom of the stairs and watched me descend. I swallowed hard as our eyes locked. Leo's green eyes were so much flash, it was hard to tell what, if anything was behind them. Mason's eyes weren't as good at hiding secrets; not from me. The intensity there burned like hot ice, sending a delicious shiver down my spine.

I paused, took a breath, then continued to the landing. Mason stared at me the whole way, a host of emotions crossing his face. Then, something seemed to click with him. It was as if he'd finally processed I was the same girl, and that slow, steamy smile of his unfurled just for me.

I moved in on him fast before he could get a good look at my flaming cheeks. Fussing with his tie just like they did in the movies, I said, "All things considered, Mason, you don't look half bad." He must have heard the quiver in my voice.

He slid two fingers under my chin and raised my face to his. "Not as good as you."

I shifted my focus right back down to his tie, which was already perfectly straight, then lost all concentration when I felt his gaze drop to the low-cut neck of my dress. I froze, my hands still on his collar.

"You afraid to look at me?" he asked.

"No," I managed to say. Heart pounding, I slowly looked up.

"I missed you all this time," he said, something inscrutable flickering in his eyes.

I missed you, too. I don't think I even realized until then just how much I'd wanted this.

He leaned in a little closer, so delicate with me, like he was afraid to scare me away. Our eyes half-closed, his lips nearly touching mine—I almost died when his fucking smartie clattered on the table in vibrate mode.

Mason broke away immediately to check it. After a moment, he shook his head in exasperation, pushed one of the buttons on the gadget and said, "We need to get going."

I stared at him, hurt by his brusque, all-business treatment, and questioning whether I'd read the whole thing wrong or not. All I could do was shrug as if I couldn't care less about what had just happened.

He opened the door for me; I stepped into the hall.

As Mason fiddled with the key in the lock, I suddenly remembered him wearing a similar suit with Louise standing next to him in a fabulous blue satin dress. A blinding flash showed him kissing the side of her face while she looked down, laughing. I guess I'd taken the pictures that night. I hated that I remembered something like that; it made me jealous and it made me question Mason's so-called justification for dating her instead of me if he ever really had any feelings for me then.

Mason headed for the car, turning when I didn't follow. "Rox? I—"

"Yeah. Sorry. I'm coming."

"No, it's just . . ."

I waited for him to finish his thought, my heart beating madly. I didn't know exactly what I was hoping he'd say; something to bring back the magic.

He held up his reader. "It's just, please don't touch this again."

I didn't know what I was hoping he'd say, but that certainly wasn't it.

NINE

The office building's security guard looked up from his newspaper and smiled. "Hey, Zaborovksy. Looking good." Then he buzzed open the security door and went back to his article.

I looked at Mason in wonder. He just shrugged and pulled me through the gate. "I don't know him," I said—but even as I said it, I thought, *Except I guess I do. Sort of. Now. Fuck. Mind overload.*

The eeriness of all of this changing reality was getting to me. I wanted the people I thought I knew to know me, and I didn't want to be reminded of my awkward place in this situation by all the people I didn't realize I knew who now seemed to know me. They were wandering around the various floors of the building in party gear.

I had no idea where we were going, but Mason seemed to know the floor plan like the back of his hand; we took an elevator to the sixth floor, then he walked us farther and farther into the guts of the building, eventually winding us through a cubicle farm. The farther along he dragged me, the stranger

I began to feel. I might not have remembered the security guard, but he had certainly seemed to know me—and that probably had something to do with why I imagined or remembered flashes of things as we moved along.

"Where are we going?" I mumbled to Mason as we walked. I stumbled, my eyes fixed on the office art lining the hallway. It was rather distinctive stuff, not the sort of works you order in bulk and have printed up for all of your satellite offices. Before, it had been the unfamiliarity that got to me; now it was the familiarity that had my skin crawling.

My hand slipped from Mason's grasp, and just as I had on the first night he came back into my life, on the next step I smoothly swiveled around and started walking back the way we'd come. Fear rippled through me.

"Roxanne—whoa, there." Mason grabbed my hand and wheeled me back around, pulling me up so sharply I fell against his chest. I looked him straight in the eyes.

"Why am I so scared?"

"We're near a sweet spot," he said. "And we have a big opportunity here."

"Wire crossing, red-lighted, layers, sweet spots . . . you've got to give me something more," I said, my frustration audible in my voice.

He looked up at the ceiling for a moment and tried to find the words to explain. "Every time Leo makes a move, we make one to cover it. But time is still going forward, no matter which part of your life you're living in. Eventually, Leo's moves and my covers will be so close in time . . . it can't go on forever."

"Thank God," I muttered.

"There's always a final move, Rox. When both parties know exactly what they want and the two sides are opposing, we've got ourselves a final step, which means there's a winner and a loser. You know, in a game of chess, where the true expert can look at a move and see that it sets the stage for a checkmate so many turns ahead? Sometimes the other player can get out of it. But sometimes the expert is right. Sometimes he knows many moves prior that what he has just done has locked in the fate of his opponent."

"Sometimes you can make a move that doesn't end the game but that makes the outcome inevitable," I repeated. "Then it becomes less about if and more about how."

Mason nodded. "This isn't the end of the game, but we're near a point where we can lock things in. That's a sweet spot."

"That doesn't explain why I feel so . . . bad."

He looked at me, and I saw about a hundred different things in his eyes, I couldn't make sense out of any of them. Did he pity me? Because that was just intolerable. Was there sympathy? Envy? Respect? I couldn't tell. So far, he'd simply made me a pawn, and I'd spent most of our time together being dragged behind him.

"Let's get this over with." He pulled me to another cubicle farm, turned, and then suddenly wheeled, blocking me from entering the workstation ahead of where we stood. "Rox . . ."

I waited.

"Brace yourself."

Excuse me? I stared at him. He stepped aside, and I slowly entered the work area. My shoes were killing me, but I would have taken a seat anyway; my knees went weak.

I knew without Mason having to say it that this was my office—if you could call a space this small and out in the open such a thing.

"Oh," I said. It was the only sound I could manufacture. Everything I had thought was missing from my home office after the computer theft had never been in my house at all; it had been in this building where I worked. In this version of reality, anyway.

It was nongeneric stuff. Job-specific stuff. But almost more convincing than that, it was personal stuff. I sat down in the task chair and looked around. There was a photo of a bunch of college pals, me and Kitty goofing off in the middle. A collage of cool pictures cut from magazines and pinned to the cubicle wall. A fun collection of small toys maybe I got from cereal boxes and fast food restaurant promotions. Wait a minute! Cereal companies and fast food restaurants didn't give away rubber rats. I scanned the assortment of windup toys and plastic action figures, and in the back of my mind—

"Aw, Rox. You still have him." Mason leaned over and picked up the rat by its tail.

I just stared at the toys; some of them seemed particularly familiar. Just like the ones Mason used to stick in my bed or slip into my bookbag. Oh my *god*. I was suddenly certain they were the same ones. How absolutely mortifying he'd caught me with them now. "They're toys. They're fun. Why wouldn't I keep them?" I mumbled. I pushed away the rat Mason was swinging in my face and tried to focus on the big picture.

There was a life here, a life I couldn't really connect to my brain but that seemed a lot more positive than I remembered. Of course, it didn't mean that what I was looking at was the real thing. Maybe this was just a reality relic, as it were, something that was still in my brain but that had no meaning for the long haul.

I swiveled around and pressed the space bar on the keyboard. The screen flickered and came to life, and I saw the mirror on the side of my monitor. I looked into it at Mason. "What should I be looking for?"

He sighed and I knew he still wasn't sure. "Just describe to me what you see and if anything surprises you," he suggested.

"I see a desktop with the usual shortcuts and a couple of zip files. Looks like I downloaded a virus program. Nothing unusual there." I clicked on My Documents. The file hierarchy matched the one I'd set up on my computer at home.

"What?" Mason asked. "Is something wrong?"

"It's exactly the same," I said, clicking on the first folder, labeled *AHOT*: *Hot* meaning my most pressing projects. The *A* would alphabetize the folder to the top, just as I'd always done on my home computers. "That's what's wrong. It's exactly the way I organize my files at home. The labels are all the same."

"What about the contents?" he asked.

I clicked on *AHOT*. The folder was empty. I looked over at Mason and he shrugged. "Click around and see if anything jumps out."

I clicked around, then swiveled around to face Mason. "I recognize the labeling system and the preferences are the ones I always set. But I recognize none of the projects." I pressed my index finger against the screen atop the list of documents. "Never heard of it. Don't remember it. Maybe I worked on this, but maybe I didn't, can't . . ."

Mason nudged my shoulder, prompted, "What?"

I stared at my finger pressed against the glass. "It's weird, Mason. This is me. This is my work. So, what's back at my house? Who's living there? Who's working there? We just came—"

Mason took my finger off the glass and curled my fist closed. But he didn't answer. He had no answers for me.

"Go ahead and disconnect the external hard drive. It's a backup. We'll take it with us just in case. Then fry the hard drive on your computer and we can go."

I checked to make sure the external hard drive had been doing what it was supposed to do, then disconnected it and handed it to Mason. I was tempted to smash my fist into the monitor, but that wouldn't fry the information. Instead, I erased the main hard drive's contents, then set the computer to reformat.

"It's doing its thing," I said numbly. "We can go."

We took the elevator back downstairs, the external hard drive's cords dangling from Mason's grip. I suppose he knew the best way to conceal a crime is to walk out in the open with it.

Mason stopped at the entrance, where the office party was now in full swing, and he turned to me with a crooked smile. "We have time for a drink. I had you get dressed just in case."

I turned away from the look in his eye. "I just want to go home," I mumbled.

He looked disappointed, but he put his hand on the small of my back and steered me to the exit, holding the door open. I slipped by him into the cool evening and we headed around the building toward the parking lot, me trying not to fall into the landscaping as I balanced on my killer heels.

Mason grabbed me by the elbow as I almost went down. But even when I was steady he didn't let me go. He just stood there, chewing his lip. "I'm sorry, Rox," he said. "I'm sorry for putting you through all this."

I blinked back tears. "Yeah. Me too. So . . . the hard drive. Do you think what you want is on there?"

He shrugged. "The odds aren't particularly good, but we'll see."

" 'The odds aren't particularly good'? Is that like a no?" A bitter laugh escaped me, and I leaned back against the wall surrounding the edge of the building. "How will we know when it's enough?" This hell seemed never ending.

Mason flipped the top of his phone and held it out to me. My name was still at the top of his list, the DEFCON number or whatever the hell it was still blinking red. "Apparently HQ has reason to believe this isn't the clincher."

I swore, and was just about to break down when I saw Mason lose patience with me. He perched the hard drive on the top of some shrubbery and stuck his hands on his hips. "You know, there are people in situations like yours who have the bad luck to find themselves having to take part in a civil war or kill somebody or whatever. I asked you to look on a computer and then asked if you wanted to get a drink. You want to explain to me where the big problem is?"

I opened my mouth to reply, but he overrode me. "I'm going to do what it takes to get you out of the red, Rox. I'm not just about this case. You should know that. And if I ask you to go to a party and take your dress off and . . . and dance in your panties with a fucking lamp shade on your head in order to help me, then that's what you should damn well do!"

"I'm not wearing any panties," I snarled.

The look on his face went from anger to confusion to a kind of horror. But he was definitely turned on. And I liked it.

I shrugged innocently and said, "The woman at the store said that because of the way this dress is cut I'd have panty lines. She told me just to go with the garter belt and stockings and bra."

Mason gulped.

"Black. Black lace garter belt," I said, sliding my tongue over my lower lip.

Mason seemed to have lost the ability to look me in the eye. He didn't know where to look. He didn't know what to do. And turning him on was turning me on. I felt powerful and sexy and in control of something for once.

"French stockings, I think," I said, putting the last nail in the coffin. "The kind that are so delicate you can wear them only once."

Mason grabbed me by the shoulders and backed me into the shadows of the building. His eyes bored into me. I could practically see the wheels turning in his head. Mason wasn't stupid at all. He wasn't the dumb jock with the transparent pea-size brain that I'd once thought was banging Louise; he was the chess-club genius, forced to play every moment out far, far in advance.

What's the move, Mason?

If I'd been scared walking into that party, it was nothing compared to what I felt now. And yet, of all things, the words that came from my lips were these: "I had a friend in college who always used to say to me: 'Just remember, Roxanne, it can't always be about tomorrow. Sometimes it's about right fucking now.' "

I'm not sure what it was, maybe the phrasing I'd used. Mason's mouth came down on mine, his hands plowing through the silky fabric of my dress. I could feel his fingers verify the description I'd given: the lace, the tiny clips from the stockings, the satin. He buried his face in my neck while confirming for himself the audacious lack of panties. As he touched me there, we gasped at the same time. His fingers streaked away, leaving damp trails against my thigh. He loosened the front of his trousers and I knew he was either going to ask or beg off.

"Yes," I said preemptively. I wanted this.

He hooked his arm under my thigh and lifted my knee. I looked at his hand sliding up the length of my leg, the silk stockings, the garter ribbons peeking out where Mason had moved my dress away, the stiletto heel. I'd never felt so hot in my life.

"Roxanne," he said, looking straight into my eyes as he entered me. "Roxanne . . ."

He fucked me hard against the wall. It went fast. I loved the rawness of it, the unabashed sexuality. I hated that he made me come so fast and followed right after. He never took his eyes away from mine. And that alone . . . that alone was just about everything.

TEN

I sat in the passenger seat of Mason's Mustang with my elbow sticking out through the open window, not daring to look at him for fear of giving away too much of what was in my heart.

"Hey, Roxanne," he yelled over the wind.

I looked at him, knowing that I was grinning like a fool. He grinned back.

"What?" I yelled in response.

"Nothing!"

We smiled at each other like a couple of lunatics.

"Are you sure?" I asked.

"I was just wondering . . ."

"Yeah?"

"Do we need to have a conversation about what happened?"

I just kept grinning. "No!"

He nodded. Then he shook his head with mock incredulity and yelled, "Okay!"

We were both laughing and stealing glances at each other, letting the wind whip my hair to shit. He shifted again and changed lanes, his foot glued to the accelerator. All I could think was that a speeding ticket would be more than worth it for feeling like this.

Our destination was on the other side of town. We'd have to pass my neighborhood on the way over, and Mason checked his handheld for the umpteenth time before pulling over to get some gas.

He eased up to the pump and hopped out. I sat in the car and stared down the street to the spot where I'd first come across Mason and Leo what now seemed like a million years ago. There was no reason really to feel this way, but dread tickled lightly up my spine when I looked over at the nearby 7-Eleven. Part of what bothered me so much about all of this was the simple fact that I was beginning to anticipate things. I stared at the shadowy figure of Naveed behind the counter, wondering if now that I knew more of the story, I'd be able to recognize any clues I'd missed if I saw them now.

I swung the car door open. Mason was still holding the pump up to the car. I answered his questioning look by cocking my head in the direction of the 7-Eleven. "Want anything?"

"A Coke would be great."

I nodded, hopped over the low cement barrier dividing the convenience store from the gas station, and pushed through the door.

"Hey, Naveed!"

He looked up from wrestling with the cash register tape and smiled. "Good evening, Roxanne. You look very nice!"

"Thanks." I eased over to the candy rack en route to the refrigerated section in the back, glancing automatically up at the round security mirror to see if the storekeeper was watching me this time. Maybe there'd be something here. Some kind of trigger I missed or just wasn't ready for. I peered down the massive row of sweets. Was I looking for a message attached to the Gummi Bears rack? A note written on Pixy Stix?

"This is ridiculous," I muttered. Mason would laugh his ass off if he were watching. I gave up and grabbed his soda and a bottle of water from the refrigerator and went to the counter.

"How's the family?" I asked as Naveed rang up the purchase.

"Excellent, excellent. My son just returned with his report card." He beamed at me. "All As."

"Fantastic. How's the little one?"

"The little one?" He tucked the change in my hand.

"Your daughter," I said, pocketing the money.

Naveed burst into peals of laughter. "What would I do with a daughter? When my wife gets pregnant again, I will tell her I want another son."

I slammed my hand down on his so fast that he must have thought I was about to rob him. "I would love to see your family picture," I said, trying not to lose my shit.

Naveed's look of surprise faded. He put his hand on his heart. "Roxanne, I am flattered you are so interested." He took out his wallet and handed me the photo. Dad, mom, son. No daughter.

"You have a lovely family," I said, my voice hoarse. I backed away from the counter. "If you ever have a daughter, I'm sure she'll be a genius."

I stumbled out of the store. Mason was leaning on

the side of his car, his hands folded across his chest. He saw me coming and moved to get back in the Mustang, but he must have seen my face. "Roxanne?"

I couldn't even articulate the rage I was feeling.

"It's okay," he said, in that too-calm voice guaranteed to drive a not-very-calm person over the edge.

"You don't even know what you're talking about," I said. "It's *not* okay. You killed Naveed's daughter."

The look on his face was priceless. Surprise. Guilt. Confusion. It was all there, and I'd nailed him but good. "Naveed doesn't have a daughter," he finally said.

"He did," I insisted. "She was getting bigger. She was going to be a genius."

"He didn't. Not anymore."

"Not *anymore*. So he did."

Mason sighed. "Um, for all intents and purposes? No."

"I don't *understand*." But I did understand. Obviously something Mason or Leo had done while crossing wires and altering fate had changed certain realities in such a way that Naveed either got home too late that night or his wife had such a crappy day that she wasn't in the mood when he did get home. There was no daughter. And there had never been a daughter. Anymore. And the only person in the world who was missing her was me.

"Are we really the only ones who know she's gone?"

"I'm good at what I do," he said with a cocky smile. "It was a seamless splice, and a damn fine wire cross."

I wasn't impressed. "Okay, so that's why Naveed doesn't know. Why do I know?"

"Because you're the Major on this wire, remember? It would be very, very difficult for a Major to miss all of the evidence before it morphed into her understanding of current reality. Even the best of us can't do it with most Majors. And I have to say, you have an unusual capacity to keep one reality separate in your mind from another. I guess that's what comes from living inside your head so much."

He took the water bottle out of my hand and opened it, handing it back without a word. I drank it down.

"I still don't understand why *I'm* the Major," I mumbled. I'd never been a major anything. I'd never been the point, the center. I'd never made a meter go into the red, and I was never the cause for alarm. I just flew under the radar, and when I was feeling particularly morose, it sometimes crossed my mind that the world wouldn't miss me at all if I up and disappeared.

I thought again of my so-called family. I hardly existed to anyone, and I hadn't mattered to anyone for a long, long time. Until now.

Then I thought of Mason and me up against the wall and indulged in the thrill the memory ran up my spine. I guess I mattered to him, and that was a lot.

"Roxy?"

"Yeah."

"I know this looks bad, but there's something I want you to consider." He had his palms up in a defensive posture. I narrowed my eyes as he stumbled over his words. "All you know is that Naveed had a daughter in another version of your reality. You don't know anything else about his life. It's entirely possible that in this version, Naveed is living a better life."

"That's a convenient way to look at things," I scoffed. "You can't just do that to a person. You can't . . . It's just not right. She never had a chance to grow up and do anything! She didn't get a say."

I looked back over my shoulder at the store. Somehow I felt like Naveed's loss was my fault. "Do you know anyone whose life improved in a subsequent version?"

"My girlfriend."

For a moment I couldn't breathe. I should have known. I should have known that this oversexed lady-killer I remembered from years ago couldn't have changed that much. It was all I could do not to humiliate myself by crying in front of him. It made me sick that I'd had sex with him and he could brush it off as if it were nothing. There wasn't even an ounce of remorse on his face. He just calmly drew a squeegee over the windshield of his car.

I stared at the squeegee and then the water trough, and then at his face, wondering why he was squeegeeing so carefully and precisely, until it dawned on me that he didn't have the balls to look me in the eyes. So much for mattering.

You thought you had me figured out. Miserable fuck. You thought that you could use me and I'd just fall at your feet and beg for more like one of those girls who invite their boyfriends to treat them like shit. But the thing about me that you obviously don't understand is that I am a highly evolved human being, able to build exponentially upon what-

ever units of intelligence enter my brain. And I know when I've been had.

I carefully stuck the Coke and the water bottle on top of the refuse can. Mason tossed the squeegee back in its trough. "Roxanne, look. I've thought a long time about what I should tell you and what I should keep to myself. It's very complicated and—"

I had to blink a couple of times to see through my rage. "You miserable, piece-of-shit liar."

"It's not like that, Roxanne; I swear. It's—"

" 'It's not *like* that'? Don't even try that one."

"*What* one? Sorry, but I don't under— Wait, I don't want you to think I was apologizing right there. I meant 'sorry' in the 'I didn't understand what the hell you meant by that' sense. Not sorry as in 'I would take back having sex with you.' Because I'm not totally in the wrong. I'm not that kind of sorry."

I backed Mason up a couple of steps, and when he stopped moving I came right up to him and stuck my palm flat on his chest. In different circumstances it might have been a nice moment. "I understand the type of sorry you are," I said. "You're one sorry piece of crap. You're sitting there, lying to me, doling out little meaningless tidbits of information, trying to play me for a fool. Which I obviously am. Thinking I knew anything about you. Letting you manipulate me. Letting myself care about you. You are scum, Mason. You are a miserable, miserable excuse for a human being. You are . . ."

He let me yell. Mine was a beautifully delivered soliloquy with just about every clichéd term for Mason being a jerk I could think of. It went on for quite a while. I thought I might get tired, but, no, I didn't.

"Roxanne—"

"If you say what I think you're going to say, I'm going to lose it." I stepped away from him and crossed my arms over my chest.

"Roxanne—"

"Don't say it, Merrick, I'm warning you."

Mason lifted both hands, palms forward, all innocent-like. And then he went and pushed the button: "It doesn't mean what you think."

"Dammit, Merrick!" A lot can happen in the blink of an eye. One minute I was staring at his face; the next minute I'd hauled back and slammed my closed fist right into it. His head snapped backward. His right arm flew back, making a nasty cracking sound as it hit the gas pump. I stood there in total shock, staring at my fist.

I don't do that . . . do I? Since when did I do things like that? *I'm not a badass. Am I a badass?*

A weird keening sound from Mason, who was huddled down by the wheels, pulled me out of my daze. For good reason. There was blood everywhere, all over his hands, pouring from his nose. I went down on my hands and knees alongside him and touched his cheek to try to see what we were dealing with here. He swore up, down, and sidewise, cringing away from me like he wasn't sure if I was going to help him or try to punch him again. I leaped up and ran into the 7-Eleven as fast as I could, grabbed a roll of paper towels from a shelf, and ran back out the door.

Mason was still kneeling, all off-kilter, delivering a stream-of-consciousness litany of curses I obviously deserved for having hit him like that, regardless of whom he didn't tell me he was also sleeping with. I ripped the plastic off this huge roll of brand-new paper towels and flailed around, trying to get the plastic to stop sticking to my bloody fingers. Mason was doubled over at this point.

Whether I really was or wasn't the sort of person who went around punching people in their faces, at this particular moment I was definitely out of my element. I did the best I could, jamming wads of paper towel up his damaged nose, unwinding the paper towel in one ridiculous contiguous piece, and slapping it against his face to sop up the blood. Tears streamed down his cheeks. I knew that later he'd try to explain them as involuntary, that the pain was simply acute enough to draw them from him without his having a say-so, but I didn't plan on bringing any of this up later anyway.

"I'm not sure what to say here," I said nervously.

He glowered at me. "I'll start," he croaked. "I have two things to say. One, please get me to a hospital. Now. Two, don't fuck the moment up by saying you're sorry. Now, *you* go."

I tried to think objectively. I tried to think about it all from Mason's point of view. What would Mason Merrick say at a time like this? What would he say if he'd punched Leonardo?

"Suck it up and take it like a man," I blurted.

He looked at me, then delicately pressed the paper towel to his nose. Aside from the fact that I could tell he kind of wanted me dead, somewhere in there I think he was also impressed.

ELEVEN

I tucked Mason into the car. He held his arm to his chest, wincing, and I almost felt guilty when I took the keys from him; I had to work hard to conceal the sudden thrill that shot up my spine as I walked around the car and took control.

We got to the hospital and they took Mason almost immediately, probably because the amount of blood from his nose made the injury look worse than it actually was. The nurse came back to get me after about fifteen minutes and led me to a room where Mason sat on the examining table, his back slumped against the wall and his face contorted with pain. His hurt arm was cradled in his hand.

"Hi," I said.

"Don't even think of asking if I'm okay."

The nurse gestured for me to come back outside the room with her. "He's a bit surly," she said, handing me a clipboard with some paperwork. "He took a good one."

"I didn't mean to hit him so hard," I said, sounding more bitter than I'd meant.

The nurse lifted an eyebrow.

I shrugged my shoulders resignedly and signed the bottom of the document. "He told me he had a girlfriend after we'd already had sex." *Not to mention he disappeared my local convenience store manager's infant daughter, which I find, to say the least, heartless.*

I handed the clipboard back. The nurse's eyes were narrowed. "Men. What do you want to bet that by the time you get home he'll have a perfectly reasonable-sounding excuse, in spite of the fact that there is no such thing as a reasonable excuse for this sort of thing."

"Yeah," I agreed. We swapped a couple more girl power–centric complaints against cheating men, and I kind of enjoyed the camaraderie of the circumstances, in spite of the fact that my real experience with this sort of thing was limited to this one thing with Mason.

We went back inside. Mason was testing the range of his hurt arm, checking out the still-functional musculature and poking gingerly at the array of tender spots on his face. The nurse put her hand on my shoulder and whispered, "Don't you worry, honey."

A good person would have asked her what she meant, particularly in light of the evil glint in her eye, but I didn't. A good person would have clarified things when she said, "I'll bet a light sedative would be helpful. And let's make sure we stabilize that arm, shall we?"

I didn't. "Let's," I said.

The nurse gave me a smile, picked up an enormous needle from the side table, and turned to Mason.

"Now, Mr. Merrick. If you could just turn around . . ."

Half an hour later, I was helping a glassy-eyed Mason to my living room couch. He lay there looking totally lobotomized, his right arm completely encased in a massive plaster apparatus. It was significant enough to be called an *apparatus*. Apparently my jilted nurse friend had released her aggression by encasing Mason's right arm in enough plaster to redo the walls of my place. The end of the construction in particular was a masterwork: she'd triple-wrapped it. And I'd essentially okayed this construction of a club limb.

Shame filled me. I was still incredibly hurt. I felt betrayed and sort of disgusted that I'd actually thought I'd pierced Mason's armor the way he had mine, that I meant something more to him than the other girls he'd screwed, but this was a petty, petty thing I'd done. And it did beg the question: when had I started being the girl who fucked guys against walls, punched people out, and took revenge by conspiring with the medical community to immobilize the limbs of cheating boyfriends? When had I started being the girl I'd sort of fantasized about being? And in reality, was it as good as it sounded?

I sat down on the couch next to Mason, whose head was lolling back, and I pushed play on the DVD player. A movie started up where I'd left off, the girl on film kicking the shit out of some bad guy, wearing a nasty pair of boots and some sort of figure-enhancing catsuit, and armed to the teeth.

Mason made a gargling sound. I looked over. "Do you want something to drink?"

No answer. I fast-forwarded. The girl was talking into a headset as she crawled through the bushes with a huge machete.

Reality is such a relative thing.

I sighed and flipped the movie off, tossing the remote to the side and feeling totally unsettled. I looked over at Mason and felt tears pinch at my eyes. It was no good; I was crappy at revenge. To successfully achieve revenge, you had to be unhampered by feelings of regret. I was soft. I'd always been soft. I leaned over and pushed my hand gently against Mason's chest. He was malleable in his drugged state and slumped gently into the cushions at his back. I lifted his legs up and arranged his bulbous cast in the most comfortable position possible.

Checking my watch and remembering what the nurse had told me, I calculated that Mason's sedatives would wear off in about twenty minutes. He'd take a moment to orient himself and a minute to freak the hell out that we were supposed to be somewhere we weren't. *Sigh.*

I went upstairs and lost myself on the Internet for a while.

"Roxanne! Roxaaaaaaaaaaaanne! I'm going to kill you."

I took a deep breath and went downstairs. Mason wasn't on the couch. He was in the kitchen. A half-dressed Mason, his suit jacket hanging loosely off the side of his frame. Which was, of course, because he couldn't get the enormous bulb at the end of his plaster cast through the right sleeve. His smartie was jiggling in vibrate mode on the countertop.

Over the grinding whir of my electric carving knife,

Mason turned furious eyes on me. "It was a sprain, Rox. Not even a sprain. A bad, bad bruise. A bruise, okay? You left the paperwork on the table. And was it necessary to tranquilize the piss out of me?"

Maybe what I'd done wasn't so bad. Maybe total regret and massive guilt weren't entirely necessary under the circumstances. Maybe I was being too hard on myself. My mouth twitched.

"It looked pretty bad, Mason," I said as seriously as I could. "And let me tell you, it sounded extremely bad. I was almost certain something had cracked. I figured I should err on the side of caution. After all, I did throw the punch."

He gave me a look of death and went back to his attempts at drawing the carving knife through the white cement.

He gestured to his smartie with his chin, and through gritted teeth he hissed, "We've got to get going, and I can't go anywhere like *this*."

I shrugged. "Then maybe this isn't as important as you make it sound."

He switched the knife off and laid it very precisely down on the table as he mustered as much dignity as a man with a nose bandage, wearing half a suit, using a meat knife to attempt to remove a plaster-of-paris club limb could possibly muster. "This, L. Roxanne Zaborovsky, is the most important event of your life."

The words hit hard. "Okay," I said. "Okay." I walked over, ducked under his arm, and switched on the knife. He used the draping side of his jacket to cover my dress while I worked the meat knife in and managed to get just enough plaster bulb off the top of the casing to get his arm through the sleeve.

Once the jacket was on and the last of the plaster particles removed, I smoothed his hair down, straightened his tie, and tried not to stare at the purple bruises settling in around the bridge of his nose.

"Roxanne."

I looked at him, surprised by the intimate tone of his voice.

"When this is over, I think you at least owe me a moment to completely explain myself."

Do you mean, to excuse *yourself?*

"You totally misunderstood. I don't have a girlfriend now. I had a girlfriend."

"Uh-huh."

"I just don't think of her as my 'ex,' you know, because we didn't break up. But, I don't know how much to tell you. I don't want to mess things up."

My blood started to boil. "I think we're a little beyond that."

"The thing is . . . Leo disappeared her."

I looked up at him, totally startled. He was either a really good liar and knew exactly how to push my buttons . . . or he had lived through something really hard. I knew how upsetting it was to discover that a convenience store manager's kid whom I'd never even met didn't exist anymore because of an artificial shift in reality; to lose someone you really loved to such a thing and to be so cognizant of it . . . that had to be truly horrible.

"It's why I got into this line of work," he said, suddenly looking overcome with emotion.

I didn't know what to think. I wanted to believe him. He was totally believable. Under the circumstances, what he'd described was totally believable. I wished the nurse hadn't said what she'd said. And I sure as hell wished I hadn't let her do what she'd done.

I could have touched him, maybe touched his shoulder or put my hand on his good one. I could have said that I was sure we'd work things out. I just didn't have the balls. I was afraid he was lying, and I was afraid he would reject me.

"Let's go," I said, breaking the moment. "This is the most important event of my life."

TWELVE

Mason and I walked to his car, and I tried to feel like he really, really deserved it when he forgot that he was substantially handicapped and probably still had enough sedative in him to make driving illegal. He managed to wedge himself into the driver's seat but couldn't figure out how to hook the tips of his fingers far enough around the stick shift knob to drive the car; I hadn't cut the plaster down far enough.

I kept my mouth shut as I walked around to the driver's side. Mason got out of the vehicle and came around to the passenger side. "Shit. Are you kidding?"

"What?" I asked.

He slid into the seat, then reached into the back with his good arm and pulled the hard drive onto his lap. Glaring at me he muttered, "I can't believe you just left this in the car."

"I'm sorry."

"101 South," he said sulkily. "Let's go."

"Sure thing," I said. Gunning the engine, I headed for the freeway on-ramp.

Halfway down the block, I knew we had a situation. Mason was leaning over me, practically, his good hand curled tightly into a fist and white around the knuckles. I felt quite sympathetic actually. The poor guy really did want control back. Every time I shifted gears, he'd wince slightly, or make a sound like a sudden sucking in of air. From my peripheral vision I could see his feet working in the footwell, one on the imaginary brake, one for the imaginary clutch.

"Everything okay over there, Merrick?" I asked.

"Fine," came the reply, followed by a fake, rigid smile.

Poor sap. We weren't even on the freeway.

"You didn't complain about the way I drove you to the hospital and back."

He glanced at me. "I was preserving what was left of my nose."

I hit the on-ramp and stepped down on the accelerator in what I considered to be the appropriate way to merge: actually at or exceeding the speed limit. Mason blanched, and I saw his bad arm swing out away from his body slightly, subconsciously trying to shift.

Now didn't seem like an appropriate time to mention that I hadn't driven in years, nor that my license had expired accordingly. I floored it, the roar of the engine and the way we basically blew out onto the freeway making me feel naughty. Now I was full-out grinning, taking the lanes past 80 mph, weaving in and out of traffic in the worst possible way. At some point I was going to have to suck it up and tell Mason I at least understood a little bit why he had such a thing for this car.

Apparently, I wasn't the only one experiencing a rush from freeway driving that day; in the rearview mirror a black sports car followed my pattern of feint and parry. Still feeling the pleasure of the ride, I swerved into the lane next to us to give it room to pass. It turned down my offer, leaving me stuck behind a Volkswagen van that should have been in the slow lane. The sports car accelerated before zipping in behind me.

"Merrick . . ."

"Jesus, just keep your eyes on the road," he blurted.

As the pavement unrolled rapidly in front of me, my foot instinctively pressed down harder. My hands started to sweat on the steering wheel as the needle shifted past eighty-five. "Merrick, you see that black sports car?"

He checked his mirror. "The one practically up our ass?"

"Yeah. Was he already on the freeway when we got on, or did he get on the freeway with us?"

Mason squirreled around in the seat and stared out the back window. The rearview mirror reflected the guy so close on our tail that Mason could have exchanged phone numbers by holding a business card up to the glass. He turned back. "It's Leonardo. We need to get away from him. Now."

"Leonardo Kaysar? You're kidding."

"Does this seem like a smart time to kid around?"

He looked so longingly at the steering wheel it was almost painful. I wasn't sure what the sports car wanted me to do, and I'd long since stopped feeling like I knew what I was doing. I was beginning to wish Mason were driving almost as much as he did.

I couldn't see our pursuer's face clearly, but I could see he held a cell phone up to his ear. Kaysar's nonchalance under the circumstances infuriated me. "He's going to kill us if he's not careful."

Mason looked at me like I was insane. "Do you actually think he's trying not to?" He pulled his handheld out and started madly texting, then switched to voice. "What do you got? Uh-huh . . . uh-huh . . . still red, then. Jesus. Keep an eye on the GPS and have a taxi waiting at the endpoint." He hung up, slamming the smartie's clamshell casing closed.

"I think Leonardo wants us to pull over," I said, speeding up more.

"Don't," Mason said.

I took the Mustang to ninety. Leonardo kept up. I drove even faster. Mason was about to have a stroke, sitting there next to me as I jumped in and out of the lanes, trying to get lost in traffic.

Swearing continuously under my breath as if the word *shit* were some kind of mantra, I gripped the steering wheel and held on for dear life. Mason started to yell at me, choosing this moment to become a backseat driver, but the sledgehammer sound of my heart beating at three times the normal rate drowned out his exact words. I wiped the sweat out of my eyes with my sleeve, which apparently incensed Mason even more, although I wasn't sure why.

The sports car touched my back bumper so gently that I couldn't help but be impressed. I lost control of the car for only a second, and swerved. Mason leaned over, still shouting driving instructions.

The sports car touched the bumper again, this time not so gently. I lost control of the car again for a moment, this time Mason's car coming off the two right wheels for a second, the entire vehicle almost airborne. The sports car had sort of latched on to the back, grinding and bumping and sliding our car and trying to manipulate my driving.

"You wearing your seat belt?" I asked Mason in a voice that was almost normal—save for the hoarse quality brought on by the lack of saliva in my mouth. He had no time to answer; Leonardo forced us forward and a car on either side sandwiched us in. A monster construction vehicle loomed into view up ahead, and there was no safe way to slow down.

Mason rolled down the window with his left hand and, with an insane amount of calm, threw the external hard drive we'd taken through the window into the path of an oncoming vehicle in the opposite lane. I heard something hit, maybe crush, and then stopped caring. A series of mathematical calculations zipped in one ear, through my brain, and out the other as we stared at the back of the braking truck ahead, into which I was being forced.

I screamed, let go of the steering wheel, and clawed my fingernails into Mason's thigh. He took me by the scruff of the neck and jammed me down in the footwell of the car. We were going to hit the back of the truck and go under.

A huge impact rocked the car, drowning out the sound of the engine and slamming my head against the bottom of the steering wheel. The Mustang careened violently to the right before swaying left again.

I screamed over and over, unable to wrap my tongue around any other noise. The high-pitched sound of metal scraping metal like the worst case of fingernails on blackboard you've ever heard filled the air, followed by shattering glass, sparks, and a horrible anticipatory feeling that "it" hadn't happened yet, but would. The top of the car was tearing away.

I shifted in the well and moved my hand away from my face for a second to eyeball the scene around me, then covered it quickly, protecting it again. Crap was flying everywhere. Grit, gravel, dust, exhaust . . . car parts? There was the hulking shadow of the truck above. Then came the lunging and retreating sensation, like we were caught on something that was giving way. Mason's good arm flailed up out the well. A good sign. He seemed to be trying to reposition himself.

He turned to me and yelled something. My throat wasn't working. I just shook my head and mouthed, *What?*

The car lurched forward and we both ducked down again. He moved sideways instead of upward as much as he could to get near me. I heard him say very faintly, ". . . come out the other side. Be ready. . . ."

We were jammed underneath the truck, and the lurching sensation was the Mustang trying to break loose. As it inched farther under the truck toward the front, and sparks shot out from the metal contact points, it occurred to me there was at least a fifty percent chance that between the truck's gas tank and our own, something would blow.

The truck eased up, the driver undoubtedly realizing that something unusual was transpiring under his vehicle. I didn't think he was in cahoots with Leonardo, but I didn't know for sure. The Mustang continued to wiggle forward. I peeked over the dashboard through my fingers and looked down a seeming tunnel toward a light.

The car jolted forward again and lost contact with the truck. For a second I thought we were going to get sucked back in, but the Mustang finally broke free and to the right. Mason yelled, "Drive!" at the top of his lungs. I wrenched myself back into the driver's seat, floored the thing while crossing over several lanes of traffic, and exited the freeway at top speed. We careened around the off-ramp, scraping the entire left side of the car along the metal ledge protector, but when we finally made it to the relative safety of the gas station just off the exit, I stepped on the brakes with all of my strength.

The car finally stopped shuddering. I leaned back against the seat with the back of my hand pressed to my nose against the smell of burning rubber. Mason leaned back against his own seat. We looked around at the twisted metal in which we were sitting. I had to make a conscious effort to relax the six hundred–odd muscles in my body that were still clenched.

Finally Mason looked over at me and said, "You okay?"

I held up a defensive palm. "Fine. Just need to rest here . . . few minutes," I croaked. Actually, I didn't feel fine. I felt like I was going to throw up or pass out or possibly both, and I didn't want to do either of those things in front of Mason. I leaned out of the car and spit down the side. I cleared my throat, trying to get the exhaust and dust out, and spit again, then leaned back against the seat.

Mason made like he was moving over to check me out and see for himself how I was, but I turned my head away from him to stare at what used to be the car window. He climbed over the car door on his side. He walked slowly around the front of his car, mouth hanging open like some cartoon character's, hugging his messed-up arm to his body for comfort. I blinked wearily, my eyes dry and gritty. I felt bad. I mean, I felt good that we weren't dead and that I'd come through in a pinch, but in a way, I really felt *bad*.

As Mason walked around his car, I realized that I'd basically killed his puppy, and that wasn't the least bit funny. I didn't know what to say. I didn't even know exactly how bad the damage was, but considering that at the very least the entire top of the car was sheared off, it had to be bad. So I stammered the obvious. "Sorry about your car, Mason." I really meant it, but my words sounded almost flippant.

Mason closed his mouth, a tight, grim slash, and just looked at me. For once in his life, the guy had nothing to say. It was like the calm before the storm. I figured he was going to start yelling at me about how women are such crappy drivers and why didn't I do X instead of Y and follow it up with Z.

He walked around to my side of the car and leaned over me, and I thought, *Oh, here it comes*. But he didn't look mad anymore, and by the time I realized that, he'd already started fading from view, become just a silhouette against a darkening sky. Odd. And here I'd thought it was such a nice day.

THIRTEEN

"Come on, Rox. Wake up."

I opened my eyes just in time for Mason's palm to clap the side of my face. I'd fainted again?

"Wake up, now. That's a girl. We've got to get out of here."

Mason put his arm around my waist, heaved me out of the wrecked Mustang and to my feet. Still bleary, I just looked at him and let him rush me to the waiting taxi. He got in after me and I ducked my face into the warmth of his neck.

Mason wouldn't let me rest, though. "Rox, listen to me. Focus. We're too far behind. Leonardo will be on us any second. I want you to remember something." He looked back through the rear window, then shouted to the driver, "Go faster!"

"Remember what?" I asked, lolling against the seat back, doing my best to focus on Mason's face.

He looked flat-out panicked. Bruised, bloodied—panicked. "Nothing is absolute until the last possible moment. Until we reach the sweet spot and make that final move. Until then, it's as simple as stopping an old lady from stepping into oncoming traffic, and as complex as making sure your code stays out of Leo's hands. And this goes on every day, every minute, every second. Bump into the kid and make him drop his soda. Run into a woman on her way to a meeting and stall her while pretending we know each other. Head off Leo's splices at the pass so that what's truly real can still happen."

He was talking a mile a minute, and it was a struggle to keep up. "This seems like more than a bump or a stall," I croaked.

"This one is. And sometimes the good guys lose. Sometimes we can't pick up the thread for a splice somewhere else, or to do so would create an even worse situation. There's always a best sweet spot, Roxanne—the moment where if you act, you limit the ripple effect and provide your opponent with the fewest number of opportunities to splice reality to their benefit. When you find it for your desired outcome, when you've truly found that sweet spot . . . well, whoever gets to theirs first, wins."

I stared at him, uncomprehending. He hastened to elaborate more than ever before.

"What we as wire crossers do is lay out wire between the infinite number of possibilities for outcomes. Fate is the straight line between now and the end. Leo wants to splice reality, splice the wire, to link to an outcome to suit his own needs. I want to splice the wire back and try to re-create the original path. While nothing is absolute until the last moment, until one of us finds the right sweet spot, what we do has its limitations."

He looked behind us again, then turned back to

me. "Think of it as Leo and I standing on opposite ends of a field holding a section of wire. There's a limited amount of wire, which means there's a limited amount of splicing that can be done. Splicing reality uses up wire, because as Leonardo and I move closer to the sweet spot on any given case, we're getting closer to locking in fate. It's all about making it to the right sweet spot first. That's where a Major's fate is decided."

He was speaking faster and faster. I focused hard on every word. Why was he explaining this now? Everything hurt, and it was hard to concentrate, but I didn't dare miss out on a piece of the puzzle; he'd said this was important. "A case with a finite solution in a life of infinite possibilities. And no do-overs?" I mumbled, my head lolling to one side against the vinyl seat back.

"No do-overs. Well, before we hit the sweet spot, we can take our final length of wire and gamble on a reset. But I've never resorted to that."

I wanted to ask him more, but the taxi stopped and we were home. Mason handed the driver a bunch of money and pulled me out of the backseat. I stumbled, my head throbbing, and Mason awkwardly picked me up in spite of his cast and climbed the stairs with me in his arms. Always looking out for me.

He managed to get the key in the lock and kicked the door open. If the whiplash from the car accident hadn't been enough, I got a second serving when Mason suddenly lurched forward as though he'd been shoved. I went flying out of his arms over the threshold into my apartment.

I untangled myself, and was in the process of cataloging the various aches and pains in my body when I saw a hand come down on Mason's shoulder and spin him around. Leonardo Kaysar. He began to punch the crap out of Mason. To my horror, I realized that Mason was at a disadvantage with his cast—that damn cast I'd put on him as a kind of joke. It was far from funny now; the plaster might be a good bludgeon, but it was obviously heavy and slowed him down.

"Leonardo, stop!" He ignored me. I stared at him, the picture of concentration as he held Mason's collar with one hand and systematically rained blows on Mason's face, adding the odd knee to Mason's gut in between.

I thought about shutting the door on them, just shutting the door on the whole thing. I even crawled to the door and grabbed its corner. Mason managed to get his good arm hooked around Leo's leg. He tried to pull it out from under Leo, but I knew it was futile from the beginning.

Mason bellowed with rage, and from the chaos, a gun went spinning out onto the hardwood floor. Leonardo lunged for it, his foot hitting the door. I had to leap back to avoid getting smacked.

Mason managed to hold his rival back from the weapon, and it was clear I had an opportunity. The gun lay near the threshold to my apartment. I could have easily reached out and grabbed it, but I didn't, muddled still with sudden indecision and fear, and all I could do was start to cry at my inability to rise to the occasion.

"Rox, we still have a chance," Mason said, his

movements sluggish and his voice weak. "We're near a sweet spot. Do you understand?" Blood poured from his brutalized nose, but he never gave up, not for a second; he kept struggling. "Rox, pick up the goddamn gun and shoot him."

Leonardo paused as Mason writhed in pain at his feet, then casually reached over and picked up the gun. I fixated on the spatter of blood on Leo's crisp white sleeves and sat there, frozen. "Roxanne," Leo said to me. "Do you remember how I warned you about Mason?"

Mason was putting up a good fight, but he was definitely on the losing end of things. I had the ability to save him now.

I looked between the two men. Leo waited patiently, massaging his shoulder with his opposite hand as he continued to hold the gun on Mason.

"You can't decide?" Leonardo asked. "Let me help you."

I looked at him in disbelief.

"I can help you, Roxanne. I *understand* you."

God, *I* didn't even understand me.

But Leonardo simply smiled knowingly and said, "You try to keep your feelings far inside you, but one cannot stay hidden all of the time. And there is one thing you are not so skilled at concealing; the body never lies. I know this and Mason knows this, and he took quite some time to study the things that make you tick."

"You're disgusting," I said uncertainly. "He never tried anything on me all those years ago. You, on the other hand, you touch me and whisper in my ear, and then you use it against me."

Mason suddenly groaned in pain. I wanted to go to him but Leo grabbed my arm, holding me fast. "You can't imagine I would be attracted to you?" he asked softly. "You think my interest in you is all head and no heart? Perhaps you accuse the wrong man. What do you think Mason is doing? Your history together doesn't mean as much as you think it means, no matter how he tells the tale."

"How can you possibly know what it means?"

Leonardo gave a languid shrug of his shoulders and let me go. "He didn't want you in the past when he was flaunting his relationship with your lovely roommate in your face. Are you so sure he wants you now? After all, you said yourself, 'he never tried anything on you all those years ago.' Did he tell you he was afraid of impacting the case back then? Impacting your future? It must have been so difficult for him to resist, poor fellow," he said sarcastically. "But how thoughtful of him. So very thoughtful to think of you before himself."

He must have read the expression of horror on my face. With a look of pity that made me want to be sick, he went on, "I told you, Mason and I have worked against each other on many cases, Roxanne. Has he been as forthcoming with information as I have been? I think not. I told you the truth of this the first time we spoke. Mason kept secrets from you. It is his modus operandi. You look at me as though you can't understand how I know these things, but it would not be untrue to say that I know him even better than you do."

I'd explained Mason's relationship with Louise away in my head because I wanted to believe that it meant nothing to him. But maybe it wasn't how I remembered it. So many things weren't how I remembered them. Maybe the pranks and the jokes weren't the flirtation I'd imagined. Maybe they were his way of creating a history for us, the "thing" between us he was taking advantage of now. He'd said he'd been working on my case since sophomore year, and in light of Leonardo's explanation, the sterility of those words Mason had used to describe our early connection was painful.

"I can prove all this," Leonardo said.

It was the phrase I'd been longing to hear all this time. I stared at Leonardo, not daring to say a word, not daring to make a move. I wanted proof more than anything.

I waited to see what he would do, but he simply folded his sleeves. The stains on them of Mason's blood vanished from sight. With his free hand, Leonardo pulled his cellphone from his pocket and fiddled with it, using his thumb. I saw then that it wasn't just a cellphone—the same way as Mason's smartie. They both had the same advanced equipment, the same impossible technology, and it couldn't be a coincidence.

I turned and watched Mason make a feeble effort to crawl forward, but was too disoriented. Tears pricked my eyes and I had to look away. Mason had never proved anything.

Leonardo finished with his smartie, tucked it in his pocket and looked down at Mason. With a look of disgust, he took Mason's pistol and stuck it in his waistband, making it clear that he didn't see Mason as a threat anymore. The he reached one hand out to me. "Come here. I told you Mason would be the first to hurt you if it would serve his purpose, and I know how I will prove it. I will show you the truth."

"No," Mason moaned. I wasn't sure how he meant it, because it sounded odd. Resignation, despair. Not so much the lilt of a villain, but not entirely innocent either. Was it that he knew he was about to be exposed?

"She's not trained for that, Leo," Mason said, wobbling to a kneeling position.

"Trained for what?" I asked.

"She can't get her heart rate up high enough . . . and if she does, it won't be good for her."

Leo smiled. "It will be good for her. Trust me."

Which one to believe? I studied their faces for clues; it was like watching a jungle cat squaring off against an alpha dog on a chain. Leo murmured my name again, and it occurred to me that though we'd been too close for comfort once before, I'd never really had a good look at him out of shadow and darkness.

I glanced at his outstretched hand and this time went to him voluntarily, though almost as if he had me under some kind of spell. He brought me close. All of the details I'd missed before were incredibly vivid. The longish hair that curled over his ears, the lock that skimmed his eyelashes. His white linen shirt billowing over naturally tanned skin.

And then I couldn't see anything at all. All I could do was feel Leonardo Kaysar's lips on mine, his tongue sliding sensuously into my mouth. He was kissing me as if we were lovers who had all the time in the world on a calm, Sunday afternoon. My body just couldn't fake nonchalance. I went hot; my limbs buzzed with excitement. I seriously thought I might have a heart attack. I'd imagined many times what it would be like for Mason to kiss me, and the reality had been so much better, but Leonardo Kaysar . . . my fantasy had never really extended to this. Never. And I knew this act was meant as much as a slap in Mason's face as anything else.

He let his lips slip away from mine and I gasped for air. Leonardo brought his palm up to caress my cheek, then down again. His hands slid over my shoulders and down, his fingertips grazing my breasts. I just stood there under his spell, the faint sound of Mason yelling somewhere in the back of my mind while Leonardo's lips followed the curve of my ear. I could feel the heat of his breath as he whispered, "Open the door, Roxanne."

What door?

My heart raced furiously; from the corner of my eye something metal flashed in Leonardo's hand. "A punch," he murmured, as if that explained anything. I felt a prick on my neck.

I staggered back, my weight suddenly unsupported as there was nobody around. There was just me . . . holding a plastic bag with a goldfish in it and feeling a sense of certainty that the doorbell had just rung.

FOURTEEN

Kitty's goldfish. Kitty never came back from Europe. Or at least, she never came back and called. I'd never pursued it. The goldfish—Existential Angst—and I had reached an understanding, and he lived with me for several more years.

I felt a strange pang of loss. Kitty had been my best friend. I'd never had a close friend like that since. Not really. Why did I let us lose touch?

And why the hell was my graduation gown out on the table, still unopened, wrapped and folded in its plastic square?

The phone was ringing.

The phone was ringing; the doorbell was ringing. . . . Last time, the last real time—*God, what do you call it, even?* In my memory, I'd gone to the phone first, thinking it might be my interviewer needing to reschedule.

Existential Angst swam merrily around in his tiny plastic confines.

"I don't want to open the door," I said to him.

But I reached out and opened the door.

"Mason," I said. It was as if the weight of the world slid off my shoulders. The sound of my inhalation filled the room. Mason Merrick stood on the threshold, the raised collar of his motocross jacket scraping the side of his jaw as he looked down at me.

I smiled, knowing that my feelings for him were plastered all over my face, and in this moment, however the wires might cross, the closed part of me just opened wide. Leo was wrong about him.

He looked at me, his eyes blank.

I tried to say something, but it was almost as if the energy had been completely sapped out of me. As if I were in a coma. I wanted to say, *Mason, it's me. It's me. That's not how we look at each other. Tell me it wasn't all a bunch of lies. You mean something to me.*

Thoughts in my head raced so quickly, but there was nothing in my body that could keep up. His eyes narrowed. And this man whom I'd become closer to than anybody else in the world . . . Mason Merrick raised his gun and shot me.

I felt the bullet enter my flesh. It was loud, and it took forever. Like a graphic: The Travels of a Bullet through the Human Body, from one of those forensics shows. The metal ripped into me, into my arm, and I toppled back, spread-eagled, the bag flying out of my hand. I hit the ground and lay there for a moment, then painstakingly turned my head and watched Kitty's goldfish flop desperately on the wood floor, the water from the bag mixing with the blood trickling across the boards. I couldn't move more than that; I couldn't lift so much as a limb. All I could do was watch the backs of Mason's shoes as he walked away, watch the splash of goldfish water mingle with my blood and tears.

I remembered this now, my life: I never made it to the interview. I never got the job. That was why I worked for an agency doing freelance.

In my mind, I feebly reached out to Existential Angst, but all that really happened was a faint twitch of my fingertips. His little fishy body heaved one last time and he went still.

Kitty's going to be so sad. It was my very last thought before the sound of my breathing and the wail of sirens drowned everything else out.

FIFTEEN

"Roxanne?"

The male voice sounded friendly, but I was clearly in a hospital, and there's just nothing friendly about that. It smelled like antiseptic and some sort of indefinable nastiness. I sat up and reached out, saw the IV in my arm, and immediately became nauseated, falling back to the bed without achieving my goal.

"Roxanne, would you like some water?"

A male voice. British accent. I slowly turned my head to stare directly into Leonardo Kaysar's eyes, trying desperately not to see him as a bad guy. Mason was the villain. The thought of it made me want to cry. The last time I saw him—before he shot me, anyway—he'd begged me to believe him. He'd appealed to my heart, not just my mind. Of course, he'd also played me before and I'd punched him in the nose for it.

Leonardo smiled sympathetically. *Mason can't be the bad guy*. I pressed my hands against my face and squeezed my eyes shut, not wanting to believe. But Leo had found a way to give me proof, and I'd seen the truth with my own eyes. We'd played a real-life game of what-if, and the answer to "What if Mason Merrick needed to kill you to get what he wanted?" was obviously: "He would." Mason wasn't here to protect me; he was here to use me, and if he couldn't get things to suit his needs the way things stood, he was willing to kill me to make them turn out right. I'd seen that permutation.

Leonardo sat in the guest chair by my hospital bed looking down at me, resting his chin on his hand. He looked entirely comfortable, as if he could wait all day for me to start talking. And, in fact, I realized it had been some time since we'd been staring at each other without saying anything at all.

It was obvious what he was doing here. He wanted to talk—about business things, about wire-crosser things. I didn't want to hear them. I really didn't think I could handle it. Still staring at him, I burst into tears.

Leonardo stood up and put aside a pair of leather driving gloves he'd had on his lap. I just sort of sobbed, my exhaustion so complete that I could barely make a sound doing it. Very calmly he sat down on the bed next to me, and even though I wanted to hate him for ruining Mason for me, more than that I wanted someone to tell me everything was going to be all right.

He took my hand and cradled it between his. I wondered if it had even registered with him that I was nursing a broken heart even I'd been too blind to see coming. And maybe it wasn't just that. Mason and I had become important to each other in a way we'd never been all those years before. At least, he'd become important to me. I missed him, and something inside of me refused to accept that this was how things were meant to end.

Leonardo and I never did find the right words. He just rocked me and murmured nice things in my ear until I fell back to sleep.

"Roxanne, can you hear me?"

I blinked to clear the fog, and suddenly a woman's face was above mine. A nurse's sort of face. The bitter, vengeful nurse. I suddenly panicked, afraid that Mason was getting his revenge on me for the plaster cast gone awry, but she made no reference to our earlier conspiracy.

"How's our patient?"

"Oh, my God," was all I could say as all over again I processed Mason Merrick shooting me. He *shot* me. "Did I lose a lot of blood?"

She blinked. "Blood?"

"The bullet," I slurred.

She smiled. "There's no bullet and no blood, sweetheart. And you're not pregnant."

"What?"

"You fainted," the nurse said. "Your blood pressure was off the charts. We just wanted to make sure we covered all the bases."

I tried to sit up, but the movement triggered a whole lot of murmured protests, clucking, and a totally unnecessary tucking in of blankets. "I want to go home," I said, quickly degenerating into something wet and snotty and sniveling.

"Your friend is on the way," the nurse said.

What friend? I thought of both Mason and Leonardo and turned my head into the pillow to shut everything out. *Do I even have any friends anymore?*

I fell back to sleep.

When I woke up, a blond woman I didn't recognize sat in the guest chair reading a magazine. When she saw me, she tossed the magazine away and came over. She was working the smoky-eye look more than most mortal women should, but with the blond bangs it somehow worked.

"Thank God. You feeling okay? 'Cause I want to get you out of here. And I want to get me out of here. I accidentally passed a room where this baby was being born and nearly puked. And then they were talking for a second like maybe you were pregnant, which would explain the fainting. And, I mean, I totally had a heart attack for laughing. No offense, Rox, but that's just ridiculous. I mean, you're practically celibate. Of course, that was before I met your Leonardo, and you *so* have some explaining to do. I mean, you're going out! And *that guy*. And frankly, you never mentioned that you were on a diet, and obviously if the reason for your anemia has to do with some kind of eating disorder, totally disregard what I'm about to say, but if not, I am *so* going to kill you about that because you know how I am about discipline, and if I'd known you were going on a diet, I totally would have gone on a diet with you, and if you ask *me* . . ."

He's not my *Leonardo*. I let her go on and on as she put some clothes on me and stuffed the rest of my belongings in a bag. I looked down at my shirtsleeve. There was no bloodstain, no hole in the fabric.

I squinted up at the blonde. *Who the hell are you?*

was on the tip of my tongue, but I never said it because I knew her. I mean, I knew I knew her, even though I sure as hell couldn't place her.

". . . I'm always telling you, and you always roll your eyes and ignore me and then suddenly, boom! You take my advice. What do I always say? 'Just remember, Roxanne; it can't always be about tomorrow. Sometimes it's about right fucking now.' And you go and listen to me for one night, and snag a—"

"What did you say?"

"You always roll your eyes—"

"The part after that."

"It can't always be about tomorrow—" she began.

"Sometimes it's about right fucking now," I ended. The voice. The cadence. The motto. I stared into those kohl-rimmed eyes and almost burst out crying all over again. No *way*. "Kitty?"

It was Kitty, without the black lipstick, the multiple piercings, the jet-black hair. Kitty, who'd somehow morphed out of a really serious Goth-chick phase into some sort of urban hipster creature who could have posed in the pages of a magazine.

"When did you start calling me that again?" she asked.

"What do I normally call you?"

Her eyebrow arched. "I went back to Katherine a long time ago."

"Old habits," I mumbled.

She shrugged. "You're my oldest friend. You get to call me whatever you want."

"When did you change your look?"

"What?"

"When did you . . . become a blonde?"

She put her hands on her hips. "L. Roxanne Zaborovsky, you are scaring the piss out of me. You were there. Remember how we tried to get the black dye out by doing a peroxide thing and nearly burned the fuck out of my scalp, and I ended up greenish gray, and I was crying hysterically? And I know for a fact that you were trying not to laugh, which was really mean, but you took me to a salon and held my hand while they fixed it."

"I held your hand while they fixed it?" I repeated, oddly touched. "So, you came back from Europe after graduation."

Kitty threw her hands up in the air. "I never went. You got shot—" She stopped short and looked down at me, blinking in confusion. "You know what? I'll be right back. I'm going to get someone to discharge you before they decide to move you up to the psych ward." She tucked the sheets in up to my chin—it was funny how her mothering of me had evolved over the years.

She was as good as her word, and by the time we hit the parking lot the smell of bad cafeteria food had ebbed away. I didn't say a word as the next stream of consciousness gathered steam. There was something so comforting about the way she took our friendship for granted. I didn't feel so alone, I guess.

Obviously, she knew the way to my place. And when we got there and I inched slowly toward the door to get out of her VW Bug, I caught her staring at me like I was insane.

Her face had gone dead serious. "You're like an old person. Just wait. I'm coming up with you."

I couldn't go any faster; I just didn't have the energy. She double-parked the car and helped me up the steps, which I was kind of horrified to discover felt like trying to negotiate Mount Everest. I was out of breath by step two out of fourteen. It was as if my muscles had atrophied.

I thought about Mason's words. How he'd told Leo I'd never get my heart rate up. And then I thought about Mason. I clutched at my heart, though there wasn't any medical explanation for the pain I felt there. Kitty unlocked the door, marched me inside, and pressed me onto the sofa.

I let my head sink back into the pillows. Kitty plopped down next to me and patted my knee. "It's going to be okay. Things are already looking up. That Leonardo is so nice. I like him a lot. Got a guy who's nice to your friends, you got a keeper."

Nice would not have been the first word I'd pick to describe Leonardo Kaysar. "He's nice to me because he needs me for something. He was nice to you because you're a hot blonde."

Kitty giggled. Through the easing fog of my sedative, I started to giggle with her . . . and then I just started to laugh hysterically. "I'm a mess," I finally mumbled.

Kitty's face fell. "You are not a well individual. I'm going to go park the car. I'll be right back."

"It's okay," I said.

"It's not okay."

I watched her head for the door, overwhelmed by the joy of having a close friend again. I don't know how we could have ever lost touch. And then it occurred to me: Maybe we did, maybe we didn't. But maybe it would happen again.

"Kitty!" I shuffled out to the top of the steps leading to the walkway. "Kitty!"

She turned just before getting back in the driver's seat, her face highlighted red in the Bug's hazards. "Yeah?"

"I'm sorry about your goldfish. I just . . . I just couldn't reach." I headed down the stairs. She looked at me as if I were insane.

"Reach my goldfish?"

"Existential Angst."

"You still feel guilty about that? Please, do not even think twice. That's *so* in the past, Rox. You'd think you just had a near-death experience. Are you going to start making me go with you to beg forgiveness of everyone you ever jostled in a supermarket?"

I managed a smile. I was testing me, testing her—testing reality, I guess.

She got in the car and the window slid down. "Would you go in already and get out of the cold?"

"I just . . . I missed you. In case I don't see you . . . again . . . soon. You know."

Kitty blinked in confusion. "I'm not going anywhere."

"But that's really not necessary," I said, assuming she meant she was planning to baby me some more. "You don't have to come back."

"Uh, *I* find it necessary," she said.

"I fainted. That's all!"

"Yeah?" she asked.

"Well?" I said.

She scratched the side of her face and turned off the hazards. "Roxanne, I'm your roommate. I live here." And then she drove off to find parking.

What the hell?

I managed to get myself back into my apartment and immediately climbed the stairs to the storage room. I put my hand on the door and pushed. The door swung open. The bedroom was just as Kitty had always kept it years ago. Bed over there, dresser over there. Clothes, jewelry, shoes strewn about. And storage boxes nowhere in sight.

Kitty came up a few minutes later; I was still sitting there trying to process. "Parking karma. Thank God."

"Where are the boxes?" I asked hoarsely.

"Which boxes?"

"Like, my files and . . . stuff."

"That's all still in the basement locker. Except for what you keep in your office." She pressed her palm against my forehead, then shrugged helplessly. "I'll make some soup you can take to your room."

I stood there for another moment or so, then went out to find her. She was still upstairs, coming out of my office with a box containing a grimy old binder and a bunch of crumpled paper. She stopped and gave me a nervous sort of laugh. "I just had the weirdest déjà vu."

"Happens to me all the time," I said numbly. It occurred to me then that if I was a Major, Kitty, my closest friend—at least, in some versions of my life—was a Peripheral. She'd feel things were out of place now and then, though according to the boys it wouldn't be anything like what I was experiencing. As far as Kitty knew, this was the only reality.

But what reality was she living in?

"Your trash can was overflowing," she was saying,

skipping sprightly down the stairs. "I'll just go dump this out then start your soup."

I sighed, thinking how my trash can had been essentially empty in the prior reality in which Leonardo had stolen everything out of it, then headed back downstairs to the kitchen to have a look around. There, things were more or less the same as they had been, but there were more touches of Kitty. Or so it seemed to me. The refrigerator wasn't laden with as many menus; just one for pizza and one for Chinese. And there were canisters and things with her miscellaneous New Age paraphernalia that hadn't been around in years.

She joined me a few minutes later, pulled a can of minestrone out of the pantry, and poured it into a pot. She pulled a tin from the cupboard, sniffed the contents, then sprinkled some wrinkled dry stuff into the soup. She put the pot on the range. "Guy at the health food store said this has some really good rejuvenation properties. I think he's Wiccan, so I figured, What the hell."

"Cool. I could use a little rejuv." She had no idea. I tried to think about the last four years. What Kitty and I might have palled around doing, but I couldn't see anything. I supposed the memories would come in time.

I watched her stir the soup. "You know, you really don't have to baby me like this. I can make my own damn soup. Hell, I can *order* soup."

She didn't look up. "I make soup all the time. It's no big deal. Besides, I need to make sure you eat properly."

I laughed. "I'm fine. It was a . . . onetime thing. Listen, tomorrow why don't we go out? We haven't gone out in ages."

She looked at me as if I were totally insane. "What are you talking about?"

"I just thought . . . I mean, for old times' sake. We should go do something fun." *Create some memories I can remember.*

Kitty grabbed a soup bowl from the cupboard and ladled out a serving. "You don't go out," she said calmly.

I laughed. "Yeah, okay."

She paused, her hand gripping the soup ladle. I stared at her. She stared at me.

"Oh, come on," I said.

"What can I say? You never go out. Now, go lie down and I'll be up with a tray in a minute."

I turned and slogged my way up the stairs in a kind of a daze. *This is just ridiculous.* I leaned over the banister and called out, "Why not?"

After a moment, Kitty appeared, hands on hips. She looked up at me. "Well . . . because."

"Because why?"

"Because . . . because you're a workaholic." Then she disappeared back into the kitchen.

I slipped into my bed and stared up at the ceiling. I jumped back out of bed and went again to the banister. "I've decided not to be a workaholic anymore!" I yelled.

Kitty's head popped into view, framed on three sides by the angles of the staircase. I could see she was trying to decide whether I was serious or not. Finally, she just laughed. "That's great, Rox! When you're ready to walk around Union Square and hit the town for dinner and a show, let me know!"

Dinner and a show. *Dinner and a show?* What, like some overpriced tourist chicken dish and a seven-thirty p.m. showing of *The Fantastiks* revival? For fuck's sake. You didn't have to be a workaholic to find that totally out of the question.

Wait a minute. Was she being sarcastic?

A few moments later Kitty tromped up the stairs with my tray. She put it down next to my bed and arranged a napkin and spoon. It was a little spooky how much she catered to me. "All set," she said, slipping back out of the room. "Enjoy!"

I didn't feel much like eating. I looked around my bedroom. The shades were closed and the lights were off. It was insanely dark. I guess Kitty thought I liked it that way. I got up and pulled open the shades and had a look around. It seemed to me that things looked a bit different than usual, though of course I couldn't put my finger on what it was. This time, the strange feeling didn't feel that strange. And it scared the hell out of me.

I stared down at the soup. This was some kind of cosmic joke. It had to be. I was clearly on a different wire. Mason wasn't in my life; Kitty was my best friend again. Yet I was still a miserable workaholic who never went out. Leonardo might have proved he was telling the truth and Mason was lying, but he'd also managed to saddle me with the worst parts of the last crappy reality.

I opened the closet and shifted the hangars back and forth. No dress, no negligee. I dropped to my knees. No shoebox, no gun, no bullets. Maybe I was in the same old crappy reality because this *was* my reality. Maybe I'd always been and always would be the same and it was just the people around me and my environment that changed. But that couldn't be true, because I wouldn't know the me I was now, the one who didn't want to be a miserable workaholic who never went out.

Afraid of angering the soup mistress, I tiptoed carefully down the hall to my office and opened the door. A stack of papers sat on the desk, plastic bins full of hanging files stacked high on the floor. I glanced at the folders and the project labels. The labels made sense; they corresponded to projects I vaguely remembered working on, but none of them seemed unusual enough to be something Mason and Leonardo could be interested in.

I turned, my eye catching a slightly yellowed paper taped to the wall. An official document of some sort. I leaned in to catch the wording and shivered at what I read. It was a restraining order for one Mason Merrick, the same year as my graduation from college. My finger swept over his typed name as if I could erase it, and then I just stumbled back, nearly sick to my stomach.

"Kitty!" I yelled at the top of my lungs. I could hear her taking the steps two at a time and she was at the door in a flash. She looked at me, and I saw her body relax. "You scared the crap out of me."

I swallowed, making a concerted effort to control my panic. "Kitty, what's this?"

She looked at the order. Then she looked at me, and when I saw the fear in her eyes I knew it was true. But I needed her to say it.

"That's your restraining order," she said quietly.

"Mason . . . for the last four years . . ." I couldn't even finish the sentence out loud. "I mean, I've had a crush on him for four years, right? Haven't I been carrying a torch for him for four years?"

She looked totally confused. "Carrying a torch? For Mason Merrick?"

I just nodded.

She sat down in my office chair, shaking her head in disbelief. "Mason Merrick has been your worst nightmare for the last four years. The only torch I know of is the one *he* tried to snuff. You have the scar on your arm to prove it." I slipped my hand under my shirt and ran my fingers over my arm. I felt an unmistakable—and sort of kick-ass, actually—knotted scar just below the shoulder. Poking and prodding the spot as if to make sure it wasn't easily removable stage makeup, I could tell it wasn't a scar from any injury sustained today. It had to be from one incurred long prior. As long ago as graduation day.

Kitty followed my gaze then looked up at me with sympathy. "Are you remembering?"

In a manner of speaking, I guess.

"Oh, god. Tell me you're not becoming—" She cut off her words, going pale, and I knew she thought she'd revealed something bad. But what?

"Becoming what?"

She stared at me wordlessly, fear clouding her eyes.

"Becoming *what*, Kitty?"

"If you don't remember, don't ask me to remind you."

We stood there facing each other, silent.

"You have to tell me." And even as I said those words, I realized just how much she probably had to tell. A lot more than she'd copped to. Kitty had answers for me. "You have to tell me everything. It's important."

She raised her arms in surrender and let them fall. "Mason . . . Well, he . . ."

I wasn't sure I could bear it, but I had to know. I nodded for her to continue.

"He stalked you. And then he shot you."

I was numb. Other things were coming back to me, other memories. Horrible memories. Trying to put all the pieces together, I was just numb.

"Roxy? Don't you remember? He was dating Louise and then he . . . wasn't dating Louise. . . ." She had that look about her as if she were trying to draw the recollections out of me. "And then he wanted to be dating you." She looked at me hopefully. "And then he *really* wanted to be dating you. . . ."

This was impossible. Insane. Laughable. Why wasn't I laughing? Because I did remember. Sort of.

"Roxy?"

"Of course I remember," I said quickly, but the look on her face said she didn't believe me. "It's just very . . ."

"Upsetting," Kitty finished.

I thought of Leonardo suggesting that Mason was some kind of stalker, and Mason saying that Leo always used that line. When exactly had Leo and Mason first started messing with time, with my mind?

"*When* did he shoot me?" I asked, angrily swiping at the tears slipping from my eyes. "Exactly when? And how?"

"I told you. Graduation day. Not long after I left to catch my plane. God, you really don't remember any of it, do you?"

Yes, Mason had really shot me. It wasn't just one of Leonardo's fabrications, and it wasn't just a what-if that ended with Mason out of my life and Kitty in it. On this wire, Mason wasn't in my life because I had a restraining order against him, and if my reality never spliced this big again, that's how it was going to stay. I put a hand out to the wall to steady myself.

If you didn't know about the wire crossers, Roxy, what would you think about all this? What would a normal, uninformed person think about this?

A normal, uninformed person might think they were losing their mind. They would probably take some drugs and go to sleep and, eventually, some reality would take hold and harden and reoriented memories would lock in; they'd never have to think about what could have been versus what actually was.

I'd be better off if I didn't resist, I realized. None of this would hurt so badly. But it mattered to me. I very desperately wanted to keep the possible versions of my life straight in my mind. I had a feeling I might need to compare them later. That, if I had to choose a reality, it would be important to be able to separate one wire from the other. Because when it came right down to it, I didn't want to be the girl who couldn't pick up the gun to save someone worth saving. I couldn't believe that was the girl I was.

Was I?

SIXTEEN

I stayed in my office for the next several days. As if leaving the room would force me to face a reality I didn't want, even if the truth was that the current reality I was living sounded better than the one I'd left behind.

But the inevitable came to be. Kitty knocked on my door. "Rox, it's Leo on the landline." She spoke as if it were the most natural thing in the world for him to call. As if she knew exactly who he was, as if they were old pals.

"I don't want to talk to him," I said.

Silence.

"He's asking very nicely."

"Tell him to leave me alone."

"He wants to know if you'll go to a *gala* with him." The suggestive tone of her voice was unmistakable. I didn't know exactly what she was suggesting, but she sure as hell had the wrong idea about the two of us.

"Oh?" I asked, affecting an air of indifference.

"Champagne. Fancy hors d'oeuvres," she hissed. "I asked him to be specific. Obviously, I told him you don't go to dinner or parties or any of that sort of thing," Kitty went on, "but he says he knows that and refuses to take no for an answer."

I leaped from my chair and opened the door on principle. Kitty lurched back in surprise. "Oh," she said. "Hi."

"Hi. I'll take it." I took the phone. Kitty seemed oblivious to my nonverbal cues suggesting that she leave, and she leaned against the wall, her arms crossed, listening to my end of the conversation.

"I'm taking the week off," I said into the phone, walking into my office and then walking back out again because the damn cordless handset was catching interference from my wireless Internet. The static was irritating, but not as irritating as the excessively rapturous look on Kitty's face. Somehow, this made me inclined to go to the gala even less. As some sort of statement. Although, I don't know if the statement was, "Yes, you are right, I never go out," or "I wouldn't even deign to get excited about such a thing."

The statement I said out loud to Leonardo was, "In fact, I'll be indefinitely unavailable. I'm no longer interested in the case."

He failed to rise to the bait. "Hello, Roxanne. How are you feeling?"

"How am I feeling? Numb, pissed off, pissed off some more, pissed off more than that." And sad. But I didn't say that. I figured he could hear my voice quavering anyway.

"I understand," Leonardo said quietly.

Did he? Did he really care? I'd thought Mason cared. I'd wanted him to, but in the end . . . well, if Mason hadn't cared about me any more than he did Naveed's daughter, Leo certainly wouldn't. I already knew Leo had a price when it came to getting what he wanted; I'd had a taste of it in Mason's car. When it came down to it, anything that happened to me could be written off as collateral damage. I was just like Naveed's daughter; either man could happily make me disappear.

I had so many questions that Mason couldn't or hadn't answered. Maybe Leonardo could and would. He'd been more upfront in the past.

"I'd like to take you out tonight, Roxanne," he repeated.

"Yeah?"

"If I might. It's a formal event. I think you'll enjoy it."

So like a man. He was moving on as if nothing had happened.

Of course, Kitty had said there was food. I was hungry, and in all fairness, bad news or a breakup had never had the least impact whatsoever on my appetite. The errant thought, *Did Mason and I just have a breakup?* floated through my mind, and out of a twisted respect for Mason, or maybe for myself, I said, "Listen, buddy, I'm grieving here."

"Pity. Are you quite sure?"

Was I? I had been wandering around the house telling myself I was the kind of girl who went to parties. If I was going to actually be that girl, I needed get my ass to that gala and prove it to myself and everybody else. You are what you do.

I looked at Kitty. She mouthed, "Please."

"One sec," I said into the phone. I covered the speaker with my hand. The only evening wear I owned was apparently in the closet of a different layer of my reality.

"I don't have a thing to wear," I whispered. "Will you help me? I need a dress, and I have absolutely no idea . . ."

Kitty turned pale and clutched melodramatically at her heart. "Shopping? Do you have any idea how long I've been waiting to hear you say that?"

I took my hand off the speaker. "Okay. I'll go."

"Excellent. I'll fetch you at seven o'clock."

"I'll see you then."

Leonardo hung up without further ado. I listened to the disconnect tone drone on in his wake, then handed the phone back to Kitty with a, "Thanks."

She had a huge grin on her face. "I'm really proud of you, Rox! You're really putting yourself out there. I mean, when you decide to come out of your shell, you just do it cold turkey, don't you?"

"I guess so."

"Well?"

"Well, what?" I asked.

"Don't just stand there. Grab your wallet. We're going shopping!"

Kitty acted like we'd never been shopping before in our lives. Maybe we hadn't. Or at least, maybe over the last four years, everything I'd bought, everything that was in the closet, I'd bought online. I thought maybe I remembered that.

I looked around Nordstrom's, totally overwhelmed with the prospect of decking myself out for a formal party. Luckily, Kitty was more than happy to act as my personal shopper. She loaded up my arms with dresses until I could barely stand, then sent me into a dressing room with instructions that I was to start working my way through them, and anything that didn't sag or refuse to zip was to be put on the short list for her personal consultation when she returned from Shoes and Hosiery.

At first I was the living embodiment of the eye roll, but then, as I began to work my way through the dresses, it was as if I were peeling off one skin, one personality, and replacing it with a new one—and then a new one, and then a new one.

Going to a "gala" with Leonardo Kaysar, professional sophisticate, was something I couldn't have predicted in any reality, on any wire. I was sure Kitty was simply too happy to see me going out to realize that we weren't the most perfect match. I knew what she *was* thinking, and it wasn't true—he certainly *didn't* remind me of my father, which would just be gross. But I guess Leonardo Kaysar did speak to something in me. It was his cool certainty about things that was attractive. That he had things covered, that he always had things under control. I didn't get that feeling with Mason. With Mason . . . I'd felt more on the same level in a lot of ways. Like we were evenly matched. Leonardo was over my head. He was impenetrable. And if I was trying to be someone new and self-actualized, shouldn't I allow myself to explore that? If Leonardo was my James Bond, then why not be his Bond Girl? At least for a night.

I slipped a couple of candidates that didn't sag or refuse to zip onto the far silver hook and slung the discards over the dressing room door.

"You decent?" Kitty asked from the other side.

"Sure." I popped the door open, but she only stuck her face through the crack.

"Brace yourself," she said.

I arched my eyebrow.

"Are you ready?"

"Um . . ."

"Because I've found it. I've found the one. And some kick-ass shoes to match."

"Let's see," I said eagerly.

She flung open the door and presented me with a black dress with red detailing and a pair of satin high-heeled party shoes guaranteed to put me in traction. It was *the* dress. *The* shoes.

"Are you okay?"

I couldn't form even one audible word.

"You hate it," she said, disappointment written all over her face. "Huh. I just really thought you'd like it. I mean, it's your taste, right? More or less?"

I nodded and took one shoe from the box, half expecting to find the gun or at least a stray bullet somewhere in the tissue. The box was empty, of course, save for the other shoe.

"Do you look like that because you feel sick, or because you hate them?"

"I love them," I finally managed to say. "I guess it's just so perfect . . . I'm in shock."

She beamed. "Then you're gonna love this!"

A pink negligee flew straight into my face. I peeled the too familiar nightgown off and shook it out.

"Oh, come on," she said. "You have nothing. Absolutely nothing. It's not that expensive. What if things go really well with Leonardo?"

A gargling sound came from my throat. It was all I could manage.

"Well, put the dress on and we'll see if it fits," Kitty said.

"Something tells me it's gonna fit," I mumbled, stepping into the garment.

Kitty clasped her hands together. "It's perfect."

I slipped my feet into the shoes.

"How do they feel?"

"Perfect," I said in a complete monotone. "And don't ask me to try on the pink thing. I'll buy it, okay?"

She raised her arms in victory. "Yes! Okay, so here are some stockings, and you can borrow one of my purses. And here's some other stuff." She held out a palm and counted off the inventory. "Dress, check. Shoes, check. Hose, check. Bra and panties, check. Purse, check . . ." She paused.

"Makeup," I said into the gap as I started putting my regular clothes back on.

"You're joking, right? You have four years of wishful thinking in the bathroom."

"Wishful thinking?"

She laughed and opened her mouth to explain, but I swear she cut herself off before she said what she really had on her mind. "I suppose you were wishing for an event like this one, with a guy like this," she said.

I was pretty sure she was being kind with her vague choice of words.

"This one's different, isn't he?"

You have no idea.

"Come on, fess up. You really like this guy."

I almost said yes even before I realized she was still talking about Leonardo. Wasn't that who I was talking about? "What makes you say that?"

"You're in much better shape than I thought. You've been working out in that little Bat Cave of yours, haven't you?"

I looked down at my body and smoothed the fabric against my stomach. I hadn't really thought about it. And, of course, I wasn't entirely sure what other me I should be comparing myself to. But Kitty seemed certain. "You've toned up. You've lost a little weight."

"Maybe," I said. *Running around the city with two men on your heels will do that to you.*

Kitty took the dress and I picked up the shoe box, following her out of the dressing room. "Kitty?"

She looked at me over her shoulder. "Yeah?"

"Is there stuff you're not telling me?"

We stared at each other for a moment, and I studied her face for clues.

"Fine," she finally said. "I admit it."

I held my breath.

"Those jeans totally make your butt look big."

We both burst out in hysterical laughter and were still giggling when we reached the sales counter. I fished out my credit card and asked for the damage.

"This is a great outfit," the saleswoman said with a smile. "But because of the way the dress is cut, you'll have panty lines. You should just go with the garter belt and stockings and bra."

I have no idea what that great outfit cost. I was too busy trying not to let on to Kitty that those words had scared me out of my mind. Luckily, she assumed I was just dehydrated.

SEVENTEEN

Sitting at an angle from Leonardo in a limousine that I was sure had Kitty in paroxysms of delight back home, I was reminded again of Mason, if only because of the contrast. Leonardo might lack Mason's sunny charm, but he had plenty of his own appeal. He had what could only be described as *mystère*. *Mystère*, and a hint of soulfulness underneath the ruthlessness of which he was so clearly proud. It was what had washed over me that first day in the agency.

He was textbook in his suave, smooth appeal, and it would have been fair to say that I wouldn't have had the guts to even desire Leonardo when I was younger. Of course, I felt exponentially older than I used to, just weeks earlier. Or maybe not older. Maybe . . . seasoned. I never used to be the girl who drove muscle cars at warp speed or fucked my guy against a wall after a party, either.

My guy. Dammit, Rox. Dammit.

I wanted to hate Leo's guts. I felt beyond bitter that he'd revealed Mason to be a fraud. Ridiculous, of course, since Mason being a liar and willing to shoot me certainly wasn't Leonardo Kaysar's fault. I suppose most women who'd been saved from evil clutches by a guy like Leo would have been on their knees thanking him in one way or another, but I definitely wanted to hate him. More than that, I wanted to be immune to him. But I wasn't.

The limo slowed. Leo slipped his suit jacket on and the door opened. I forgot to look at the driver. Not that I would have expected the driver to be anybody particularly useful to this mystery I was living, but I'd made a resolution, a point of consciously recording as many details about my surroundings as I could.

Leo led me forward with his hand on the small of my back. I was only about three steps in when I realized where we were: the office building Mason had taken me to on the last wire. A party was still a party, even when you had a fancy Brit calling it a gala, and this was the same party Mason had made me dress up for. The same party. The same dress and same shoes. The same building. The same damn moment in time I'd already lived through. "We're backwards," I said in a sudden panic.

Leo's hand massaged my shoulder, undoubtedly as much to prevent my escape as provide comfort. "It's all right," he crooned.

I turned on him with narrowed eyes. "Don't tell me it's all right. It's not all right. It hasn't been all right in some time. I'm not a total idiot. Did we or did we not go backward in time? Didn't this party happen already?"

I knew before he even spoke that the real answer was: *It depends*.

"It depends," Leonardo said. "I did make a very small splice. Technically we are parallel to the prior wire, but we are also slightly behind in time."

His willingness to admit that was almost more of a shock than the situation itself. I had to give him credit for not giving me a fuzzy answer like Mason would, but it was no small splice he'd made, at least not by my standards. Kitty's reappearance in my life and the new unimproved Mason were big, big things, and who knew what else had changed by tripping to this new wire.

"Let's not dwell. We should try to enjoy a bit of the party," Leo said.

According to Kitty, the way my life was going, Hell would freeze over before I got another opportunity like this. If I was trying to make the version of me I wanted, I was exactly where I needed to be.

Leo read my acquiescence and ushered me onto the scene with a graceful wave of his hand. I stepped into the stream of traffic flowing through the offices, but the minute I joined the partygoers, a wave of anxiety hit me just as it had with Mason. I made one of my famous U-turns and headed for the exit. I thought the space might close in on me. There were too many people, too many crowding bodies.

"I'm not running away, it's just . . . too much," I gasped, trying to plow my way back to the doors. But Leonardo was by my side, one hand at my waist, one on my back, steering me around. "Let's get you a drink. It will help you relax."

I concentrated on not freaking the hell out in public while Leonardo retrieved two flutes of champagne. I downed mine in one decidedly unladylike guzzle, then reached for Leonardo's partially finished glass.

"Perhaps later," he said, moving the flute out of reach.

I glowered at him. "You're a bad man." Craning my neck, I made a big show of looking for a champagne server.

Leo touched his fingers to my cheek and gently pulled my gaze back to his. "If only you could get past your prejudices, I think you'd find I'm quite good."

Oh, please. "That right there . . . was that some feeble attempt at seduction?" I asked. "The idea being that I'll swoon at your feet and do anything you say?"

"I've not had any complaints about my methodology," Leonardo said with a smile.

The nerve. "You know what? Knock yourself out. Whatever you want to do. You want something from me, go ahead and seduce me. Seems like as good a plan as any." I know what I would have replied if I were Leo: *It worked for Mason.* But Leonardo did not do what I would have done; he didn't take the bait.

I attended to the important task of delicately removing an endive hors d'oeurves from a silver tray. Chewing on the morsel, I studied Leonardo's face, trying to come to terms with the idea that maybe he wasn't as cruel as my instinct wanted me to believe. The possibility that maybe he was in the right was completely unnerving. "You *are* a bad man," I insisted as soon as I'd swallowed. "You broke into my apartment, stole all of my equipment, backup machines, and storage discs."

"Yes, about that. I neglected to ask—I requested everything be returned exactly as found. Was it?"

"Every plug, plugged in, every disc duly filed," I admitted. "Of course, there is the issue of having my privacy violated and, for all I know, my personal information copied. And then there's the issue of larceny being a crime—not to mention it's just a shitty thing to do."

"I apologize for the inconvenience. Please be assured that I had no interest in your personal files. And nothing was copied."

"It was a violation. And I must also add that it's small potatoes next to that bit where you tried to run me over."

Leo moved gracefully through the party, exchanging greetings and small talk with complete strangers as if it were the most natural thing in the world. I followed on his heels like a lap dog. "I mean, seriously, Leo. You tried to kill me."

He stopped short just behind an ice sculpture shaped like a horn of plenty and flipped the top on his smartie. "I'm terribly sorry, Roxanne, but I must pull away for one moment." With a smile, he reached out and pushed a lock of stray hair behind my ear, then turned his attention to the device. He punched in a couple of things with his stylus, then quickly tucked the device away. "Forgive the interruption. We were talking . . . ah, yes. No, I did not try to kill you. I was not even driving. That accident was the result of a miscommunication between my people that I truly regret."

"Accident? That was no *accident*. I was there. I know. You tried to kill me."

"No," he repeated calmly, slipping an earbud into one ear. "Though Mason undoubtedly *told you* I tried to kill you."

I was about to rebut when I remembered. I had never seen who was driving. Not really. Mason told me it was Leonardo, and I'd hauled ass without even seeing who was at the wheel.

"Roxanne," Leo said, again directing the seductive force of his green eyes at me. "I'm afraid that it's going to take you some time to work through all of Mason's lies. To have various . . . truths become evident and others to fade is very difficult, I know. Just try to concentrate on what you have seen with your own eyes, versus what someone else told you was there."

I almost jumped in and defended Mason. Before I could say anything at all, Leonardo murmured, "I'm sorry for your loss, Roxanne."

I froze. "I . . . what?"

"He made you care for him. And I'm sorry for it, for your sake."

My cheeks burned as I remembered the first version of this party. I wondered if Leonardo knew how far Mason and I had taken things. If he did, was it Mason who'd told him in another time, cockily describing me as one of his conquests?

I certainly wasn't about to ask. I didn't want to talk about Mason, because I knew Leo couldn't help but say bad things about him, and I also knew Mason deserved that, but I wasn't sure I could bear it.

Leo continued escorting me through the crowd until we'd walked straight through the entire party and out to a hall on the other side. I realized he was heading for the same bank of elevators as last time, and I knew we must be going up to the offices again. But experience had proved to me that nothing ever stayed quite the same, and I wondered what I would find up there. Maybe the agency in a new location yet again. Maybe something completely different. Either way, I wondered if Mason's toys were still up there like props on somebody else's desk.

Leonardo pushed an elevator button, and I leaned against the wall, trying to take the weight off my aching feet.

"I understand loss, you know," Leonardo said softly. Something flickered in his eyes. It was the most real emotion I'd yet seen from him. "There are things that run much deeper in this world than your friend Mason Merrick's obsession with what is 'right.' "

"I think Mason understands loss as well as you or I," I said. "He told me you disappeared the woman he loved."

Leo looked at me with unfeigned surprise. The elevator door slid open, and he ushered me in. "He actually told you that?"

"Is it true?" I asked.

He paused. "No. And it's a rather poor fabrication. Especially compared to what you and I have lost."

I stared at him, trying to determine if he was manipulating me the way a faux psychic tricks answers from unwitting marks. The elevator shuddered. I grabbed the railing, noticing how the movement seemed to unsettle Leonardo more than I would have expected. He glanced at his smartie, but simply continued his thought. "What Mason describes as his greatest sorrow is a paltry thing compared to what you and I have lost. His was not an irreplaceable, undying love, was it?"

"I . . . I don't know." I faltered. It couldn't have been an irreplaceable, undying love if Mason truly had feelings for *me*.

"No," Leo answered himself. "And all that remains is the idea of his loss as a catalyst. Nothing more. But you and I . . ."

I blanched. How was he planning to connect us?

"Well, your father is as gone to you as mine is to me. For all intents and purposes, he died, Roxanne. You and I have a sorrow without end. One that cuts as deeply and as painfully now as in any reality. It drives us."

He knew about my family—or lack thereof. He knew I was tender there. He knew it and he wasn't above using it on me.

"What do you really know about what drives or cuts me?" I asked.

"I know you live a life that is . . . perhaps not what you'd like it to be."

I slammed my hand against the emergency button. The elevator lurched to a halt and I turned on him. "Stop it. You're manipulating me. It's nasty and transparent."

Something of his cool façade slipped; he looked as though he truly felt my words and I couldn't help but soften a little. "I apologize if what I've said hurt you," he said quietly. "Just remember that Mason is a wire crosser because it is his job. I am a wire crosser in the name of family, loyalty, and honor."

I didn't answer. I was too stunned by the parallels Leonardo had drawn between himself and me. On the face of it, it seemed ridiculous; but below the surface, inside, where it counted, maybe the two of us had more in common than I'd ever imagined. I watched numbly as he pressed the emergency release button, and we resumed our upward climb.

The elevator shuddered again. We both grabbed the rail and I saw how white Leonardo's knuckles were. He was under a great deal of stress, even if he didn't let it show on his face. In fact, he looked irritated more than anything. The sort of irritated that I'd seen every time he thought about Mason . . . or about Mason trying to thwart him. I glanced up at the numbers. "Hey, we've passed my floor," I said, realizing. "My office is on four."

As I moved to correct the mistake, his hand whipped out and grabbed my wrist short of the panel. "We're not going to your office."

I pulled my hand away. "Then, where are we going?"

He didn't answer. Just kept his eyes on the orange fluorescent numbers above the door as we traveled.

I didn't understand at first. Then, a memory came back. There were thirty floors in this building. And the top ten required special security clearance, which—

Oh. *Oh*.

The elevator stopped at twenty with a jolt. Leonardo looked at me. "If you please, Roxanne. Time is of the essence. *Timing* is of the essence. So, if you please . . ." He gestured to a small black square with a flip-top at the bottom of the button panel.

He needed me. He one-hundred percent needed me; I had security clearance and he did not. I could use that, and I jumped on the moment. "I'm not going to do anything else for you. I'm not going to follow you, and I'm not going to listen to you unless you give me something," I said. "Just tell me why you want the code."

In his eyes was a flicker of annoyance; then, as I held my ground, something else. Something closer to respect. "What if I told you that your code already belongs to me, and I'm simply trying to find a way to get it back?"

My heart pounded. Mason had said Leo wanted to profit off me, off my code. This fit that explanation. I was getting closer; I wanted to get closer still.

"Give me more."

Silence.

I opened my mouth to launch into a tirade; he raised his hand to silence me. "We don't have time now. After. Then, when I do, you'll know you can always trust me to do what I say."

There was no good reason to turn my back on this arrangement; he could easily tell me nothing and I'd still do what he asked in the hope I'd get some more clues on my own. What else could I do? I wasn't sacrificing much.

"That's a deal," I said, holding out my hand. He took it in his, turned it over and kissed the top. I added, "Family, loyalty, honor, Leo. Don't do me wrong."

"Of course not," he said.

Of course *not.*

I only hesitated for a second before I flipped the black cover up and punched in a security code, realizing too late how odd it was that the number was at the top of my brain. I didn't even have to think about it, the way somebody who worked in an office building every day wouldn't have to think about it. A tiny red light went on and I pressed my thumb against the security panel.

The elevator opened; I stared into the dark hall for a moment, and then took a step forward, expecting Leonardo to follow me. He punched the stop button again and stayed on the threshold framed by the elevator doors.

"Aren't you coming?" I asked.

He pointed to the unmarked double-wide security doors just a short way down the hall. "I'm afraid not. I'll be working . . . elsewhere."

I felt the blood drain from my skin. "What will I be doing?"

He studied my face. "Think of it as a . . . mission."

"A mission?"

He shrugged. "Not unlike a spy mission. You'll like it."

I looked him right in the eyes, my own narrowed.

"You did more than look in my office. You looked through my whole house." *And my life.*

"But left nothing out of place."

I rolled my eyes. Still, the fact of the matter was that I wanted to break out of the life it seemed I'd led. Which was obviously what Leonardo Kaysar had counted on. "Well, let's hear it."

Leonardo gave me the basic rundown of what

needed to happen. It seemed too simple, which should have given me pause. "So . . . I go into a secured area, check out a specific storage device—a flash drive—with an alpha-numeric designation you want me to memorize, and then we go somewhere upstairs to a data bank and load it?"

"That's correct."

"Why is moving it from one spot to another in the same building a big deal?"

"Because I am concerned that we will move to a wire where one of the two does not exist. And perhaps to one where the code itself does not exist. As you yourself are aware, you only work in this office . . . sometimes."

I studied Leonardo's face and saw no evidence of a lie. And indeed, what he'd just explained was too outrageous for a lie anyway. And too confusing. "Now you're going to explain about the somewhere upstairs part," I guessed.

"Yes." He fiddled around in his breast pocket and pulled out a small notepad, foregoing his handheld in favor of low-tech.

As I'd said, I still didn't really understand. "So, we just basically get the thing and walk it upstairs?"

"More or less."

Why did I think that meant *less*.

Well, I could huff all I wanted, but I knew it wouldn't do any good. Besides, he already knew I'd do this. An embarrassing thrill edged my voice when I asked, "So, after I get this thing, it'll be like Mission Impossible—where there's one guy in a van with the computer equipment monitoring everything, and one guy breaking into the offices to steal something."

"Exactly."

"Don't you think that people with air ducts and in charge of top secret projects all over the country saw the same damn movie and are prepared for exactly this kind of break-in?"

"I'm not concerned."

It took a moment, but I resolved myself. I leaned back against the wall outside the elevator and said, "Cool. Fine. Where do I get this thing, and where's my van?" I knew I had the most ridiculous grin on my face. I was suddenly fantasizing about Leonardo doing a James Bond impression in a custom-tailored tuxedo, and me totally wired into some equipment making sure he didn't get lasered or arrested or pulverized. Except . . .

"Except for one or two details," Leonardo said. "You're not ever the 'guy in a van.' Or perhaps I should say 'limousine.' "

Oh. I blinked rapidly in a futile attempt to process. My nerve wasn't improved when he added, "And where you're taking it isn't exactly easily accessed."

I stared at him. "I don't understand. If I'm not the guy in the van . . ."

Blink. Blink. Blink. I suddenly had flashes: mental pictures of other offices in this building, offices where he might send me. "No way. Uh-uh. I'm not breaking and entering anywhere, and setting myself up to be lasered or arrested or pulverized or whatever the hell happens when you go into places and spaces owned by powerful people with ties to the government for whom security is paramount."

Leo leaned over and caressed my cheek. "Roxanne, you do have such an imagination. You will not be pulverized."

That left breaking, entering, lasered and/or arrested, and all things included under the abbreviation *etc.*

"I'll mess it up. I'm not graceful. I have a natural way of looking suspicious. I always get picked for bag searches. The dogs always spend extra time sniffing the backs of my knees, and agricultural agents never believe there are no oranges in my trunk."

He raised an eyebrow.

I don't know how I knew what I'd just said to be true, but I had a vague sense that on some wire or another, it was. "*When* I go out," I said through gritted teeth. "In the versions of reality when I go out. Okay, this isn't the point. The point is that *technology* is what I do. It would be ludicrous to put you on the tech end and have me pretending to be some kind of spy."

"Yes, well, it's not ideal," he agreed.

"But?"

"But you're smaller."

That was it? I was going to risk getting arrested, maimed or terminated because I was smaller? Maybe if I lopped off a couple of his limbs, he'd be small enough.

"That and, as we've already determined, you have the security clearance I don't have. If I went, I'd be thwarted by security before I ever made it anywhere. That is simply not going to work." Leonardo consulted his notepad again. "Now. Please let me know if I lose you somewhere," he said, obviously not clueing in to the fact that he'd already lost me somewhere back around "pulverization." I peered down at his carefully penned illustrations, obviously diagrammed to scale, with attractive flourishes around the F's and the P's of the labels.

He removed a pen from inside his same pocket. I meant to ask him if he had condoms, a fishing hook, and some dry soup mix in there as well, but I got distracted by the gold nib of his fountain pen as it scratched a satiny black X between two lines on his map.

"Do you see this piping?" Leonardo asked. "It runs from beneath the basement, all the way up the building. Next to the piping is the air conditioning system—a tangle of air ducts, really. The best access is on the thirtieth floor, so you must take the regular or service elevators up and only then move into the walls. With your clearance, you can use the regular elevators, of course."

I gulped and tried to focus on the route his index finger was taking toward the X.

"The air duct I marked, like so, follows *this* route, to *this* particular room. Our destination."

The air duct? I was still reeling.

"It's rather narrow, as you can see from my illustration, and it will be a rather tight fit."

A tight fit.

"I suspect it will also be rather difficult to turn around in the confines of the space, so a quick exit might be tricky, and . . ."

A quick exit might be tricky?

". . . ahead of any explosives or the like."

Explosives?!

I burst out laughing. It was a high-pitched whinnying sound. Awful, really. Not the kind of sound I normally make. It totally revealed my fear.

Leonardo took my hand in his. I pulled it away.

"Roxanne," he purred.

"I'm immune, Leo." I put my hands on my hips and did my best to look all business. "I just hope I'm also indestructible."

EIGHTEEN

When I'd said it seemed too simple, I was right. I passed through security only to be confronted with more security. Getting the flash drive Leo wanted was like going to get something from a safety deposit box, except there were a lot more cameras and security guards lurking everywhere. They asked me where I planned to work on my project, and told me I only had two hours before I'd have to bring it back and check it out again. This was obviously some serious technology I was dealing with, and it occurred to me that as far as its likely purpose, it was either going to make someone a lot of money in the future, kill a lot of people or cure the common cold.

I knew I was supposed to get right to part two of Leo's plan, but I ran to the nearest computer I could find and plugged in the drive just to have a peek. There was nothing on there. I couldn't believe it. I simply couldn't understand. But as I'd been feeling odd heat waves as I moved, I wouldn't have been surprised if by the time I got to Leo's X there *was* something on it.

I'd been heading toward X for about two minutes when I realized that being an operative wasn't all it was cracked up to be. I was on my hands and knees in an air duct with my dress hiked up around my waist, a headset he'd given me crackling with painfully loud static in my ear, and the flash drive in my bra poking into my left boob. I was wondering when I was going to wake up from this surreal dream when Leonardo swore. It scared the piss out of me, because it was the third time, now, in as many minutes, and each time I'd heard a twinge of something I hadn't ever detected in his voice before. It was the sound of insecurity. The sound of fear. It was not a sound I wanted to hear while jammed inside an air duct and wearing a high-tech earpiece, an evening dress with fuck-me pumps, and with an illicit flash drive in my possession and stuck in my bra.

"Mason's using a lot of wire on this," he said.

Static overtook our connection. ". . . major splice, bigger than he's ever done. Listen to me, Roxanne. It is critical that you finish this operation. Everything we said goes out the—"

Static.

I started freaking out. The air duct was trembling now, and the metal above me must have split because tiny grains of something were pelting down on me.

"Leo? I'm going to get the hell out of here. Leo?"

Just static.

A loud whistling sound filled the duct, the sound of my own panicked breathing. So much for abject silence. A large clump of something struck me on the head and bounced off, clattering away in front of me. *Fuck silence.* I kicked off my pumps and started turning my body around in the duct—not easy, since the thing was shaking and the falling dust was making it hard to see. I got one leg pointed up and was trying to get it over my head to turn myself around, but my neck was twisting in a really bad way.

The static cleared for a second. "Roxanne! Roxanne! Can you hear me?"

"I'm here! Make that, I'm getting the hell out of here."

"No! It doesn't have to be real if you keep going. You must proceed!"

I must proceed? I must proceed?

"Remember why you did this in the first place. You can be the person you want to be."

Could he read my mind? What exactly did he know? "It's called a fantasy for a reason! I *did* this because I was confused. Because my life is going crazy and I confused wanting to have control and be a Bond girl with the fact that Bond girls don't exist—and if one does, she probably has a shorter life span than a fruit fly."

The air duct was shaking; I was wedged with my legs over my head, dust blanketing my face and in my nose. A pastiness covered my tongue. The gig had been to silently approach a contained area without triggering security due to temperature, sound or the presence of suspicious substances. Hopefully, *substances* didn't include something like me.

"Kaysar, I'm in trouble here. I've got to go back."

"You listen to me, Roxanne. Mason has managed a critical shift in fate. I don't know what he did, but you must—I repeat, *must*—proceed with the plan and deliver that code before the chain of events he set off reaches completion and you are buried in what is essentially an archeological layer of reality."

"What the hell is that supposed to mean?" I shouted, though I grasped that, at best, *an archeological layer of reality* wasn't a good place to be buried.

"It means you'll probably die in this version of reality if you do not pick yourself up and move on. You. Must. Proceed!"

Even if I could've seen more than a foot past my hand, I would have been blinded by anger. There Leo was, sitting in his nice limousine. A limousine with wheels and a motor and the potential to get him the hell out of Dodge. I, on the other hand, was stuck—make that wedged—in Dodge. I had to believe that if I was caught this was clearly a criminal breach of security. At best.

"I'm in trouble, asshole! I'm going back!"

"The only way out is forward, Roxanne!"

Behind me, the air duct was crushing downward and the only untorn metal I could see was some sort of drainage pipe that wasn't there before. I felt a sudden chill. *What if what Leo said about archaeological layers of reality—whatever they are—is true? What if the only way out is forward?*

I had to hope to God it was true, because there was no more tunnel behind me. I heard an odd roar of twisting metal, and the sides of the duct vanished before my eyes.

I flipped my legs back to the way they had been in the first place and started hauling ass forward, down the narrow passage that was supposed to be a simple air duct and was now just some kind of nightmare. "Leo? Are you still there?" On my hands and knees I scrambled as fast as I could, desperately grabbing at the slippery metal under me, trying to gain traction.

"I'm not leaving you. I'll never leave you. Stay ahead of it. Run as fast as you can. Forget about the alarms. Forget about security. Focus on one thing. No matter who or what tries to stop you, no matter how scared you become, put the code back, Roxanne. Otherwise Mason will kill you, whether he means to or not."

He didn't have to convince me anymore; I was pretty sure that the only thing behind me was the potential to be buried alive. Scrambling, clawing, lunging, I finally saw the light at the end of the literal tunnel. Just where Leo had said it would be. The opening where I was supposed to lower myself down.

Being able to see my goal spurred me on, but it was getting harder and harder to move. It seemed like my legs were being buried, crumpled in metal that would crush me forever. There was no time for finesse, silence, grace, security, carefulness, nothing. The metal was compacting around my body and I could hardly move. I couldn't even hear Leo in my earpiece anymore.

I am alone. Regardless of what he said, I'm alone.

Sheer terror propelled me toward the light. There was so little room to wriggle that I knew in a few more seconds I'd be toast.

I reached the vent, punched it with my hand, grabbed the edges of the opening, and pulled my body out with all of my might, throwing all of myself through. I plunged down into a secret, secure, hermetically sealed, pristinely clean, pure white room where I was supposed to be completely silent and never so much as break a sweat. The grille was still rattling on its side on the hard floor when I followed it, smacking spread-eagle and face down. The alarms had started going off while I was still in the air.

"Leo?"

But my headset had fallen off and I was on my own. A video played on the wall, the recorded voice warning me that I was going to the equivalent of hell and back for breaking and entering, something about a minimum sentence of thirty-five years in prison, to cease and desist, to put my hands up and step to the wall, the whole nine yards.

I raised my arm and tried to think about what Leo had said to me, that if I just kept going I could outrun the outcome before it got to the end of the line. I couldn't pretend to understand.

Nonetheless, I had to act. I turned from the wall, put my hands back down, and pulled the tiny flash drive out of my bra. I scanned the labels lining the rows and rows of slots until I found the one matching the alpha-numeric Leo had made me memorize. The door flew open behind me. I looked over my shoulder; a uniformed security team was closing in on me, and it was all so strange because the walls of the high-tech, very pristine, high-security, don't-sweat room looked like a bomb had gone off, and the sparkling white floor I'd been standing on was nothing more than dirt.

The security guards shouted at me, still a ways distant. They pointed guns at me, and all I could do was think: *Outrun fate. That's what it's going to take.* My hand shook so badly that I could hardly hold the flash drive straight. I ducked down, punched the in/out button, and a drawer slid out with a little slot for the disk. I plugged the drive in, and even though I pushed the button again right away, it seemed so damn slow.

So slow that the armed guards had time to come up and grab me by the back of my dress and throw me to the ground, to twist my arm behind my back, to shove a boot down on my spine and get a handcuff around one of my wrists.

All I could think about was thirty-five years minimum in prison unless I managed to plead insanity based on the fact that I believed I was operating with the best of intentions for the good of a reality that hadn't happened yet, and that I apologized for any inconvenience but that a guy from the future had told me . . .

You're going down, Roxanne. You're going down.

The floor slipped out from under me and the guards went flying, and suddenly it was like freaking *Alice in Wonderland* and I *was* going down, with metal and pipes and dirt all around. The craziest part was that Leo caught me in his arms at the bottom of the rabbit hole.

He set me on my feet, and when I actually had the courage to pull my face away from his jacket, I looked around. I was in a hole. On a piece of chain link that was keeping all the dirt from caving in hung one of those supersimplified architectural renderings of the building, with a FUTURE SITE OF . . . sign and a company symbol. It didn't take a rocket scientist to determine that we were in the excavated portion of a construction project.

I didn't even consider asking Leonardo to explain,

because I already got it. The building I was just in with the security I'd just breached didn't exist yet.

"It's all right, Roxanne. I've got you."

I clung to Leo, shaking, crying. "It's over, right? I did what you said. I put it back. It's over, right?"

The look on his face said it all. There was genuine emotion there. He looked a bit stricken, really, and I knew that he didn't want to have to say anything. It *wasn't* over, because somebody got in the way.

"Mason," I said. "Because of Mason." I just about collapsed. Leo captured me in his arms and held me like he meant it, while I sobbed into his shoulder and let all the fear I'd worked so hard to tamp down come out.

The dirt on my face smeared into his delicate linen collar, my broken fingernails snagged the wool of his suit. I could feel his mouth, his lips against my ear, and it was all too much. All this emotion. I was so exhausted. So exhausted, and filthy, and my heart was practically exploding with the adrenaline.

He walked me out of the construction area. My dress was in shreds, my stockings nothing but runs. Stumbling as I walked, I buried my face in Leonardo's shoulder as he helped me toward the limousine.

"I just want to go home," I wept more than said.

Suddenly, Leo stopped. He lifted my chin and looked me in the eye. "I'm going to take care of you, Roxy."

He'd never called me that before. But I didn't dwell on it. I just closed my eyes and let him lead me out.

I wasn't even conscious of the drive home, simply faded in and out of a kind of groggy haze. He carried me up the steps to my apartment and brought me inside, then carried me up to my bathroom. The house was quiet. I guess Kitty was out.

He sat me down on the edge of the bathtub. I said, "This is too much for me, Leo. I can't do this. My brain was not designed to process all of this. I'm tired of crying. I'm tired of blacking out. I'm tired of trying to keep an open mind and accept the impossible."

"Shush, Roxanne." That's all he said. He turned the water on in the tub and let it begin to fill. Then he took a towel, ran it under warm water, and gently wiped the dirt from my face.

"Shush," he said tenderly, wiping my arms next. His fingers ran over my dress. I grabbed at his hand as it touched my side.

He looked in my eyes and shook his head a little, then smiled. It felt good to have him touch me this way. To have *someone* touch me. Concerned, caring, attentive. I had somebody's full attention—Leo's full attention—and it felt incredible.

I let my hand fall away from my side and he slowly pulled on my dress, revealing more of my skin by the inch. I stopped being self-conscious or afraid or angry or anything, and I just let myself feel.

"Come," Leonardo said, holding out his hand. I stood up and my dress slid off my body. He pulled slightly on my hand and I stepped out of the fabric.

He led me to the bathtub and supported me as I climbed into the warm water. I eased back and let the warmth overtake me, the water stinging the tiny cuts and scrapes on my exposed skin. Leonardo rolled up his sleeves. He pulled a clean cloth from the towel rack, rubbed it with soap, and began to wash me clean.

He murmured things to me, words of encouragement, words of comfort. "You did well, Roxanne," was the last clear thing I heard. I felt him press his lips against my neck, and then he wrapped me in a towel and carried me to bed. All things considered, this was not a bad way to get over a guy. I just wished that, with all Leonardo's attention and care, my last thought before drifting off hadn't been of Mason.

NINETEEN

Kitty came home from work the next afternoon, rattled about in the kitchen, then walked into the living room with a vase and a bouquet of flowers. She looked down at me where I slumped back on the sofa pillows in surprise. "Roxanne, what are doing?"

"I'm sitting in the living room." It was what I'd been doing all day, somewhat shell-shocked. I hadn't seen Leo.

Kitty put the vase down and looked at me for a moment, then started to remove the plastic from the flowers. "How was your night?"

I would love to tell you all about it. Not.

I sighed. "We . . . talked. Went to a party." It was too much work to explain, and she'd just think I was crazy.

"Oh." Kitty wrinkled her nose. "I guess I hoped you two would come up with something more exciting." She cocked her head and looked at me, and I guess she read that I wasn't in the mood to share. "Any plans for tonight? I was thinking about ordering a pizza."

I turned my head. "Sounds good to me. I'll buy if you fly."

"Duh. You never fly."

I sat up straight, inexplicably angry. "What does that mean?"

She looked a little startled. "Uh . . ."

"I don't do dinner? I don't go out? I don't fly?"

"You don't fly," she repeated with a rather deer-in-the-headlights look.

God bless her, but I just totally lost it. I jumped up and grabbed her by the shoulders, causing her to nearly fling the flowers away, scattering water droplets everywhere. "Kitty! Stop telling me what I don't, can't, or won't do. Because I'm doing it, okay? You wouldn't believe what I'm doing! And going forward, I'm going to do even more. I'm gonna pick up that goddamn gun and I'm not going to let people make decisions for me or tell me what to do!"

I had her in shock—in almost as much shock as I was. I removed my hands and stepped back from her, holding my palms out in the air like I'd just touched electricity or something. She didn't speak. I thought she was going to slap me at first.

"You didn't deserve that, did you?" I realized, my face flaming.

"Not really," she said. "I'm sorry. I just thought . . ."

"What?"

"You're different. You're really different. Something's changed and I don't know when or how, but you're really different. I'm confused, but the thing is, Roxy . . ."

"Yeah?"

"It's better."

"What do you mean?"

"I just . . . think you're better," she repeated, waving her hand in the air to suggest there was no other way to explain. She tapped her finger against her temple and studied my face. "Yeah. Different. Better. But hard to get used to."

"Look, I'm sorry I . . . manhandled you," I said sheepishly.

She broke into a smile. "No harm, no foul. Can I ask you a question, though?"

"Go."

"What gun?"

"What gun? Oh. The 'goddamn gun.' I totally should have told you. I'm keeping a gun in my closet now. For protection."

"Holy-moly. Do we need protection again?"

"Well, someone did break into the house and lift all of my computer equipment," I groused.

She started in surprise. "When was this?"

Oh, right. That was in another version of my life. The one in which you weren't my friend anymore. "You don't remember?"

She frowned as she thought about it. "No. Ohhhhhhh. Ohhhhhh." She looked at me meaningfully. "Okay."

"Okay?" I wasn't sure what she thought she'd figured out.

"Yeah. No problem. As long as it's not loaded. Oh, and one more thing," she added, turning back to the flowers she began arranging in the vase.

"Fire away."

"What's with the handcuffs?"

I'd forgotten. I'd been wearing them so long I'd gotten used to them. "Well, with Leonardo here last night—"

I was stopped by a full-blown, high-octane screech as Kitty wheeled around, her mouth wide open. "Oh. My. God. Ohmigod, ohmigod, ohmigod!"

"What?" I asked, starting to totally freak out. "What happened? What's wrong?"

"Oh. My. God. You did more than talk. You slept with him! Bondage on the first go? Those European men are so advanced!"

Sigh. What would any commonsensical person do in my shoes? They'd say, *Yes, Kitty. Actually, Leonardo was here last night and he stripped me naked and there were feathers and handcuffs and all kinds of . . . straps . . . and things*. Or maybe, *Gee, Kitty. Actually there's something I've been meaning to talk to you about regarding the fact that lately I've been experiencing my life in several different dimensions of time, one of which being where we don't even know each other anymore*.

I didn't relish either explanation. I didn't think my eardrums could take it.

"Well?"

"This is not going to be easy." I gestured to the chair facing the sofa.

She froze in mid–flower arrangement, seeing my face. "What? What's wrong?"

"Sit down," I said.

She did, her eyes wide, swallowing continuously as if her mouth were going dry.

"It's like this . . ." No, that wasn't a good way to begin. "The thing is . . ." *Shit. Okay.* "I think it would be fair to say that I've been acting a little . . ."

She leaned forward, waiting for the adjective.

"Um." I tapped my index finger against my temple, trying to figure out how to put it in the least bizarre terms possible. In the face of my silence, Kitty decided to fill in the blanks.

"Strange? Abnormal?" she suggested. "Whacked out? Left of center? Marching to the beat of your own truly one-of-a-kind drummer? Souped up?"

Jesus.

She frowned. "No, that's not what you were going to say, was it?"

"Not exactly."

"Oh. Sorry."

"Preoccupied. I was going to say preoccupied."

"Ohhh. Right."

"Yeah. So, I think it would be fair to say that I'm a little preoccupied with . . . things . . . these days."

"Yes. I think it would be fair to say that," she said encouragingly.

"And it's for good reason."

"Yes?"

"Leonardo is not my boyfriend, and I do not have a handcuff on my wrist from any bondage he might have been . . . performing on me."

Her face fell. "Bummer."

"Yes, well . . . I think there will be plenty of time for that in the future." I then felt ill. I could no longer use phrases like *in the past* or *in the future* with any suggestion of certainty.

Kitty reached out and patted my handcuffed wrist.

"I find that the best way to handle difficult things is to just come out and say them."

"Great. Here goes. Leonardo Kaysar is an agent from the future who has the ability to 'cross wires,' by which I mean splice reality, alter the course of fate. Sometimes I seem to go back in time, sometimes forward, and sometimes I seem to start over. Frankly, I'm never quite sure who I am. Leonardo says that Mason Merrick is a villain. Mason says Leo is. Apparently, one of the pieces of code I've been working on is really important to both guys and happens to be a major factor in the outcome of my fate. Since Mason was willing to kill me in the past, as you saw, I have to say that I have fewer qualms about siding with Leonardo at this point. And—"

"Roxanne?"

"Yeah?" I asked hopefully.

"I really have to pee."

"What?"

She stood up. "You know I don't mind listening to your theories. I just really should pee first, and then I'm all yours."

I stared in horror as she got up and disappeared. My "theories"? As in, weird conspiracy theories? Was this a usual ramble for me in this reality?

I went to the refrigerator and pulled out a bottle of chilled white wine. I pulled the cork and poured two glasses.

Kitty came back and picked one up. "Excellent idea," she said. She made a big scene of settling in for the long haul, plumping up the backrest of her chair, arranging her clothes, and then clasping her hands in front of her. "Much better. Now, what's that you were saying about Leonardo being a sexy agent from the future?"

"I didn't say sexy." I took a giant swig of wine, exactly the way you're not supposed to drink it, and sat down at the kitchen table. "I'm not joking. This is not a theory, conspiracy or otherwise. This is real."

And, of course, I then proceeded to ruin my own case by bursting out with insane laughter. *This is real? Did I actually just use that phrase?*

Kitty winced.

"Sorry," I said, pulling myself together. "Sorry about that. I'm just nervous."

She studied me intently, less of that let-me-humor-you-my-little-friend air about her. I remembered then that *she* was usually the one who believed intergalactic space travel was only moments away, in the existence of angels, and who was open to the possibility that algae scum had feelings. If anyone was going to believe me, it was my old pal Kitty.

"Can you prove it to me?" she asked.

"That," I said, "is a perfectly reasonable question, and in fact . . . I cannot."

She nodded thoughtfully. "Well, when you can, let me know."

"I'll do that."

"Great." She smiled.

I stood up and pushed my chair in.

"That's it?" she asked in surprise.

"Yeah. Until I can prove it, I see no reason to say anything more."

"Oh. Okay." She pointed at my wrist. "What do you want to do about that?"

I looked at my wrist, looked over at the electric

carving knife on the counter and then back at Kitty. "Wanna bet there's a Web site that'll show us how to pick the lock?"

She grinned. "Let's go."

TWENTY

I woke up the following morning to more complete and total normalcy. Nobody was trying to get me to do anything. I turned on my computer and went downstairs while it booted up. Kitty was dressed, making herself a bag lunch to take to work.

"Morning," she said.

"Morning." The coffee was already made and I poured myself a nice big mugful, then leaned against the counter and watched her wrap three conjoined pieces of pizza into a tinfoil triangle.

"That stuff's going to kill you one of these days," I said.

"I stopped ordering extra cheese, remember?"

It was just like college again.

"Any messages?" I asked.

"Nope."

I went back upstairs to the window and looked out through the sliver not covered by the drapes; nobody was sleeping in their car. Nobody was trying to get me to do anything illegal or trying to persuade me to believe the impossible. Maybe it would be a good day.

I went back downstairs to the kitchen. Kitty stuck a paper towel and an apple in her bag, gently lowered in the tinfoiled triangle, and folded the top of the bag over. I followed her to the door, not quite knowing what to do with myself.

"I'll see you later," she said. She stopped with her hand on the doorknob and turned to look at me, her blond hair swinging out. "You okay?"

"Everything's great," I said. "Have a fabulous day at work."

"You too," she said, and slipped out the door.

I took a swig of coffee, then went back upstairs and settled in at the computer.

It had been a while since I'd really "been to work," but it wasn't like I was getting phone calls asking where any projects were. Should I be at an office? I looked through the files in the holder on my desk, suddenly wondering if I had any outstanding projects in this version of reality. How had reality changed this time? Had it changed yet again while I was sleeping? The last few days had been impossible to plan for. A mishmash of convoluted memories were little help.

I had several freelance folders relating to the agency. I opened them up and scanned the documents. Nothing seemed new or out of place. I'd wrapped up my old projects and apparently hadn't signed on for any new ones. There was an e-mail printout from the agency asking me if I was done with my vacation, which, of course, made me snort coffee out of my nose. My time with Mason and Leo wasn't anything I'd call a vacation, but I guess someone had set up an excuse on my behalf. Maybe it had been me.

I surfed the Web for a while, but quickly tired of it. I tapped my fingers on my desk and rearranged the magnetic words on my date board. I put the mug of coffee down and went to the closet, rummaged around, and found the high-heeled-shoe box. The shoes were gone, of course, but the gun was still there, along with the ammunition.

I pushed hangers around until I found the dress. Thanks to Kitty, it was in a plastic wrapper with a dry-cleaning stub hanging off it. I pulled up the plastic. Technically, the garment was clean, but it hung limp, looking like it had been through hell and back. I almost laughed to imagine what Kitty must have been thinking upon seeing the perfect dress she'd picked out completely trashed after my "date" with Leonardo. But in quintessential Kitty style, she'd kept her mouth shut and pretended it was completely normal.

But I *couldn't* laugh. I remembered how good Mason and I looked the first time I'd ever worn that dress. That one night. It hurt to think of all the question marks I had about him, about us. And though it had been a pain in the ass and I'd flip-flopped about believing in Mason a million times, there was only one thought on my mind as I pulled the garment down again. Now that I was being left completely alone, I had to wonder: Had Mason stopped trying? Did he give up? And was I asking these questions because I cared about his work agenda or his feelings for me?

For that matter, where was Leo? He'd worked so hard to keep me in sight, to take care of me after the spying incident. And he'd seemed like he was flirting because he wanted to and not because he wanted me to do something for him. Leo had touched his lips to my skin in a more tender way than before, and though he was clearly a professional lady-killer and I couldn't trust him, there was something in him that seemed new. Different. Something I responded to.

And yet, neither man was here.

I didn't feel like working, even if I'd known what to do. All I wanted was to watch one of my movies while I stuffed my face full of popcorn and chocolate, trying not to think about Mason or Leo and me at all.

I grabbed my messenger bag, jacket, and keys and slipped out the door, heading for the 7-Eleven to purchase some sorely needed comfort food. Halfway there, almost to the place where it had all started, I stopped in my tracks. I had never considered myself a superstitious person, but I nevertheless added an extra block to the trip by heading around the back way, planning to cut through the parking lot behind the store.

I guess I picked the wrong avoidance tactic, because parked in the lot was a crappy, boxy rental car with a guy leaning against it. The guy with the two last names.

Seeing Mason under these circumstances was more of a shock than I'd anticipated. Flustered, I forgot Leo and the past few days. I forgot I wasn't supposed to care about Mason or his transportation anymore, and I almost made a friendly joke. Until I remembered what it felt like to watch him look me in the eye while he pulled the trigger and shot me.

I wanted an explanation.

Mason stood up straight and dropped his arms but didn't move toward me. He just waited next to his car, and there was something in his body language I didn't recognize.

"You shot me," I said uncertainly, my voice cracking. "I opened the door and you looked me in the eye and you shot me."

He frowned and kicked the toe of his shoe against the ground. "Yeah, well . . . what really sucks about this is that I know how it looks. It ain't good. Leo's one of the best."

It was a subtle play; he knew he had a baseline from which to work. He knew that he'd made me care about him, and he was trying to use that against me.

"So was that you?" *Was the Mason standing in my doorway pulling the trigger the* real *you?*

"Was what me?"

I knew him too well. "You're stalling," I whispered, feeling a kind of horror come over me. I needed to know: "Did you shoot me, Mason? Did you try to kill me? And was it the same when you meant to bury me alive so I wouldn't put that disk back?" It all sounded even more horrific coming out of my mouth.

Mason grabbed at the back of his neck and looked down at the ground, his face the very picture of grim. "It's not that black-and-white. It sort of depends."

"It doesn't depend," I said incredulously. "It's yes or no. Answer me straight; no joking. Was that you crossing the wires knowing I would die?"

I have to confess that the fact that he was so uncomfortable answering the question, that he had such a difficult time giving me any answer, in and of itself brought a measure of sympathy and even a little bit of doubt of his crimes. In his eyes was true pain.

"I didn't *know* you would die," he said. "In fact, I think we can both be assured of that, given that you're standing right here."

Oh, you're stalling, Mason. "Did you act," I whispered, "knowing I could die?"

He dropped his hands to his sides and murmured a resigned, "Yes." The word sounded soft coming out, but it flew across the six feet between us like another bullet.

I stepped back, unsteady. It didn't matter whether or not he felt bad about this. If I'd needed proof of who was bad and who was good, who was my villain and who was my hero, I'd just gotten it.

He reached out to me; I leaped back out of reach. "Leonardo never tried to hurt me," I said.

"He pushed us under a truck trying to get the code, Roxy. You could have died then, too. Did you forget?"

"I didn't forget. But he explained it was an accident. He wasn't driving. I never saw who was driving. You were the one who told me it was Leonardo."

"Number one, if he wasn't driving, but he had 'his people' chase you down, what difference would that really make?"

"He couldn't have known the lengths to which his people would go," I said a little desperately. "And you not only shot me in cold blood, but you admitted it and also tried to bury me alive."

"I wasn't *trying* to bury you alive. Not like you think. And yeah, I admitted it," he said, disbelieving laughter bursting from his mouth. "But that's because I'm the one who's being straight with you. Do you really understand who Leonardo Kaysar is?"

"As much as I understand who you are," I muttered.

Mason shook his head. "Remember to think of it this way. Leonardo pulls the genie out of the bottle; I try to put the genie back. I believe that what was meant to be, should be."

"But then I wouldn't be friends with Kitty again."

"Maybe you were always meant to be friends with Kitty. And if that turned out not to be the case, at least you wouldn't know. You wouldn't miss her."

"I missed Naveed's daughter. I haven't forgotten about that."

"Yes, that's weird. But we already know you're an unusually aware Major. When we get to the end of this thing and your reality locks in, that will probably start to fade. And you gotta understand, there was nothing I could do to keep from losing Naveed's daughter. Leonardo had already set that outcome in motion. He tried to cross wires to reset the fight over you we had that night. He was trying for another chance to win first possession of you. I countered his play to keep the status quo, and Naveed's daughter was a random casualty of the move—a casualty on a list I do everything in my power to keep as short as possible."

He sighed and, after a moment, glanced at my face. His eyes were sorrowful. "I do what I can, but sometimes you just have to be a little . . . ruthless. It's tough at first. It's easier to screw something up than to fix it and restore it to the way it once was. But it's better to make the hard choice with the right outcome as soon as possible. Fewer repercussions."

Anger filled me. "And if some poor sap who has nothing to do with anything happens to be in the way, well, so be it."

"Look, Rox, I don't like people disappearing either."

"But you're saying it's a necessary outcome," I said bitterly. "And you also said that Leo disappeared your girlfriend. You couldn't bring her back?"

He winced. "That's a tough one, Rox. Believe me. For one thing, if you *do* bring them back, it's rare that the relationship between the disappeared and his or her friends is the way it was before. And you have to do it in a way that doesn't substantially change fate. It's tricky."

I felt a pang of sympathy—just before jealousy and anger crowded the feeling back out. "You did manage to bring her back, but she didn't know you, did she?"

"Right," he agreed.

"You and Leo became enemies because of it."

He nodded. "It wasn't the only reason, but she's a big one. Look, this girlfriend thing. Rox, I think you need—"

I put my palm up. I didn't want to hear any more about some chick he loved more than anything in the universe, blah, blah, blah. I just wasn't up to it. The idea of it made me jealous and miserable, and the last thing I wanted was for Mason to see that.

"Aren't you supposed to be off anticipating Leo's next move?" I asked numbly.

Mason shrugged, a weariness evident in his entire being. "There isn't a next move, and I give Leo another ten minutes to come to that conclusion. He's a little slow in the head sometimes."

"There's no next move? So, what do you plan to do?"

"I'm not sure," Mason said bitterly, "which I think you should know is more dangerous than anything."

As if on cue, the squeal of brakes shot through the parking lot as a car pulled into an empty spot. Leo jumped out and made a beeline for me. "Roxanne!" He put his hand out protectively and gently ushered me away from Mason, who just looked at him with weary amusement.

Mason and Leonardo stood there facing each other. I waited for one of them to throw the first punch. No punch. I waited for someone to pull a gun. No gun. I waited for something, *anything*, any kind of action to match the intensity of my heartbeat, but though the two men faced off, there seemed to be a stunning lack of aggression.

"Is Mason going on with his sob story again? It's always his last-ditch effort. Shows an appalling lack of creativity."

"Which sob story?"

"The one about how I supposedly disappeared his girlfriend."

"Did you?"

"I told you. No. Mason's just a mercenary. He'd say or do anything to get what he wants. He loves to bring her up again at the most critical point."

So, *this* was the most critical point? "Okay, okay, whoa, there." I stretched out my arms to keep the two men apart. I looked at both. "What I want to understand is, if each of you is the bane of the other's existence, and if this is a critical juncture, why aren't you trying to kill each other? Why are we all suddenly acting like there's all the time in the world?"

Leonardo glanced at his reader. "Actually, time is running out. But then, I like a challenge," he said cryptically.

"Likewise," Mason growled.

"Stalemate is it then?" Leonardo asked him, distaste dripping from his words. He looked like he'd rather be shooting his pistol instead of talking.

Mason folded his arms across his chest. "Yup. Stalemate. I guess you could say we're back to square one." He nodded, looking as grim as I'd ever seen him.

Leo stroked his chin, studying Mason's face. Suddenly they both looked at me, and then at each other.

"Back to square one? Are you kidding me?" My sanity couldn't take much more of this.

"We haven't secured an outcome, and instead have worked ourselves to an impasse," Leo said. "And I think neither of us can take the chance that fate will give us what we want. This . . . well, this has never happened before." He looked almost embarrassed—not a look I could remember seeing on his face before, which made it all the more disconcerting.

"Meaning?" I pressed.

Leo sighed and looked at Mason. "I cannot believe I'm saying this, but if we are not willing to accept fate, then it seems Mason and I must enter into an agreement to reset the playing field or neither one of us can get what he wants."

Wow. I'd nearly died more than once. This wasn't a playing field.

"A handshake agreement," Mason said, testing the idea.

"Yes. Honor. I know it's a foreign concept for you."

"Shut up, Leo. A handshake deal's a foreign concept to you, too. And the only reason I'm going to do it is because there is no doubt in my mind that I'm going to beat you, just as I have before."

"You are so fixated on the past. What does any of it matter if you lose now?"

"Save it. Where do you want to start?"

I just stood there, watching the guys discuss my future. I would have acted if I'd had any idea what to do.

Leo shrugged. "Neutral territory."

"Fine with me."

I had no idea what *neutral territory* was, but Mason seemed to know. The wind ruffled Leo's hair, and he carefully smoothed it back down as he and Mason stared at each other.

"The only reason this is going to work," Leo said, "is because neither of us trusts the other at all."

"It's one for the history books," Mason agreed in

a murmur. "So, the deal is, we reset the playing field, and then it's each man for himself?"

Leo nodded and held out his sleek, manicured hand. Mason's rough, tan fingers closed around it. They shook on their agreement.

Then they both turned to me.

TWENTY-ONE

After arguing for several minutes about who was going to take me to wherever we were going, the decision was made that we should all go together. I didn't bother pointing out that if they really were in some kind of détente then it shouldn't matter who had custody of me on the way. This arguing suggested that neither of them meant to keep their word if it came down to the wire and they faced losing the game.

Neutral territory turned out to be in front of the inside goddamn 7-Eleven. "Why here?" I growled.

"DMZ," Mason said. "And it seemed appropriate for the reset."

"In other words . . ." I trailed off, hoping one of them would finish my sentence with something helpful.

Leonardo smiled. "In other words, we agree on almost nothing."

"Except for one thing," Mason said.

Both men looked at me.

"Which is?"

"We don't want you to die now," Leonardo said.

"We *definitely* don't want you to die now," Mason said, glancing at Leo and proving to me he'd added the word in the spirit of one-upmanship.

But . . . *now*? "Well, thanks," I said dryly. "That's considerate of you." Especially given that both of them had nearly killed me at different times.

"So, if you feel ready . . ." Leo began, advancing on me.

"Whoa, whoa, whoa!" I put up my palms. "You know what? No can do. There comes a time when a woman has to stand up for herself and take matters into her own hands. I'm very sorry if some snippet of code I wrote or will write contributes to the Apocalypse or whatever, but I'm through listening to you two. You've thrown me around, taken advantage of me, taken advantage of my lack of information—which, I might point out, is the direct result of your not telling me anything. I've almost died several times, you've made me cry, and none of it has amounted to anything. We never get anywhere. Because you do something"—I pointed at Mason—"and then you do something"—I pointed at Leo—"and both of you just keep negating the other person's actions."

"Yes, that's kind of how it works," Mason agreed, his voice low and measured like that of a hostage negotiator. "Except that usually there's no reset. I get how upsetting the idea of starting from square one must be for you."

Oh, do you, now? I almost punched him again.

"You're a highly unusual case," Leonardo said.

"You'd better believe I'm a highly unusual case," I yelled. "This stalemate is *your* problem, not mine.

I'm done with this. I refuse to cooperate. So I demand that you take me home and leave me alone." And then I waited.

And I waited.

Let's not all rush forward at once.

"I see how it is," I said, mentally weighing my options. It didn't take long. There weren't any.

"I'm not sure you do see. You're not done," Leonardo said. "You can't be done. You're not a Peripheral; you're a Major. You're the point of all of this. You're indispensable."

I leaned against the wall, wondering why I didn't just get on a plane or a train or hop in Kitty's car and disappear myself from all of this. Well, I didn't *really* wonder. I already knew that I didn't really have the moxie Leonardo had once credited me with, even if I was starting to stand up for myself. And I also knew that out there held nothing for me. At least here I had bits of the life I wanted to lead. And who knew if I could even hide from wire crossers?

I watched the men argue over procedures and who would do what, and a thought occurred to me. If I did what they asked, we'd reset to a reality where Mason wasn't my stalker. We'd end up back on that first wire, and maybe I could stop Leonardo from switching things up and making Mason the villain.

"You okay, Rox?" Mason asked, a kind of concern in his voice and eyes that just didn't say *stalker*. What did that mean to me, though?

"I don't know." I looked numbly at him. "Just tell me this is it, that this is the end. I mean, I realize we're starting over here, but in a way it's also the end, right? When this plays out, I'll be done? I can just go on with my life? I can learn from this and . . ."

An uncharacteristic look of guilt showed on Leo's face; Mason looked stricken. "I'll try to come back and fix it," he said.

I stared at him in confusion. "What?"

"Well, in a reset . . . you've been hyper-aware of your realities through the past jumps, but this time you should be cognizant only of what you knew the first time around," Leo finally said—a scary answer if I ever heard one.

"Wait a second," I whispered. What if things got worse this time around? And I'd never know the difference?

Mason selected one of the presets on his reader, Leo injected the punch, and I knew the past wouldn't wait.

We had everything before us, we had nothing before us.

I'm not going to panic . . . not going to panic . . . not going . . .

What are you doing, Roxanne?

I'm going to the 7-Eleven. People go to the 7-Eleven all the time and absolutely nothing happens to them. So, chances are that nothing is going to happen to you, which means there is absolutely no point in panicking. Keep walking.

I lost my footing and stumbled a bit. I put my hand to my forehead as if I could stop what felt like an audiotape of my very own thoughts, prerecorded, playing back without commercials.

Give me a break.

I'm going to die.

If nothing else, go down fighting.

How strange.

I stopped in the middle of the street, halfway between the 7-Eleven and my home, and looked around. How strange, indeed. I was as scared as I'd been the first time around, but I had the sense that it wasn't for the same reason; I knew why I was scared now, and it made me wonder all the more what I'd been scared of then. Unless I was caught in an endless cycle of this crap, which was something I didn't even want to take seriously.

A half block later I slowed to a halt and looked behind me toward home. A discarded *S.F. Chronicle* blew across the street. I looked forward; the pale glow of the 7-Eleven was only a block away.

I almost started to laugh in spite of my fear. They had been wrong again. I wasn't rewound to L. Roxanne Zaborovsky on the brink of her very first reality splice, before Leonardo Kaysar, before the second coming of Mason Merrick. Because if I were that person again, this moment would have seemed fresh and new and I'd be panicking the way I was before, still not knowing why. No, I was still the Roxy who was three times removed from her original reality and cognizant of bits and pieces of every single one. That wasn't what they were expecting when they'd gambled on a reset.

As I stood there staring at the glow of the 7-Eleven sign, a figure emerged from the shadows and stepped into the street. *Mason.*

I looked behind me. The figure of a second man rose up from a crouch in the shadows. *Leonardo.*

Give me a break.

"She's mine, Leo!"

I couldn't see Mason's face in any detail. I couldn't see his expression, and I'm not sure it would have mattered. My recent life had begun again, events unfolding just as they had the first time. My body began responding to invisible cues as if I were repeating a dance I'd practiced many times before.

The way I pulled at my messenger bag and started searching for my phone, the way the men started toward me, the way I dropped to the street on my knees, spilling my things; the way the pavement vibrated, the way I tried to crawl away on my hands and knees.

And . . . the way I gave up and curled my body into surrender in the street.

Mason and Leo were shouting at each other. Curled up in the street, I let my mind wander as I waited for my cue, as it were. And it was then that I realized that while the motions were all the same, I wasn't. I might be scared, but not like before. I might feel some panic, but not like before. I might find my heart beating overtime, but my breathing was measured, my mind silent of screams.

Everything around me was exactly the same, but I didn't have to be. If I could purposely hesitate or make a proactive move, if I could slip even an extra second into time or pluck one out, I could change things. Meaning, I had as much ability to create a new reality for myself as they did. And that wasn't something the guys had counted on.

They'd commented how I was unusually cognizant of the reality splice, how my transition from one reality to another hadn't been seamless. And Leo had also seemed surprised at the residual memories I'd kept from previous versions of my reality. Leonardo had said I was an unusual case. He was right. And given what they said just before the reset, even more unusual than they realized.

Silver streaked through the air, and I watched a gun flip end over end until it hit the pavement. Except, I kept my head up this time and took a closer look. That wasn't a gun; it was a punch.

Mason ignored it, barreling full-force into Leo as if the guy were a tackling dummy. Watching them closely, I saw that now they were grappling over a gun that had come from inside Leonardo's jacket. I would have bet a lot of money it was the same gun he'd give me later.

I closed my eyes and waited for Leo to come for me. He did, as he had before, picking me up under my arms, crushing me face-first into his chest, moving backward, dragging me along with him like a rag doll.

Except this time I wasn't so busy being scared out of my gourd, and this time I noticed the object in his jacket pocket bumping against my rib cage.

I knew Mason would be fighting to win the advantage all over again, and Leo for a second chance to gain *possession* of me. But it was as if they were in a scripted realm. Every cry of pain, every blow, the gun arching up in the air . . . it unfolded exactly the same way. With my eyes squeezed shut and the toes of my shoes scraping on the pavement, I heard Leo say, "This is where it ends."

I kept waiting to see which one of them would break first and change things. But as they fought on,

I figured out the answer for myself. It was going to be me. In the moment that I was supposed to wonder how a person prepared herself to die, just as the gun went off and Leo lurched sideways, I slipped the hand that was supposed to be hanging loosely at my side into Leo's jacket pocket and took his smartie.

I knew where the punch was on the ground, and when Leo let go of me and I fell away from him to the pavement, I twisted my body to face it.

"This is where it begins," Mason shouted. The two men started running, smashing together and wrestling each other to the ground.

I lifted myself to my knees and crawled hand over hand, knee over knee, grabbing the strap of my messenger bag on the way, then crawled to the punch lying in the street. I stuffed it in my bag along with Leo's reader and retreated.

Now I was as scared as I'd been the first time.

I kept crawling down the middle of the street, the gravel raking my knees and palms, the messenger bag heavy with the equipment. Blinking back tears, I set my sights on Mason's Mustang, parked just as it was before, in perfect condition.

At some point, the boys would recognize that I was stepping off the wire. My hands were shaking when I wrenched open the car door and climbed in. The heat begin to build. If Leo didn't take advantage and overpower Mason before Mason picked up the gun and locked in the sweet spot as he had before, I had only a moment or so before the reality splice.

Sweat trickled down between my shoulder blades as I hugged my knees to my chest in the growing heat. I watched the men. Mason shouted, "L. Roxanne Zaborovsky," but I wasn't where I was supposed to be.

They stopped fighting, exchanged words. I could tell by their frantic body language that they were finally cognizant of being unwired; that I'd unwired all of us.

Mason searched the ground; Leo's hands dug into his jacket pockets; then both of them started running toward the car.

"The deal is off!" Mason yelled.

"Obviously," Leo shouted back. "The reset's a bloody mess!"

I reached out to the car keys. This wasn't a simple reset if I did something before Mason spliced reality.

If nothing else, go down fighting.

I turned the key and the engine caught, blaring out with a full muscle-car roar. Hauling on the steering wheel I hit the gas and peeled away from the curb, one or both of the guys glancing off the broadside of the vehicle as I drove off batshit-crazy for home.

The heat evaporated as I raced down the street. *Oh, my God. The car.* I suddenly understood that reality had spliced the first time around while I was in the car. The heat had been insane, like it was a moment ago. But it must have been the moment at which the guys were fighting and Mason won the advantage over Leo that it was hottest; the minute the fate of the fight was determined, the splice had gone through. Leonardo couldn't do anything to change that fact, so he'd had to go off and identify a new wire to cross to put me back on track for his goal.

But I might have stopped the reset from fully going through, and so the original reality splice didn't seem like it would be duplicated. There was apparently still wire left, and I was going to use it the way *I* wanted to. If only I knew exactly how to splice things to get what I wanted.

I hit the brakes in front of my place and double-parked the Mustang, grabbing my bag and running full-speed up the stairs. Fumbling with my keys at the front door, I figured I'd bought enough time before they made it back, even at a sprint.

The door opened, and I crumpled down on the threshold and pulled the reader and the punch from my bag. Mason had explained it to me, but that wasn't the same as seeing it done.

I set the reader to ROXY'S APT and shook the punch, unsure how else to get the tiny chamber to fill with that nanobiotech stuff. *You do not know what you're doing. You don't even know if it works like this.*

All I knew was that I wanted to go home. But home to the Roxy I was becoming, not the one with the life I didn't want to live. I struggled clumsily with the equipment, punching random buttons. I couldn't figure it out, and my shaking hands didn't help.

The damn thing sprang out of my hand and hit me in the face, clattering to the ground in front of me. I cursed, pressing my palm against my forehead. If it hadn't already hurt about as much as metal on flesh could hurt, Kitty's bloodcurdling, "Ohmigod," in my ear would have done the rest.

TWENTY-TWO

"Ohmigod! Ohmigod!" Kitty dropped to her knees next to me, grabbing at my hands. "I shouldn't have left. I just figured that was part of it, you know? That I shouldn't be here and it was all your own doing. Look, it's really okay. The important thing is that you opened the door. Right? That's all that matters. We'll cross the stupid threshold another time. Don't think of this as a setback. It will come. In a couple days when you feel better we'll go back to the 7-Eleven and kind of start the last part again. This is just one step back, two steps forward."

I stared at her. What was she doing here? Hadn't the reset gone through? Had I effected some sort of change with the punch and the smartie?

All I said was, "What the hell are you talking about?"

She frowned and sat down. "What do you mean?"

"What do *you* mean?"

"You *know* what I mean," she said. "You panicked."

I shook my head, trying to clear it. "I just hit myself in the head. That's all. I mean, believe me, I'm pretty fucking tense, but that's not what you're talking about, is it?" We eyed each other. "What do you know that you're not telling me, Kitty?"

She swallowed hard and didn't answer.

I forced myself to remain calm. "I cannot stress to you how important it is to tell me the absolute truth right now."

"Wait a minute. You *don't* know what I mean." She looked at me with pleading eyes. "Don't make me tell you," she whispered.

My God. Tell me what? "I'm making you. I'm begging you."

She looked down at her hands and said, "You're agoraphobic. But since you hit your head maybe you're an amnesiac agoraphobic," she said.

I rolled my eyes. "I'm not an amnesiac." *Well, not exactly.* "But what do you mean, I'm agoraphobic?"

"You're agoraphobic."

I started to laugh.

"It's not funny," she said. "You're scaring me." She got up on her knees, took me by the shoulders, and forced me to look at her. "You're begging me to tell you the truth, and that's the truth. You're agoraphobic. You don't go out. You work from home. You don't date. You compulsively buy makeup online for nights out and great parties that you never attend. You watch spy movies about people living exciting lives of adventure you will never even come close to experiencing. You're agoraphobic."

She was serious. She was totally, completely, unequivocally serious. But the person she was describing wasn't me. It had been once; I remembered. But not anymore.

"Come on," she said. We went into the house and she led me upstairs to my office. I looked around. It didn't seem particularly different from the first time I'd walked this wire—well, there was an empty box on the ground and a thick red binder sitting on top of a pile of papers. I remembered Kitty coming out of my office with a full box and a red binder on top. She'd taken a bunch of stuff out of my office that time around.

"Look," she said, tapping her finger on the stack of paper sitting on the desk.

I scanned the contents of the binder, then quickly looked through the papers. *Oh, my God.* It was a mass of material on the subject of agoraphobia. Research, descriptions of symptoms, lists of online support groups, and one in particular caught my attention. " 'Tips for Desensitizing to Shopping'? "

She shrugged. "You don't remember. You must have hit your head really hard. We just finished our whole sequence, including some practice runs to the 7-Eleven, and you were going to try to do your first one alone. Obviously you didn't quite make it. But it's nothing to worry about. Now I'd like to take you to the hospital."

"Why? I'm completely fine."

"Well, this fainting has happened before, and I thought it was just some typical panic from your condition, but . . . but now I'm thinking maybe it's something else. Maybe you're not getting enough iron or something."

"Maybe I'm pregnant," I said darkly, thinking about the nurse who'd assured me I wasn't when I'd been in the hospital just a few days ago.

Kitty burst into hysterical laughter.

"Nice," I mumbled. "Wait a minute. You told me I was a *workaholic*."

"No, I said agoraphobic."

"I mean before."

"Before when? I mean, you *are* a workaholic, but so what?" Kitty sighed. "Maybe I did the wrong thing here. Maybe I shouldn't have said anything at all about your problem." She suddenly looked horrified and covered her hand with her mouth. "I'm an idiot. I *shouldn't* have said anything at all. Agoraphobia feeds on itself. One little panic attack becomes one big panic attack. One big panic attack becomes lots of big panic attacks until one day you can't leave your house. Until you don't even want to open the door. Maybe telling you will trigger the problem again. The mind breeds fear, Rox. Now that I've said something, maybe this will become a self-fulfilling prophecy. That's how you once described it to me, anyway. The way the condition just sort of took over. I'm so sorry, Rox. I'm such a fool. Amnesia is way better than agoraphobia, as far as I'm concerned." She peered closely at my face. "You don't feel panicky now, do you?"

"No. Just completely freaked out. But it's not your fault."

She frowned. "I totally should have lied. You weren't ready to hear the truth."

That's why on that last wire you said I was a workaholic instead of what I really was. And being a

Major, I was experiencing a whole jumble of bits and pieces of the different wires crossing. Being an agoraphobic wasn't one that stuck with me. So you lied the first time around. But it doesn't matter.

I said, "You did the right thing. I promise. Now, help me piece all this together. I wasn't phobic in college, right?"

"Right."

"But Mason shot me on graduation day and—"

"What?"

"Mason Merrick shot me—"

Kitty burst out laughing. "Through the heart with Cupid's bow, maybe."

"Mason Merrick wasn't stalking me?"

She sat down in the task chair. "If anybody was stalking anybody, I'd say it was more like you stalking him," she said with a small smile. "As the song goes, 'There is a light that never goes out. . . .' I've been saying for the last four years that if I could get you to put that torch down for one second, I think we might actually get you out on a date. Of course, that would require you to actually leave the house."

"Four years?"

"Four years of 'Mason Merrick this,' 'Mason Merrick that.' " She rolled her eyes. "I mean, the guy was hot and everything, but I don't think he was worth the kind of brain space you've been giving him."

I looked up at her, wincing at her description of me and the fact that the song she felt best described me was an anthem of a terminally depressed, angst-ridden eighties band. "I've been carrying a torch for Mason Merrick for four years?" And Mason wasn't a stalker in this reality because Leonardo never kissed me and made the splice to convince me Mason was the bad guy. Now we were getting somewhere. What about the fact that Kitty and I hadn't spoken since graduation day?

"You and I . . . we said good-bye on graduation day. You left . . . and then what?"

"Graduation day? Oh. Well, I called you just after I got in the cab and it pulled out, intending to tell you I thought I might have left the heater on in the bathroom."

"That's it? You thought you left the heater on in the bathroom?" I actually giggled. It was so . . . minor.

The phone rings. It's Kitty calling to tell me she left the heater on. Then the doorbell rings. . . .

"So you called, and?"

"And nothing. You didn't answer. I was almost at the airport when I got a call from Mrs. Bimmel." Kitty shifted her weight, looking about as uncomfortable as I'd ever seen her. "You sure you want to talk about this? You always said you didn't want to talk about it."

"I don't remember that either," I said, trying to crack a smile. "Start from the moment you walked away from the door."

"Like I said, Mrs. Bimmel calls and tells me you were shot. Obviously, I thought it was a bad joke. But she wasn't laughing. When I realized it was true, I made the cab turn around. I never went to Europe, and I've been here ever since."

"Who shot me?" I asked, mentally crossing my fingers.

"We don't know." She shrugged. "Some random guy."

"Not Mason?"

She sighed impatiently. "Not Mason. Mason had nothing to do with it. Just some weirdo we think saw me leave with my luggage and meant to rob the place. They never caught him and that was that."

Tears came to my eyes. I blinked them back. She couldn't have known how I felt about Mason now. Not just a crush or a torch. It was something much, much more.

"So you turned around and came back from the airport. . . ."

"Of course. And thank God, because when you got out of the hospital, you became afraid to open the door. I thought it would pass. It didn't. Things got worse. You developed a fear of a lot of stuff, and eventually it just took over and it's only during this last year that you really decided to try to overcome it once and for all."

"Which led to my going out at two a.m. to the 7-Eleven to practice going shopping."

"Well, this time you were just going to try to get through the door by the counter, and if things were going really well, maybe buy just one thing before turning back, so I wouldn't call it shopping. That's how it works. One baby step at a time until you stop being afraid."

"Why two a.m.?"

"Because you said there wouldn't be as many people in the store. Fewer things to panic you."

"But then Mason and Leonardo come out of the woodwork, and Mason walks me home, and I have no knowledge of what I went out for in the first place."

"Mason and who?"

Oh, yeah. She hasn't lived through my "date" with Leonardo Kaysar. She doesn't even know he exists. "Nobody. Nothing. Go on."

"Well, Rox. Obviously, you never made it to the 7-Eleven." She checked her watch. "You wouldn't have had time. I just found you on the ground about to pass out from your panic attack."

And you wanted to take me to the hospital, where a nurse would tell me I hadn't been shot and I wasn't pregnant. Something occurred to me. "Hey, what exactly are you doing out so late tonight?"

A sly grin came over her face.

"Booty call?" I guessed, laughing a little.

"It happens," she admitted, laughing too.

"Kitty, one more question."

"Sure. I've told you the worst, and there's nothing I've left out."

"Why have you stayed here with me through all this crap? I must have been an unbelievable pain in the ass."

"You're still an unbelievable pain in the ass." She smiled.

"No, seriously."

"Well, Roxy, we've always been like sisters. Since college. And you didn't have anybody else. I mean, when your family didn't even try to call you after I told them you'd been shot . . ."

I was pathetic. No family, no friends except for Kitty, who'd basically done everything for me the last four years. No life.

"You've just humored me for all these years? Don't you ever get the urge to just . . . move out?"

She smiled wide. "Nope. This is my home. Besides, you just don't turn your back on your sister when the going gets rough."

I almost burst into tears.

"Oh, shit. Don't cry, Roxanne. This isn't the time for the weepies."

"I'm not going to cry," I said, doing my best. "But . . . thanks. I know it's completely insufficient, but thanks."

"You're welcome. If you have any other questions, I'll be in the living room. I've got to go look up some kind of spell or chant or something to try to deal with this weird déjà vu I've been having." She went into the hall and turned at the banister. "I hope this doesn't come back. If I were the kind of person who didn't believe in the impossible, I'd say that an instant recovery like this was . . . impossible. So, don't succumb to that self-fulfilling-prophecy stuff, Rox. Pretend you never had agoraphobia and you never will."

I watched her disappear down the stairs and looked around my office at the evidence of my former illness. It explained Naveed's weirdness that night. He was probably surprised to see me wandering around the store with no problem, since I'd only ever been in the store with Kitty before and she'd probably told him all about my struggle with mental illness so he wouldn't ask me about anything or panic me.

I got up, walked out into the hallway, and peered down at the front door. Funny how I'd fainted in the same spot where I'd fallen after being shot, as if the present were literally a layer right on top of the past. If reality had spliced in the car . . .

I went back into the office. First I checked for the restraining order, but of course it was gone. Thank God. Thank *God*. I turned back to my desk and started going through the papers piled high on every surface until I found the folder I was looking for. My agency project folders. At the very back, where the oldest stuff was, there was an info sheet for one Kaysar Corporation. The company I had scheduled an interview with on graduation day four years ago.

The phone rang. After a moment, Kitty yelled up, "Rox, you're not going to believe this. It's Mason on the phone. Mason Merrick! How's *that* for a coincidence?"

I grabbed the landline. A weird forgiveness came over me. "I'm so sorry. I'm sorry I ever thought you'd really do that. Hurt me. Leo must have—"

"Stop. It's okay. Listen to me. You got us pretty tangled up. I've been running in circles here, trying to block Leonardo, and I'm still not even sure if he's going to try and use more wire now to see this thing out. But I'm headed your direction, maybe ten minutes away. If Leo gets there first, for God's sake don't open the door. Just hold tight." He hung up. I slowly set down the phone and went downstairs to the kitchen, where Kitty was putting some weird brewer's yeast concoction together in a canning jar.

"What's wrong?" she asked.

My mind reeled. I tried to separate all the wires, all my feelings, but things were impossibly fuzzy. "Um . . . don't open the door. You seen my bag?"

Kitty stared at me, the jar lid clutched in her hand, which was frozen in midair. "It's on the sofa."

In a daze, I walked to the living room and pulled

out the punch and the reader. The wood beneath me trembled as Leo and Mason came pounding up the stairs. I held the punch up to my neck like a suicide gun, watched as dark and light flashed through the crack under the door when Mason and Leo both hit the landing.

Flinching as one of them hit the door, I soon could tell they were scrapping again. But I felt better this time. While it seemed to me that Leo was right to boast—he was a more talented wire crosser—he sure couldn't beat Mason mano a mano.

"What's that ruckus?" Kitty asked, appearing in the foyer. She froze when she saw me with the punch against my neck. Her eyes suddenly narrowed, her arms folding across her chest. "L. Roxanne," she said crossly. "What is that? A staple gun? You take that thing away from your neck right now."

I stared at her. "No offense, but this is a really bad time. Could you maybe go upstairs?"

The thumping and yelling on the other side of the front door continued. Instead of going upstairs, Kitty flounced past me and threw it open. The men let go of each other, breathing heavily. They looked disoriented by her presence.

"Hi, Kitty," Mason finally managed to say.

"Mason? Wow . . . nice to see you." Kitty looked back at me in confusion. She looked blankly at Leo, then back at Mason. Then she looked down at the gun Leonardo had drawn and let out the most blood-curdling scream I'd ever heard in my life. I'm sure it scared the crap out of everyone present.

We all stood frozen in the silent aftermath, my arm beginning to flag with the weight of the punch I was holding up to my neck. Kitty collected herself with a dramatic breath, squared her shoulders, and stepped forward with her hand out. "Empty the gun or you will rue the day you were born."

Both men looked over Kitty's shoulder at me, and I readjusted the punch to place it against my temple, going for a fearless look to mask my mounting hysteria. "Kitty, I swear to you, they are not going to pull the trigger. I swear it." I raised my chin and glared defiantly at the men. "Now, *I* might pull *this* trigger, but they are not going to shoot. They can't. I guarantee it."

Of course, I *couldn't* guarantee it, but I had what I needed to trip a wire, and Mason had already told me there wasn't much wire left. They simply couldn't afford to run out now.

"You *swear it*, swear it?" Kitty asked.

"Absolutely."

"Okay, then."

I thought she'd step away; I should have known better.

"The bullets," she said, jutting her hands forward. I watched in disbelief as Leo emptied his gun and spilled the bullets into Kitty's open palm. She curled her fingers around them and jammed them in her pockets. It was working. I couldn't believe it. She was clearly a reality variable they were unable to take a chance on. "Put the gun on the floor and take one step back."

Leo cursed in his typical English fashion and laid his gun on the threshold of my apartment. Both men stepped back, and Kitty picked it up. The minute she had it in her hand, she lunged forward and slammed the door in Leo's and Mason's faces, immediately locking and bolting and chaining it.

The boys started pounding and yelling, and Kitty turned around, spread-eagling her body across the door. Her face was white, her earlier bravado evaporated as if she'd just registered the seriousness of the situation. "For God's sake, put that thing down and call the police. I am not letting this happen to you again."

An incongruous bubble of laughter formed in my throat. Kitty somehow thought one or both of the guys was the stalker from long ago, back, ready to finish what they started? That was ludicrous. No more ludicrous than anything else I'd been experiencing lately, but still. Even better was the fact that they'd done what she told them.

"Mason's here to help me, Kitty. I swear it."

We both jumped back as the door almost buckled. We looked at each other for a moment; then a polite knock followed in the subsequent silence. "It's Mason. Let me in. Leo's out cold. You've gotta let me in."

Kitty shook her head, but I ignored her and swiftly unlocked and opened the door. Mason leaped over the threshold and locked up again behind him.

"We're running low on wire. There's still some left because the reset didn't go through, but time is running out."

"What happened to stalemate?" I mumbled.

He gave me a funny little smile, a perplexed laugh. "You took care of that. Didn't count on the Major crossing the wires. Now, listen to me." He shook me, begging me to focus on his words. "You don't have to be anything you don't want to be. You got that?"

I stared at him. Mason stared back. "Whatever happens, you know . . ."

I swallowed hard. "I know what?" *I know* what, *Mason? If you really care about me, just say it, won't you?*

I could interpret that crooked grin however I wanted, I guess, but I wished he'd have said the words out loud. Love is the kind of thing that gets left open to a whole lot of misunderstanding.

I saw a flash of silver in one hand and I knew what it was all about, but I felt his other arm pull me toward him, crushing me into his body, and I knew what that was all about too. He was preparing me to wire cross, but he also wanted to kiss me.

I closed my eyes as he kissed me like he owned me. The intensity, the rawness of his tongue pressing into my mouth, his teeth biting at my lower lip felt like nothing else. He kissed me like he meant it, like he'd been born to it, and not just to get my heart rate up. But the other thing was, he kissed me like it was good-bye.

At last, too soon, Mason pulled away. He took me even tighter into an embrace, his faltering sigh burning hot against my cheek. I felt his punch go in; I heard Kitty shriek in horror. A tear slipped down my face as I waited for the words Mason would say seconds later:

"Open the door, Rox."

TWENTY-THREE

Phone. Door. Fish. My graduation gown still wrapped and folded in its plastic square.

Slip a second in, pluck one out . . . I knew Mason couldn't possibly shoot me this time; he'd crossed the wire himself. So, then, the phone first.

The goldfish bag swinging from my hand, I bolted for it, grabbed it, and shouted, "I'll be right there, Kitty!" like a complete dork, then ran for the door. Sweat prickled along my spine as I curled my fingers around the doorknob, pressed the phone against my chest to block out the sound.

And then I opened the door.

Leonardo stood on the other side. *Mason, what are you* doing*?* Juggling the goldfish and the phone, I tried to slam the door shut again, but Leo's forearm rammed against it. His face frozen like a mask, he brought up a gun with his free hand and pointed it at me. I stood there, paralyzed.

"Hello? Rox?" Kitty's muffled voice leaked from the phone. "Is anybody there?"

Roxanne, don't be weak. Do something. Do *some-*

thing. But I just stood there like a coward, clutching the phone and the fish, and let Leonardo shoot me.

I fell backward, a sharp pain permeating my breastbone, and the phone flew out of my hand. The goldfish bag burst open on the ground. Crashing spread-eagle to my apartment floor, I lay there as water soaked into my hair.

The fish was still in the bag, flopping around in the small amount of water that was left. *You can't breathe either*.

It was as if I'd taken a sledgehammer to the gut. Each breath was painful, barely squeaking enough oxygen into my body to count. Tears spilled down my cheeks as I rolled over and slowly clambered to my hands and knees. Leonardo was gone. The fish wasn't flopping anymore. I could see his tiny little body still fighting for air inside the bag. The water had all but seeped out.

Get up. Just get the fuck up.

Sobbing and gasping, I stood, grabbed the bag off the ground, and lunged for the counter in one contiguous motion. I grabbed the flowers out of a vase, threw them aside, and dumped in the fish.

Please, please, please, was all I could mouth, watching the cloudy water.

And after a moment, Existential Angst wiggled his tail and decided to make it. "I'll change the water in a second," I whispered.

My hands were shaking so badly I couldn't have done any business at the moment anyway.

I turned back to the mess on the ground and the open door, tried to put all the pieces together in my mind. Where had Leo gone? My chest hurt badly. I looked down; a tiny streak of blood stained my shirt. I pulled the fabric up and gasped. A huge bruise was developing on the left side of my chest, a small bleeding welt in the center, just over the heart.

So minor. How so minor?

A tinny voice cut through the silence: "If you'd like to make a call, please hang up and try again. . . ."

I looked at the phone on the ground, a bullet buried in the handset.

"Roxanne, I called nine-one-one." One of my neighbors stood in the doorway. "You're not okay, are you?"

I think he caught me as I fell. The next thing I knew, I was lying on my couch in the living room and listening to the accompanying sounds of someone emptying a dishwasher in the kitchen.

It took me a second to process before I sat bolt upright, completely freaked out. I clutched at my chest and got up to look at the vase of flowers on the table. Different flowers. Different vase. There was no fish. No fishbowl. On the edge of panic, I called out, "Kitty?"

"Yeah?"

Thank God. "Where's the fish?"

She appeared in the doorway of the kitchen, blond again, with a scrub brush and an empty fishbowl in her hand. I was back in the . . . present. "In the kitchen with me."

"Existential Angst? He's still alive?"

She looked over her shoulder, then turned back to me and said with one of those deadpan looks, "He's insulted by your question—I'm just cleaning his bowl. Of course he's still alive."

"Where's the pink vase?"

"In the sink with the fishbowl. Those old flowers were starting to stink. Are you okay?"

"Yeah . . . just tired. I'm going to nap here for a minute."

"Sure." She disappeared back into the kitchen.

Mason. What did you just do? I knew better than to think that everything was fine or normal just because Kitty and her fish were still here. After all, he'd gotten Leonardo to shoot me, which was pretty shocking. What else was different remained to be seen.

I let my head fall heavily back on the couch. So much for my moment of self-empowerment. Stealing Mason's car and driving off had been just a new method of running away and hiding. I'd stood there and let Mason stick me again. And I'd stood there and let Leonardo shoot me. I'd just *stood* there. And here I was again with Kitty cleaning up after me in the kitchen while I was sitting on my ass freaking out.

Kitty came out of the kitchen with the fishbowl and stuck it on the counter. I watched Existential Angst swim in circles for a while, running time lines through my mind and trying to figure out where the guys were likely to be and what they were planning. Since there wasn't much wire left, they couldn't afford to mess around with more reversals and forwards.

Kitty returned with some fish food, which she tapped into the bowl. "I thought you said you were going to be done today."

"Huh?"

"I thought you said you were going to be done with the Zapper."

"The Zapper?"

Kitty raised an eyebrow. "You've been obsessing about it for months. You've been living it for months. You're sick of it. I'm sick of it. We were supposed to pull a cork and celebrate when you were done, and that was supposed to be today. So did you turn it in or what?"

I sat up. "What's the Zapper?"

She stared at me. "You're seriously asking me? I think you're more than just tired, Rox. Are you okay?"

It was not the time for being mothered to death. "I'm fine. Just . . . humor me, okay? Tell me what I told you about this Zapper thing."

"All you said was that you got a project for this device thingy. It was months ago. Some sort of next-generation handheld. They asked you to write some code or some nonsense. You said it was a sort of GPS thing for an alpha model, and I told you I only spoke English. Remember?"

"Oh, yeah," I said, not remembering at all.

Kitty relaxed a little. "Yeah. So . . . well, you know, you always name your projects some random name, and this one we just called the Zapper. Remember?"

"Absolutely. That's a funny story. I totally remember!" *Sigh*. "So, I said that I was supposed to be done today?"

She cocked her head. "Don't even try to tell me you're so sick of this project you've developed amnesia. Of all your procrastination techniques, that's without a doubt the lamest. You said you were done and just needed to have me drop the documents off this afternoon, and then we . . ."

I was already halfway up the stairs. I dashed into

my office and poked furiously at the keyboard to wake up the computer. I went through the file hierarchy until I reached the folder called *AHOT*. Inside *AHOT* I scanned a series of project folders, ending with the last one, called simply Z. I clicked through, and sure enough there were a huge number of files with names all including ZAPPER in the title. I sorted the files and looked at when I'd last updated them. Most had been updated yesterday. I found the master document, a sort of template I'd developed for turning in projects to the agency, and just as Kitty said, I was done. I was done with the code and was turning it in to the agency today.

I headed back down to the sofa in a daze and plopped onto the cushions. My future, the future Leonardo wanted, was right here on this wire. It was here and he wanted possession of the code, which meant that he'd be along any minute, Mason on his heels. I could just make myself comfortable until the doorbell rang, and then we could all have a nice, polite discussion about who got what or . . .

"Screw that!"

Kitty's head popped through the kitchen door. "You talking to me?"

I leaped off the couch. "Yes, yes, I am. Screw that." I ran upstairs to my office and started looking through the files, looking for something more about Kaysar Corporation or anything at all about Mason Merrick that might be on the machine from one reality splice or another. But no answers spontaneously appeared; they were stuck in a different time on a different wire. If I hadn't found answers before the code, and I hadn't found answers now that I'd written the code, then they weren't in the present. Maybe the answers were in the future with Mason and Leonardo. . . .

I knew what I had to do. I downloaded the contents of z to a flash drive; then, with my finger twitching nervously over the keyboard, I finally dragged the z folder to the trash can and clicked delete. Grabbing an old manila folder, I dropped the drive inside and ran back downstairs to the kitchen.

Kitty was washing a small green apple in the sink. "You want half?" she asked.

"No. The thing is . . . I just wanted to say goodbye."

"Bye," she said, totally focused on scraping the little oval sticker off the apple skin.

This was serious enough to worry about not coming back. *"Kitty."*

"Mmm?"

"If I don't come back, I want you to know you've been a great best friend. The best. You are a *sister* to me. I mean, you're my entire goddamn family. So, thanks."

That got her attention. Her left eyebrow went up. With a chuckle she asked, "Where exactly are you going?"

Oh, hell. "The future. It's basically"—my mind grasped for a way to frame my intentions that she could understand—"a mission of sorts."

"A mission." She took a huge bite of apple and with her mouth full asked, "Can I come?"

"Are you serious?"

"Well, yeah, I'm serious. I'm not doing anything."

She believed me. More important, someone was on my side. Mason and Leo wanted something from me, but Kitty wasn't like that. She was an unbiased observer and she wanted to help me. I was really touched. Even if she didn't have a clue what I was talking about, I was really touched. This was who she was: a kind, generous person.

"You have no idea how much I'd like to have you come with me, but I don't want you to get hurt," I said, suddenly sad. "This could be dangerous. In fact, it's very likely to be dangerous."

She took a final bite of apple, then stepped down on the trash can pedal and tossed the core inside. "Don't be silly. I can hang with the best of them." She leaned against the kitchen counter and grinned. "If it's that dangerous, if I kick the bucket, be sure to call my mom and dad."

"Jesus. Let's be morbid, why don't we." I threw up my arms in resignation.

She gave me a wink. "So, when's this going down? And what kind of costumes?"

"Costumes? Okay, look, Kitty. I totally appreciate your . . . your interest. But I've got to get going."

She followed me upstairs, then peeled off and went into her own bedroom. I found my messenger bag, and stuffed in the manila folder and the punch, the gun, the reader, and a handful of paper clips and ponytail holders that I included for no reason other than that they were the sort of items that in a movie were always useful in a pinch.

I ran down the stairs, and Kitty followed right on

my heels wearing some sort of ridiculous hat that had springy antennae with stars bobbing on the ends. "I'm ready," she said, sticking her fist out in a go-get-it manner. "Let's go to the future!"

I shook my head, bemused. I headed for the door, then stopped and gave Kitty a big hug, then went for the doorknob. "Hopefully, I'll see you very soon," I said.

"Roxanne!"

The completely freaked-out tone of her voice stopped me in my tracks. I turned and looked at her.

"What are you doing?" she asked.

"I'm going outside."

Her jaw dropped.

I stuck my hand on the doorknob and felt the most incredible force of panic well up inside me. "Oh, God," I said as my head nearly exploded from the rush. I was still agoraphobic. No wonder she'd seemed like she was just playing with a child.

I swayed backward, and Kitty was there in a second, wheeling me around and marching me over to the couch. She sat next to me, staring at me with huge eyes. "Were you actually going to open that door?"

All I could do was nod. My heart pounded so hard I felt like I could feel the beat in every part of my body. I'd never felt such panic before . . . except . . . except for maybe . . . It was the kind of panic I'd been talking myself out of on the way to the 7-Eleven that night at two in the morning. *Say it isn't still so.*

"Why didn't you go through the steps of your routine the second you felt it welling up?"

"My routine? What? No, I-I just . . . It happened so fast. And I really need to get going."

"You were really planning on just going out there—just opening the door and wandering out for a stroll?"

"This isn't a stroll. This is an emergency."

"Well, that's all well and good, but you've got a serious problem."

She didn't have to say any more. I knew what was happening. I was agoraphobic. This was the original version of reality. Kitty *had* existed then. Well, she'd existed the night I'd left my house on a mission to cure myself through a strategically planned set of visits to the 7-Eleven. This was the wire I'd been on when I'd left the apartment that night. But then reality had spliced—roughly, as Mason pointed out—and when I opened the door to Mason's car and spilled out onto the pavement, I'd already been on a different wire—one in which Kitty did not exist.

"If the game is outside, I'm going to have to go with you," she said. "And I'm really not sure how far we're going to get. I mean, we always go straight to the 7-Eleven, so maybe if we go that—"

"But that's where I'm going," I yelped in relief. The 7-Eleven represented a sort of portal. That was where the guys had taken me for their reset, so I figured that if the *where* mattered when it came to planning a leap to the future, then the intersection by the convenience store was my best bet.

"Okaaay . . ." Kitty said. "I'm willing if you're willing."

* * *

Ten minutes later, I wasn't quite as willing. I'd been literally leaning on Kitty the entire way over. I'd thought I might throw up at least three separate times, and it was like a giant, persistent panic attack the whole way. *This is what I'm really like*, I found myself realizing. *This is what my life was really like. This is who I was.*

But this is not how I plan to end up. If there's even one length of wire left from this botched reset, I'm going to use it, because there is no way I'm going to end like this.

It was unusually cold out, one of those sunny days that looked warm from the inside of your place. As I stopped at the intersection of my reality, at the very spot where this crazy situation began, I was struck not by melancholy but by the realization of all that I'd become in my best moments on the wires where I didn't have prior knowledge of this version of myself. There was a future yet to be won.

"Did you want to keep going?" Kitty asked, gesturing to the 7-Eleven.

Naveed. "Yeah, let's just stop in for a second." It was hard to be around people on the sidewalk, and it was hard to stand at the door of the 7-Eleven and want to go in. It took a couple of tries, and a lot of patient coaxing from Kitty, but I finally thought about Mason's admonition not to let myself be what I didn't have to be.

As we entered the store, Naveed looked at me with wide eyes. I knew his first instinct was to make reference to my condition. Instead, he just said, "Good day, Katherine. Good day, Roxanne."

"Hey, Naveed. How's the family?" I asked.

Naveed beamed as he always did. "I told you my wife was having another child?" he asked.

I just smiled, ignored the roar picking up steam in my head, and plucked some spearmint gum from the impulse-buy section, placing it on the counter with a grungy dollar bill from my pocket. He swapped the bill for my change and leaned forward over the counter.

"Twins!"

"Is one of them a girl?" I asked.

He cocked his head to one side as if to say, *So be it*. "Yes. But I think she will be very smart. As smart as her brothers."

"Oh, my God," I said, grabbing his hand and pumping it up and down in congratulations. "That's unbelievable. I mean, fantastic . . . and terrific. I am so happy for you." I scooped up my change and the gum. "A genius," I called out as I walked to the door and the bell chimed. "I think she will be a genius."

He smiled proudly. "I will see you soon."

I waved back at him. *Thanks, Mason.* I just knew he'd worked that.

Kitty and I walked back outside, and I stopped at the intersection. "This is where we say good-bye," I said, my voice clogging a bit with tears. This was where it got real. The last wire I ended up with might not include her.

Kitty crossed her arms over her chest. "I'm not going anywhere," she said.

"I am," I explained, pulling the punch and smartie from my bag. I set the reader, praying I was doing it right. I let the punch's chamber fill.

Kitty was talking a blue streak, arguing. "Roxanne," she said, "don't you dare go out without me."

I should have ignored her. I should have just punched myself. But in the end, I didn't want to go alone. I punched us both, hoping we could fix things together.

TWENTY-FOUR

I came to, sweating and wincing on my hands and knees with lumpy bits of gravel pressing into my kneecaps. Next to me, Kitty sat on the pavement struggling to get her sweatshirt off. *The heat*, I thought. *She's not used to the heat.*

I looked around and it wasn't at all what I'd expected. We were sitting on the pavement of what appeared to be an inner-city playground. It had clearly been neglected for a number of years, all faded lines and divots, but someone had taped off the ground with the lines of a basketball court. The pole supporting the hoop was tilted at an unplayable angle, and from it hung a dirty net.

I guess I should have been panicking, but for some crazy reason I felt a sense of relief. Relief at the empty space around me, relief at the silence. Even if it was the sort of weighty silence one normally referred to as the calm before the storm.

I looked up. We were surrounded by a spiderweb of freeways and transit tracks that spiraled above and around the city. I could see blurs of color shift and stall and accelerate, tram cars or whatever moving along the tracks. I was again reminded of Mason's deejay metaphor: how the crossing of wires on a case was like a club deejay scratching a record. Back, forward, hold, forward, hold, back . . . And yet, for all my experience, the sounds were nothing more to me than dull static.

Kitty and I looked at each other, her eyes huge, dominating her pale face. She hadn't believed me. She stood up, wobbling a little, and headed for a water fountain.

An electronic gong sounded from different places around and above us; people poured out of the neighboring buildings, and the usual hustle and bustle of city life crowded out the quiet. I stood and peered through the hurricane fence surrounding the playground. The men and women wore a mishmash of formal businesswear and leather catsuits; from what I could tell, it seemed that cars on street level got only one lane—probably for emergencies. Pedestrians and bicyclists on a variety of traditional and mechanized rides took the rest of the space.

No, this was not a homogeneous group of people, but one thing struck me that they had in common: their obliviousness toward the people around them. They all worked their cell phones and handhelds. They were jostling and bumping one another shoulder to shoulder, but each was in his or her own individual world.

"Hey, Rox," Kitty hissed.

"What?"

"I thought we were doing pretend, but this isn't pretend." She hovered over the water fountain, using it to support her weight as she bent at the waist.

"Are you okay?" I asked.

"No."

She gasped for air, and I recalled how winded the first reality splices had made me. But that didn't seem to be the whole of it. Kitty's tan seemed to have faded a couple shades, and I realized that believing in the possibilities of swapping jokes with algae scum, natural healing from brewer's yeast, and intergalactic space travel were substantially different from the reality of leaping into the future.

"All this time, you still thought I was joking," I said. I knew, but was a little annoyed. "Didn't you think it seemed rather bizarre? And elaborate, all of my explanations?"

"You've never dated anyone who's taken you to a *Star Trek* convention, have you?"

I was overcome by a memory of one of her dates. "Point. The thing is, I've been completely serious about it all. And you must have realized I was completely serious. But you didn't believe me?"

"Yeah."

"And you played along anyway."

"That's what friends are for." She said it matter-of-factly, standing upright, staring wide-eyed at the sky with her hands on her hips.

"Well, now you see I'm not crazy. Are you okay with it?" I asked kind of lamely.

She turned to me, and I could see the barely contained hysteria written all over her face. "Am I *okay* with this? Am I *okay* with it? Are you joking? I realize that I'm a go-with-the-flow, up-for-any-adventure, fairly Zen kind of person—"

"Now, don't get angry, Kitty."

"I'm not angry! Do I seem angry? Because I'm not angry. I'm just totally freaked the hell out!" She closed her eyes and took another deep breath, and I think what she murmured was, "Inner peace, inner calm . . ."

"Kitty?" I asked, tentatively reaching my hand out to her shoulder.

She stuck her index finger up in the air, and I retreated and let her have a few more moments. Then her eyes popped open. "It can't always be about tomorrow. Sometimes it's about right fucking now. And tomorrow is today. This is now."

I don't think I'd ever admired her more than I did at that moment. "When this is over, my friend, I am so going to owe you."

She joined me at the fence and managed a weak smile. "I'll take you up on that."

"Do you want to sit down? Do you need something to drink?"

Kitty raised an eyebrow. "*Drink*-drink? Do we even have the correct currency? And for all we know, ten bucks isn't even a penny in this age."

"I've got a credit card on me," I said flippantly. But I hadn't really thought of money. I hadn't thought of a lot of things.

"Is it illegal to exist in a place you're not supposed to exist? I wonder if they'll be able to tell where we came from. Or what we've done to get here." She suddenly perked up. "Maybe we'll be celebrities."

"Celebrities or felons," I muttered.

"Looks like the mandarin collar's a big fashion do," Kitty said, observing several passersby. I stared at the people—our people—and noted how all looked oddly formal.

"What year is this?" Kitty asked. She looked around, probably for a newsstand, but there wasn't anything of the sort. Everyone likely had a gadget in their pocket that fed them the news twenty-four hours a day. I doubted newspapers even existed anymore.

"So, what now?"

I swallowed, working hard on not revealing to Kitty that I hadn't a clue. I stuck my hand in my bag and rummaged around for the manila folder, wanting to be sure I still had the one remaining source of this code that was ruling my life and the version of life I would end up living.

"No!"

Kitty squealed in horror as I shook the envelope upside down and yelled once more at the top of my lungs.

"Is there a problem?" she asked timidly.

I looked up at her. "I don't believe in coincidences."

"I know," she said.

"It's gone. It's gone, and I don't believe in coincidences."

"What's gone?"

"The code for the smartie."

She looked at me blankly.

"The Zapper! The Zapper code is gone!"

Kitty just looked at me helplessly. "I'm sorry."

"It was in this envelope. . . . Hey!" I examined the envelope a little more closely. It was the envelope I'd received at the agency. The same damn empty envelope with the same roughly opened top. "Well, what do you know."

"Not a whole lot," Kitty muttered. "Would this be an inappropriate moment to ask you if you have a plan?"

I lifted my head. "A plan? Absolutely I have a plan. We're going to the agency." I shook the envelope in the air. "We'll see if they know who L. Roxanne Zaborovksy is this time!"

I looked at the city bustling around me. Ahead, I saw it: the tip of a spire. The ferry building. The ferry building not far from where the Bay Bridge used to be. I couldn't see much behind and among the sky-clogging freeway system and the dense collection of skyscrapers, but I saw the tip of that spire between a set of buildings. And since the ferry building marked the east end of Market Street, the location—the *original* location—of my employment agency, I swiveled around and marked that general area in my mind.

The odd diagonal of Market Street, oft maligned because of the near impossibility of turning left off certain stretches, was a blessing to me now. "We have assessed," I said to Kitty. "And now we proceed."

I started toward the spire, retracing my steps to the location of the agency.

"Um, not that I'm doubting you or anything," Kitty said, "but how do you know where to . . . proceed?"

I recalled Mason once describing to me how a three-dimensional desk from a different point of view was just a flat rectangle. Leonardo had warned me of being buried in an archeological layer of reality. I had a mishmash of memories in my head, some from the past, some never to be, but if I had my geometry right, I had our destination right.

"Trust me."

Fifteen minutes later, Kitty and I stood outside the agency doors, staring at a sign that read, THE MERRICK AGENCY: FREELANCE WIRE CROSSING. I burst into peals of what probably qualified as maniacal laughter. The building was the same. My humor didn't come from the surreal comedy of the name; it was that I'd been working for *him*. On the wire where I'd been doing freelance work from my room, I'd somehow been getting my assignments in the present from Mason's agency in the future. I guess on the wire where I was working in an office building, I'd been doing government work. I'd been fated to write this software. I wondered when I'd first become Mason's case. Clearly before I'd become his employee.

"Let's not go in just yet," I muttered. I wasn't sure what I wanted to ask. I didn't have all the puzzle pieces.

Kitty leaned against the wall and watched people go by. I could hear little gasps and squeals burst forth every time she saw something unusual, but I was busy trying to work out Mason. He must have been keeping tabs on every project assigned to me, watching, waiting, hoping to be there before Leonardo when the one project everyone was waiting for came to pass.

Yeah, he and Leo must have been eyeing each other, fingers twitching, ready to pounce for years. Leo came off the mark first, playing offense, Mason followed, and the case with me on the wire as the Major blew wide open one fateful day at two o'clock in the morning.

But now I was in control of my own fate. Things were different, anything was possible, and I knew that Mason would be a villain in my world only if I let Leonardo Kaysar make him one. "Let's go."

"Okay," Kitty said, starting to walk away. I grabbed her by the back of her jacket and wheeled her around. "Let's go *in.*" I marched her through the doors of the agency.

We approached a receptionist wearing an outfit that reminded me of something more appropriate for a cruise ship purser. Kitty was probably fascinated by the duds, but I was more excited about the fact that the man was sitting in what had to be the most ergo of ergonomic chairs I'd ever seen. It was made of a clear, flexible rubber, and I wondered how many decades it would take for the thing to be invented, because I definitely wanted one.

"May I help— Oh, my God!" The receptionist leaped from his chair, ran around to us, and engulfed me in a huge bear hug. He finally pulled away. "Hello, Rox. I should tell everyone you're here. Mason didn't tell us; I suppose he had a surprise in mind."

Hey, Rox. Hey, Rox? *Not "L. Roxanne Zaborovsky, I presume?" Or even, "Who the hell are you?" He knows exactly who I am.*

"We're here to see Mason Merrick," Kitty said cheerfully. Then her eyes bugged out. "Ohmigod, look at that crazy tape dispenser!"

I watched the slow arch of the receptionist's eyebrow.

"Kitty," I said with measured politeness. "Why don't you go outside and get some air? I'll be out in a minute."

She narrowed her eyes at me but walked back out the door. I nodded at the receptionist. "Nice to, er, see you too. Is Mason around?"

"Unless he slipped in, I don't think he's even on this layer." The clerk pressed a button on his earpiece and said, "Dial Mason Merrick." After a moment he looked up. "I'm sorry; he's not answering. Do you want to just wait in his office?"

Well, that was easy. "That would be great."

He pressed a button and released the lock on a nearby door. As I passed through the waiting area, I compared the space to what I remembered from the agency layout before. The room wasn't configured in exactly the same way, but the basic shape of the place where Leonardo had first intercepted me was the same.

A couple of women in ridiculously short skirts and formal suit jackets with mandarin collars came out of a second white and unmarked door, holding it open for me. From the corner of my eye, I saw them do double takes, pause, then decide not to stop me. *Everyone knows who I am . . . and they seem . . . pleased to see me.* It was odd.

Behind the door was a hall with glass siding through which I could see banks and banks of people with headsets and microphones and monitors with lists of names and world locations, like a kind of airport arrival-and-departure scheme. It reminded me of traffic control crossed with public television pledge week. The names and locations on the monitors looked exactly like the listings Mason had shown me on his reader. Green, red, and gray dots blinked and pulsed, disappeared and reappeared in constant motion. The hubbub on the agency floor was similar to the chaos of a stock exchange floor as runners with headsets moved through the area.

This is who Mason talks to with his reader. It's what he's always checking. Leonardo has something similar. Who does he talk to? They were tracking cases and wires, giving statuses, alerting users to potential moves.

For me, Mason had played the role of technology company employer; to someone else, he was probably something else.

I wandered down the corridor, checking the names on doors until I reached the very end. *Wouldn't you know it, a corner office.* I tapped lightly on the door. When nobody answered, I went in. It made me smile, being in Mason's office. I could definitely feel him here. Sports paraphernalia was in the bookcase, a pair of basketball sneakers hanging by the laces off a hook in the wall. It felt impossibly familiar. I sat down in his desk chair and my heart just about stopped.

On his desk, in a large silver frame, was a picture of Mason pulling a girlfriend close, his lips planting a big, goofy kiss on the side of her cheek. She was wearing a blue satin dress, and she wasn't Louise. She was me. On one wire—on one layer, at least—Mason and I were meant to be.

I pressed the picture to my heart, then put it back on the desk and headed to the receptionist. "Hi. Question. How long has everyone been working on my case?" I asked.

"Since you disappeared, of course," he replied with a warm smile. "You were one of the few Peripherals I know of to become a Major—to have a dedicated project team." He shook his head in disbelief. "I can't believe it's over. We're going to have a hell of a party." He leaned forward. "Obviously, behind closed doors we talked about what might happen if Kaysar closed the case and won. Most of the files are classified, of course, but rumor had it you were the last one left on a case with very little wire left. Of course, the personal element made the situation even more meaningful to all of us."

"The personal element." I swallowed hard, took a deep breath, and asked just to be sure, "I was Mason's girlfriend, and Leo made me disappear?"

The receptionist didn't answer; it was as if something in his brain suddenly clicked. "Yes," he finally said. Then, "Did Mr. Merrick bring you here?"

"Of course," I said breezily. "He just hasn't finished explaining everything. So, uh, how do I relate to the case?"

The answers were coming more slowly now, and his easy, upbeat demeanor was fading rapidly. Still, he said, "You're part of the chain. Without your code contribution, the smartie wouldn't have been developed by the government at the particular time and place that it was. Kaysar Corporation would most likely have developed the technology first, except this time they would have controlled both the juice and the tech before we— Mr. Merrick *does* know you're here, yes?"

The juice and the tech. The punch and the smartie, to be sure. "The juice was developed by Kaysar Corporation? And the reader was developed by . . . the government?"

"Yessss." The receptionist had gone rather chilly. He pushed the button on his earpiece and said, "LRZ status, stat."

"Tell Mason to meet me at Kaysar Corporation," I blurted, pushing my empty manila envelope at the receptionist. Then I turned and burst out the door. On the sidewalk I found Kitty leaning against the wall, staring upward with her mouth slightly open. I grabbed her by the wrist and started booking down the street.

"So far three people have asked me if I'm visiting from the suburbs, and one even asked if something was wrong with me," Kitty said. "People are so *nice* in the future! Oh . . . hey! Don't squeeze my fingers so hard."

"We need to keep moving," I said.

"Did you find out anything?" Kitty asked.

"Yeah. What time is it?"

Kitty looked at her watch. "It's about five o'clock. Why?"

"Shit. I don't know . . . I mean . . . if this is a parallel wire, a layer superimposed on the past, then that explains why nothing is over."

"Uhhhhh . . . what?"

"Sorry. Thinking out loud. The thing Leonardo had me put into the computer on the top of the building during the gala, that was the code. He'd gotten us to the place where I'd written it, and he had me put it in the building in the present because he didn't own the building then and didn't have the security clearance I had. He must have known something about that particular computer. Maybe he bought it later or something, but the important thing is— Wait! He put

Kaysar Corporation in the exact same place. He spliced me forward and I loaded it on *his* machine. Those were his guards. This is some kind of cross-over on parallel layers. But . . . Mason messed with the time line as I was doing it. Leo was thwarted." I was thinking fast and furious.

"Well, once more we've reached a point where I've written it. Given that I don't have it in my bag—where I just put it . . . after I spliced reality to get us here—we must be somewhere in between me writing it and me putting it in the building at the gala. Which means that once the gala happens, if nobody makes a splice, the second I put the code in, in the past, that's the second Leonardo will be able to take it here in the future. I think."

Kitty blinked rapidly.

"I don't blame you," I said. "If I were you, I wouldn't understand either. The thing is, Leonardo and Mason have been laying down pieces to a puzzle, and every time there's a splice, the puzzle board changes a bit and they have to take out pieces that don't fit and put new ones in. But I'll bet you anything there's only one piece left. That flash drive is inside Kaysar Corporation, where I put it during the party in the then layer, and we need to get it out before the party starts in the now layer, if you get my drift."

Kitty cleared her throat. "So . . . what do we *do*?" she asked.

"We need to get to Kaysar Corp. fast, and this isn't fast." I stopped and grabbed a startled pedestrian by the sleeve. "I'm sorry to bother you, but what's the fastest way to the Kaysar building?"

"I'd take the motoway to get just about anywhere from here. The nearest entrance is to the right, about one block and around the corner." His hand swished in the air to describe the route.

"Thanks."

"So *where* are we going?" Kitty asked.

"To my office," I said, leading her around the corner.

"We're going home?" I could tell by the sound of her voice that she wasn't sure whether she should be relieved or disappointed.

"No, my office here."

"I know you know that I have no idea what you just said," she remarked, stopping in her tracks.

I looked around for something that would match the description of a motoway entrance, then at her with complete sympathy. "I'm sorry I got you involved. I'll get you home as soon as possible, but there are answers for me here. I'm starting to understand why I'm so important to these two guys. But I need to be sure which side I think should win."

"Don't you want Mason to win?"

The easy answer was yes. But this was the new me who took nothing for granted. I said, "I *want* to want to. But I need to see what there is to see here."

Kitty chewed on her lower lip and looked around at the familiar yet unfamiliar people swirling around us. "I don't think it's a good idea to know things out of time and place. It just seems to go against the rules of the universe or whatever."

I put my hands on my hips. "And what are the rules of the universe?"

She blinked at me. "Well, you know." She waved her arms in front of her. "The rules of the universe."

"Uh-huh. Well, here's the thing. Both Mason and Leonardo have shown me a version of my reality in which the other is willing to take my life in the name of this case."

"Ah," she said. Then, clearly unable to process that, she said, "How can you have an office here? I mean, do we even really exist in this time, much less keep offices?"

I looked up at the tip of the ferry building spire for reference again, then back at Kitty, smiled, and said, "Yes and no. It will depend."

TWENTY-FIVE

The motoway entrance turned out to be fairly obvious at the spot the pedestrian had described. People crowded together in a mob that dispersed several yards later into different lanes, like lines for an amusement park ride. Beyond the crowd was, at first glance, a sort of blur. Kitty and I joined the crowd and watched the blur. It wavered and flickered and began to take form. I thought I saw wheels. But my view was blocked as the mob suddenly surged forward, and Kitty and I were swept into a sea of leather, padding, and helmets.

Aside from the attire, the people looked regular, with briefcases, loads of laundry, bags of groceries, and, of course, the ubiquitous earpieces and smarties. The line proceeded in a fairly organized manner, without yelling or shoving. One couldn't even hear specific voices; with everyone on the phone doing business or talking to friends and family, the rising sound was a cacophonous murmur.

The crowd moved forward again, passing under an archway that supported the transit structure. I glanced over at Kitty to see how she was coping. She was coping fine, was actually flirting with the guy in the line next to us. "Are you from the suburbs?" I heard him ask, his glance flickering over our clothing.

I stuck my head between them. "Yeah."

He smiled apologetically. "I'm afraid they won't let you on without regulation attire."

Kitty and I looked at each other. The guy pointed kitty-corner to a storefront. "There's a rental depot right there."

I smiled and grabbed Kitty's hand. "Thanks." I dragged her across the street, hesitated with my hand on the glass for just a moment, then pushed my way in.

The man at the counter was wearing a suit and tie, a somewhat incongruous combination given the nature of the garb on racks running the length of the store. One glance into the adjoining room revealed a stockpile of weapons. "You can rent a grenade?" I said in disbelief. The storekeeper smiled. "What can I help you with?"

"We need . . ." What did we need? "Regulation stuff for the motoway."

"Two sets of leathers?"

Kitty and I glanced at each other. "Everything we need for the ride. If you could just fit us out with the whole shebang."

He smiled. "Of course. Right this way." He ushered us to the racks, gave us the expert once-over, and pulled two leather jackets with matching pants and what must have been the rental serial codes imprinted on the cuffs. He brought them to the counter and then gestured to the armory. "Pick out what you like. You can get helmets at the terminal."

"Helmets?"

He raised an eyebrow. "They haven't let people go without in years. Where are you girls from?"

Kitty looked at me with alarm. "The suburbs," I said.

"How nice," he replied, then disappeared into another storage room while Kitty and I picked up our leathers and stepped into the armory.

"Oh, my God. What should we take?" I asked.

"What should we take? Uh, how about *nothing*?" I didn't miss the tone of Kitty's voice, suggesting impending hysteria. But I didn't have time.

"I think we need just a couple of weapons. Something . . . minor," I said.

"Weapons? Who are we thinking of killing?"

"I dunno." I cracked a smile, because if you can't laugh at yourself . . . "Maybe Mason and Leo?"

Kitty raised an eyebrow, but didn't respond to my clearly rhetorical question. Instead, she held the leathers to her body to check the sizing and shrugged. "These go over our clothes, right?"

"I guess so. I mean, I don't fancy the idea of leaving my underwear with the store clerk."

She laughed and climbed into the pants. I did likewise, but my attention was on the grenades, rifles, and assorted other weapons in the room. I had no interest in actually using them, so it seemed stupid to take anything except maybe a knife and a pistol. I stuck a knife in Kitty's boot and cradled a gun in both hands. It was like the pistol in my closet. Well, it was the same kind, and like the shoes and the dress that moved in and out of my life as Leonardo and Mason played deejay to my record, it could have even been the very same one. I slipped the pistol into a side pocket with a strap that seemed designed as a kind of holster.

"Hey, Rox?"

"Yeah." I glanced up and nearly choked. Kitty was holding an enormous gun up alongside her body.

"Does this semiautomatic weapon make my butt look big?"

We both giggled. "No, that semiautomatic weapon does *not* make your butt look big."

Kitty laughed and threw a sock in my face.

Twenty minutes later, decked out in the leathers and some lug-soled boots, we trundled back to the counter. I felt ridiculous. I slapped my credit card down. There was a pause. The salesman looked at it. Then he poked it with a mix of confusion and distaste. He looked at us. "One of you did remember your smartie, yes?"

"My smartie. Right. My smartie."

He nodded and held out his hand. I looked at it, then at Kitty, who gave me a how-the-hell-would-I-know look, and then I slowly pulled Leo's reader from my pocket and laid it on the counter.

"Marvelous." He took the smartie-cum-reader, and while he was busy scanning infrared over the bar codes imprinted on our rental equipment, I stuck my credit card back in my pocket and tried not to think about the fact that Leo most likely could track us through this. Perhaps it wouldn't matter.

The clerk handed the device back to me. "All set."

"Thanks." We turned and started for the door. I stopped short. "When we're done with this stuff?"

"Just turn it in to the nearest rental depot," he said, pulling out a cloth and wiping the smudges off the glass countertop. "We all have reciprocity."

Kitty and I stepped out of the shop and headed across the street to get back in line for the motoway. "This is really hot," she said, tugging at her collar. "I don't get why we have to wear it."

I didn't have the heart to point out that the use of leather, plus the prefix *moto* in motoway, implied something other than the sort of transportation the word *subway* implied. The guy moving next to her had the top of his leather jacket open, beneath which I could see his charcoal pin-striped coat, that usual mandarin collar, plus a crisp white shirt and a tie. I hoped that meant this was safe.

"Where to?" said a man who clearly worked for the motoway.

I gave him the address for the office building where Mason and Leonardo had taken me. Apparently the address existed, because he didn't blink an eye when he said, "Smartie, please."

Aside from the likelihood of Leo tracking us down through this smartie, I realized that it was entirely possible somebody would notice the discrepancy between me and its supposed owner. But it wasn't like we had a choice.

I handed the motoway attendant the reader and he casually flipped it in his hand so it pointed the other way. "Tandem?" he asked, pointing between the two of us.

Kitty looked at me. I nodded. The guy waved it

over some red bars as if he were checking me out at the supermarket and handed it back.

Wow. This smartie was turning out to be quite the all-purpose piece of equipment, a smart chip on steroids. Everyone had one; and from what I could tell, the wire-crossing GPS Mason and Leo and I were using to travel through time and splice reality was just another program loaded onto it. Simple. Too simple. No wonder the government had hired Mason to keep the code out of unauthorized hands. As I looked at the teeming mass of people around me—a fraction of what was surely an enormous world population by now—it was clear that if everyone had the ability to cross wires, the potential chaos would be almost unimaginable.

Clearly Leonardo wasn't too concerned with the outcome of such a situation, but I still couldn't exactly fault him for wanting to make the tech available. He wanted to change the past, maybe even to bring his father back, which was understandable. In fact, he wasn't so different from Mason. Both had been motivated by the loss of someone they loved. I'd never thought about how that might work. Was it wrong to want to change fate to save someone?

The motoway line was moving quickly, and within a few minutes I could see the big picture: tricked-out motorcycles moving along a kind of conveyor belt.

"Oh, shit," Kitty said.

Oh, shit, indeed.

She looked at me. "You are *so* driving."

I swallowed hard as the number of people in front of us winnowed down to one couple. Both grabbed helmets from a rack, ripped off plastic sanitary ribbons, fit them on their heads, and jumped on waiting motorcycles. There was a funny little tug backward and then the guy, motorcycle and all, shot forward into a tunnel.

"Does this strike you as insane, or is it just me?" Kitty asked.

I picked up a helmet, ripped off the ribbon, and pushed it into her gut. Then I picked one up for myself, did the same, and put it on.

The woman in front of us climbed on her motorcycle, and I saw her plug the end of her reader into the dashboard, then press a button. She pulled back for a second; then she too shot into the darkness.

The conveyer belt trundled onward, drawing up a motorcycle with a seat large enough for two. A tandem.

"Oh, shit!" Kitty said.

"Get on," I hissed, climbing onto the moto.

Kitty stood mesmerized, her eyes huge behind the visor of her helmet. The guy behind us poked his head up. "You from the suburbs?" he asked.

Oh, for God's sake. This was getting ridiculous.

Kitty just nodded.

"First time, huh?"

Kitty nodded again.

"You'll be fine," he said, patting her shoulder. I slanted the guy a beseeching look, and he gave her a little push. Kitty lurched forward and climbed on.

"Ready?"

"Absolutely not."

I plugged in my smartie and pushed the button. The backward pull nearly dumped Kitty off the back. She grabbed my waist as we shot off into a tunnel, letting out a piercing scream that lasted as long as the breath itself. The only reason I didn't scream was because I was holding my breath. We must have blasted through this tunnel for five minutes, my back and neck cramping up from crouching low over the vehicle, but I figured it was preferable to having my head lopped off by some accident.

"How does it know where to go?" Kitty yelled.

Excellent question. I guess I should have been scared out of my mind. But after I got used to the moto, I felt a sense of freedom and an incredible thrill. Some mechanism shifted beneath us; the black became gray and then white, and then we lurched sideways as the moto split off from the tunnel expressway.

Kitty squeezed tighter, ducking her head into the back of my suit. The moto's dashboard lit up, and the words PREPARE FOR RELEASE, REDUCE SPEED FOR MERGE flashed in alternating red and white, accompanied by a polite female voice piped through the helmet speakers alerting me to the same. There was a click, like a train router, and the moto sped free of the belt. We careened unsteadily into bright sunlight onto a seven-lane highway.

For a moment I thought the freeway was empty, but the streaks on all sides of me morphed in and out of car shapes as they slowed and accelerated. *I've been here before. Déjà vu.* I blinked hard to clear my vision. I looked in my rearview mirror and saw a black car on my tail. My heart started pounding. *No, not black. Just blue. It's blue.* All I could do was pray there were exits nearby, because there was no possible way I could change lanes.

The dashboard blinked and presented a map. I followed the route and headed down the appropriate exit ramp into a thick stream of traffic. The dashboard flashed an alert.

I followed more instructions and drove carefully to the back of a slowing line of other motos. Everybody was swiping smarties at a tollbooth, after which some people drove to the side and turned their vehicles and helmets back in. Others checked in and kept going. I glanced down at the GPS; there was no indication I was supposed to turn in our moto.

I paused at the tollbooth, swiped Leo's smartie, and had a quick look around. Spirals of similar speedways were layered high above the city on all sides.

A light on the tollbooth turned green. I pocketed the smartie and took a deep breath before driving into the single lane of traffic at street level. "Here goes."

I think I gritted my teeth the whole way, because when we finally stopped at Kaysar Corporation I could barely speak for the tight pain in my jaw. "I guess we can leave the helmets with the bike," I said.

Kitty put her hands on her hips. She opened her mouth to say something but thought better of it. It didn't matter, because the tight line of her mouth telegraphed her feelings on the matter loud and clear.

"I've come to a decision," I said. I'd considered it earlier, but my mind was made up. Once he got what he wanted, Leo had no incentive to make sure that I was still the best possible version of myself: Roxy-plus. Leo was about himself, first and foremost, whether he disguised it as family loyalty or not. When Leo was through with me, I might be a version of myself I didn't want to be, and he'd just consider it a cost of doing business. "Leonardo Kaysar is a bad man. We should avoid him at all costs."

Mason couldn't give me everything I wanted, either; well, he couldn't guarantee anything. But in my heart I knew he'd do the best he could. After all, this was his doing, and he'd let me keep my best friend and had reappeared Naveed's daughter. I'm sure he thought hard about it first. And to the extent that he could, he'd also let me stay the girl I wanted to be—the girl he wanted, too. But I knew you couldn't predict everything, and whenever he gave me what I wanted, he risked sacrificing something else. He had a kind of . . . moral compass that guided him, which was why he was working to maintain time's integrity. That made him trustworthy, respectable. It had once cost him his girlfriend—me. Now I hoped it would put us back together.

Kitty seemed to be struggling with her ability to process the details around us, her face a contortion of confusion and attempts to find a certain Zen in all of this. As I watched her fight panic, it made me think of myself and how I'd stopped the automatic onset of that feeling. I'd changed. I'd changed myself.

The building in front of us was the same building I'd broken into for Leonardo, a future incarnation of the same building from the early excavation I'd fallen into the bottom of. Yes, Leonardo had made me break into the present-day layer of a floor he would eventually own.

Pieces from the past, present, and future: they were all telling one story. No matter how the boys moved the pieces around, no matter how they recut the pieces to fit.

We'd circled the entire building, sweating in our heavy leather suits. I was afraid to take mine off; I wanted us to look as normal in this time as possible.

I followed Kitty into a sliver of shade and stared the building up and down. We could go straight inside to the receptionist's desk and attempt to bullshit our way past whatever security they had, but I doubted very much I had clearance in Leo's version of the building here in the future. The other option was to break into the underground garage and work our way up through the guts of the building in some sort of . . . as yet undetermined manner.

I tried to remember the details of the layout—the elevators, the piping, and the air ducts—that Leo had shown me when he sent me on my mission the first time around.

"C'mon," I said, heading for the garage gates. "Okay, so, here's what we're going to do. We're going to stand here on the side, looking as if it's the most natural thing in the world for us to be here, and we're going to have a conversation."

"About what?"

"Well, we can pretend. We just need to look as innocent and normal as possible. And then, when someone comes through the gates, we'll saunter in before they close."

"Saunter?"

"Yeah. Saunter. It's important that we affect an air of nonchalance."

"Good god," Kitty muttered, rolling her eyes.

"You ready?"

"Uh-huh."

We stood there for five minutes discussing the merits of organic fish food before someone finally drove out. Then we sauntered. The gates closed behind us, and we stood in the dark garage.

Kitty unzipped the neck of her catsuit and sniffed herself. "Yikes. Sweat."

"Sshh. Someone's coming."

Two men in light blue cloth jumpsuits and huge belts laden with construction tools of every possible purpose had stepped out of the service elevator. I forgot about nonchalance and innocence, and froze.

"Hi," Kitty chirped.

"Hello," the portly guy on the left said, his eyes brightening as he took in the vision that was Kitty. His thinner coworker couldn't get beyond a stupid grin. They took off their toolbelts and began reorganizing the contents, swapping back tools they'd apparently borrowed from each other.

"What now?" Kitty whispered.

I wasn't sure. These guys could give us access to the elevator. That'd be much better than working our way up through the ventilation system. "What would a Bond girl do?" I asked.

Kitty looked at me. "Cleavage."

I looked at her in horror. "You're kidding."

"Oh, please, Roxanne. If you can think of a more intellectual way of getting them to let us in without I.D., by all means, share."

I, of course, had nothing to share.

Kitty unzipped the neck of my suit and dragged me forward. She launched a barrage of perky chatter while I did my best to stand there and look appealing. The weird thing was, they were looking at me as much as her. I started working it like a Bond girl would. And within a few minutes, they'd swiped their readers and we were in the service elevator on the way to the thirtieth floor.

Rattling and shaking, the elevator took forever to climb. It stopped with an old-school *ding,* and the door opened with no trouble at all. I pressed the open button as the door tried to close. I could feel Kitty watching me, but I needed a moment to collect myself for what we might confront. Finally, I took a deep breath, looked at Kitty as if I hadn't the slightest reservation about our situation and said, "Shall we proceed?"

"Sure. Do you know how to get from here into the room you're looking for?"

"You could say that," I said—and that was all the explanation I gave her. There was no way in hell I was going to use the term *air duct* before it was absolutely necessary.

TWENTY-SIX

I'd been right about the geometry of my present resembling a layer under the future, and it had gotten us this far. If I could remember Leonardo's instructions when he talked me into and through the air duct, I figured I could use my memories of our little *Mission Impossible* scheme to my advantage. Kitty and I would simply go in the way I had before. Things would go even more smoothly without the dress and heels. And this way there was no need to get involved with the kind of front-desk nonsense that could, if Leo was looking to do it, get a person arrested in the wrong theoretical time.

Kitty actually didn't need much coaching. I think she'd gone to a place in her head where she was at a science-fiction convention and was reenacting one of the exploration sequences from *Lord of the Rings*.

When I saw what we were facing, my heart sank. The room wasn't like the one I'd been in before. It had a different layout. In this layer it was . . . off-kilter. Obviously, they'd redecorated this level several times over, but I'd still expected it to basically match.

"Does your neck hurt?" Kitty asked.

"Huh?"

She tipped her head sideways, and I realized she was mimicking me. I tipped mine back straight. "The vent was on the left of this wall, I think." Instead, there was a heavy metal racking system laden with boxes of ancient computer parts, spilling over with wires, cords, and plugs that looked long-since forgotten. I looked through the bits and pieces: maybe I shouldn't have been surprised that this stuff hadn't been touched in a long, long time.

"Well . . . let's do this. Can you give me a hand?"

Kitty paused for a moment, but just a moment. I knew hard labor wasn't her thing, but she put what she had into it, and shoulder to shoulder we shoved the rack. She said, "I'm only doing this because I think it will be helpful for both of us to understand the full extent of your insanity."

"Thanks," I replied. I turned around and put my back into pushing. The rack moved. I cleared away some grime on the wall, looking for anything, a crack even, that would indicate a vent.

Nothing.

I shifted my weight, and there came the strange groan of unsupported wood beneath me. I tapped my foot lightly, and a hollow sound confirmed the truth.

"This is so Nancy Drew," Kitty said.

Just as she said that, I saw what I was hoping for: the lines of a trapdoor half covered by the rack. The good news was, they probably weren't even using this air duct for its purpose anymore. The bad news would be if it ended up being completely blocked on the other side.

"Cellars make me think of slasher movies," Kitty said nervously. "Trapdoors make me think of theater deaths."

"Help me push this all the way off," I said, ignoring her and getting into position.

Kitty dug her shoulder in and we managed to push the shelving back off the square.

Unfortunately, the trapdoor had a different-looking locking mechanism from the grate I'd opened with Leo.

"Bummer," Kitty said, summing it up just about perfectly.

I pulled Leo's smartie from my pocket and studied the gizmo, wondering if there was anything in the device that might be helpful. I tried not to think about the outcome of my last foray into this exciting world of security breaches. How would my new equipment help? Could it?

Crack!

Kitty had tired of waiting. She'd taken a long piece of metal and pried the lock off the trapdoor. Along with the sound of straining wood had come a strange electronic beep. She spread her hands out and looked at me like, *Whatever*. "Well, it's unlocked now, I guess."

I stared at the door.

"Well?" Kitty asked.

"What if we open this door and it blows?" I hissed. "What was that beep?"

Kitty eyed me, picked up a foreign-looking piece

of equipment from a box beside us and peered down, perhaps wondering if it could be used to test the trapdoor's safety. A shower of brown dust sprinkled everywhere. "Ew." She put the object back and apparently noticed I still hadn't done anything. "Then it blows," she whispered back, letting her hands fall loosely to her sides. "Look, I didn't expect to be gone this long. I've got a shift this afternoon."

Right. In a parallel dimension. If she was lucky, she'd end up back home independently wealthy.

"Okay, okay," I said. "Here goes. I'm ready now." I grasped the trapdoor's handle. "If it's going to blow, it's going to blow."

"Roxanne, do what you have to do and let's get on with it. I think this dust is affecting my asthma."

Huh? "Since when do you have asthma?"

"I don't. It just sounded dramatic. Look, if you don't do this, I'm going to do it for you."

I elbowed her out of the way. This was the new me, the take-charge me. "I'll do it."

I pulled gingerly on the handle; a small hiss signaled a release of pressure. The door raised slightly on its own. I pulled the lid back and we both poked our heads into the space. My breathed hitched when I saw them lying there, covered in dust: my high-heeled shoes.

"Hey! Aren't these the same as the shoes we picked out for your party?" Kitty cocked her head, processing the implication of their presence here in the duct in the future. After a moment, she let out a low, "Whoaaaa. That's heavy."

I held my breath, waiting for security warnings and sirens and scurrying personnel, but all was silent. "Here's how it's going to go down," I said, secretly taking great pleasure in being able to use that phrase. "You're going to follow me. And when we get to the end of the duct, I'm going to go into that room and you're going to stay up so you can pull me back when I'm done."

"What should we use to reach?"

I looked around and pulled a giant, tangled handful of old USB, LAN, and long extension cords out of the box. "MacGyver it."

Kitty interrupted a close examination of the fatal scuffing on her suede boots to shake her head in weary resignation. "You've been waiting to say that all your life, haven't you?"

I gave her a huge smile. "Absolutely. So, you ready to be stealthy?"

"No problem."

"It's important that we remain completely silent," I pressed.

"No problem." Kitty exuded such calm confidence that I immediately worried she'd mess up.

"Okay, then. You take this and stick it in your pocket."

I handed her Leo's reader, then began tying the various extra cords end to end in a mass of knots it would have taken an entire troop of Boy Scouts hours to loosen. I fixed them around my body just the way I'd seen it done on TV, then looked over at Kitty, who was studying the bags under her eyes in the reflection of Leo's smartie. "You ready?"

"Mmm."

I swung my legs over the side of the trapdoor and eased my body down until I felt the bottom of the passage. Bending down to my knees, I studied the dark, narrow vent, then popped back up. "Maybe you wait until I get to the end of the cord. When I wiggle it, that means you should follow. If the cord is taut, and I wiggle it, start lowering me down very slowly. Very slowly, got that?"

Kitty nodded.

"I'll pull once sharply on the cord when I want to come back. Got it?"

"No problem," she said serenely.

"You're in your Zen happy place, aren't you?"

"Why, yes, I am."

"Fabulous," I muttered. In college, when Kitty went to her Zen happy place it usually meant she was nervous beyond functioning. But we'd done okay so far. "You ready?"

"Ready."

I got on my hands and knees in the duct, then turned back to look over my shoulder. "From here on out, we are completely silent."

"Completely silent."

I crawled forward, then looked back. "You know what you need to do? A wiggle means you start lowering me. Do a kind of . . . I dunno . . . a sort of creep-lower, creep-lower, creep-lower." I used my hands to demonstrate how she was to slowly follow me in, allowing slack as she moved.

Kitty nodded vigorously. "Creep-lower. No problem."

The more I crept along the duct, the more I loosened up. This wasn't hard; this wasn't scary. This totally rocked. I was Rox. I was living the me I wanted to be. Here I was, orchestrating my very own mission. I was team leader and I had a . . . a squad. Sort of. Well, I had an underling. At least I had an underling. And here I was, already nearing the light. I was past the point where things had gone horribly awry the first time, and there was no collapsing tunnel. And here I was at the opening. And it all had gone so smoothly and simply.

I carefully unhooked the vent cover and laid it flat on the surface behind me, then peered into the room. I was in luck: it was laid out precisely in the manner I'd seen before, with the exception of some minor equipment and several locking mechanisms. But I was pretty sure the slot I needed was unlocked, because I'd unlocked it during my trip here with Leo. I prayed our realities were working the way I believed.

So, I had to get down. It was just a matter of wiggling once.

I did so, and I heard a slight squeak and then a small, "Oops." But then a tiny amount of slack allowed me to swing my legs through the vent opening and lean slightly forward. Another small amount of slack followed, this time without the squeak.

Creep-lower, creep-lower. I began to sink slowly into the pristine air of the white room. *Nice, Kitty.*

And then . . .

Ring!

Ring! Ring!

Oh, shit. Turn it off, Kitty. You're too close to the room. The sound!

A huge amount of slack sent me careening toward the floor. I stopped short, spinning in midair.

"Hello? Oh, hi, Mason!" Kitty said loudly.

After another huge lurch, Kitty's head appeared, framed by the square sides of the vent opening. "Mason wants to talk to you."

I swallowed as I swayed gently above the glossy white floor and shook my head.

"What? Don't you want to take it?"

Goddamn Zen happy place. I craned my head sideways and glared at her.

"Oh." She put the phone back up to her ear. "This is not a good time. We're in the silent room."

"Not anymore," I muttered.

"He says no is not an option."

"Ask him what he wants," I hissed, trying to focus on the bank of drives along the wall in a desperate attempt to avoid motion sickness.

"He wants to know what the fuck we're doing in the lion's den."

I grabbed the cords binding me, signaled to Kitty to pull me back up, and waited for her to retreat so she'd have better leverage. After a few moments when nothing happened, I climbed hand over hand back into the duct where Kitty handed me the phone.

"For God's sake, what is she doing here?" was the first thing Mason said to me.

I looked at Kitty. Behind the mellow facade she was clearly scared out of her mind. It had to be a huge change of dynamic for her.

"You still using her as a security blanket?" Mason asked. "Send her back before she totally loses her shit."

"I'm going to," I said, all huffy because I knew I

should never have brought her. It was always easier to do the hard things with someone else. Then again, I'd been literally lost without help before. But now things were different. I was handling this. No, I was *rocking* this, and it was totally selfish not to send her back.

"Good. Listen, I'm less than ten minutes away. I'll be there as soon as I can. Don't move. Or if you must move . . . hell, I don't know, go hide somewhere."

Hide somewhere? Was he joking? We both knew that if Leonardo didn't already know I was in his building, he'd know soon. "It's not real convenient at the moment. I'm in the supersecure room about to steal that code back."

Mason swore so loudly I almost dropped the phone.

"Isn't that what you want?" I asked.

"I also want you not dead," he said. "Listen, Rox. You touch that code, you're going to throw things off the wire. It's a paradox that we can't possibly predict the outcome of. You're not supposed to be here. You're the freaking Major. The idea of you purposely messing with reality across these layers is totally—"

I hung up on him and turned off the phone. "Okay, Kitty? We're changing plans. Here's what's going to happen. Fuck the silence. Fuck creep-lower."

"Fuck creep-lower?" she repeated in a small voice.

"Right. We're going to get down there fast, we're going to take the code, and we're going to get the hell out of here. Got it?"

Her eyes were so big I thought her head might explode. But she nodded. I unwound the cord from myself and tied it around Kitty. Then I pointed to the vent opening. "Go."

No Zen happy place now.

"Go."

"Blurgh."

"Yeah, I know. But if you don't go, I'm going to push you through without the rope."

She went. I gave her the creep-lower treatment at high speed, and she hit the ground lightly. I grabbed onto the side of the vent opening, lowered my body until I was hanging off the side, and let go, praying I wouldn't break something. I didn't.

Kitty stood in the middle of the room, totally paralyzed. I moved quickly to the storage bank, aware that this all seemed too easy. Still, what could I do?

My fingers searched the row of drives until I hit the box that matched the one I recalled. I popped the eject button, and my flash drive fell right into the palm of my hand. I had my code back, and if I figured things right, I had it back before Leo could make use of it.

Uh-oh.

I felt the air tremble a bit, and I knew what was coming. I threw myself at Kitty, taking her down under me, but my heroic rescue was negated by the intense blast of heat that followed, sending us flying. When cool air finally touched our sweaty skin moments later, Kitty and I were sprawled on the other side of the room in a mass of tangled limbs and cords.

"This is not good," I said, fixating on a blue light

suddenly strobing silently from some sort of fiber-optic tubing that ran around the edge of the ceiling. "We just did something."

Kitty disentangled herself from me, muttering something about not needing to be a rocket scientist to figure that out; we were fucked. But it wasn't like we'd suddenly woken up in a version of reality that resembled the bowels of hell or something. Everything in this room minus the unnerving light was the same. At least, I thought it was. Maybe this had just been a brilliant move on my part and . . . Hey. Maybe I was getting good at this. I'd have to seriously consider a career change if I never got back home.

Or . . . Mason was right. I was a wire crosser's worst nightmare: a Major changing reality by taking action in the future on a directly connected wire. Pretty unsettling for everybody involved.

I looked at the tiny drive in my hand, just stared at it. Had I fixed things? Was this over? I looked around the room. Had I finally hit the sweet spot just right?

I didn't think so. It didn't *feel* over. It just didn't feel over, which was probably because I'd changed only one thing. And whatever I'd changed, that wasn't the point. It was still uncertain whether Mason would get my code and turn it over to the government, out of reach of Leonardo's plans to rewrite history for his benefit alone, or whether Leonardo would get it and have his way. It would be over only when I gave it to one of them.

But there wasn't much wire left now. The case was already closing; the door was open only a crack.

"Did whatever you needed to have work, work?" Kitty asked, looking wildly around.

I don't think so did not seem like an appropriate answer under the circumstances. "We need to go," I said, pulling so hard on Kitty's arm that I almost pulled it out of the socket.

We ran to the spot under the air duct vent and stared up at it. Kitty turned her head and glared at me. "What now, MacGyver?"

The cords were with us, and we were down here. There was no way we'd be able to get back up. *Nice going, Rox.* I unknotted an extension cord and put it in my bag. Then I pulled out Leo's smartie. I was aware that I was surrendering my team-leader status by doing this, but I had to call. Mason would help. Except . . . I didn't know how to reach him. This was Leo's smartie, and he didn't seem to have Mason's number programmed into it. I was on my own. And I was responsible for Kitty to boot.

Flash-flash-flash. Kitty flinched from the strobing blue light on the wall, her lips moving silently.

"Everything's under control," I said. "The best way to avoid detection is to do everything calmly. Like we're supposed to be here. We're just going to step out the door and walk to the exit. I have a reasonable memory of the floor plan, and whoever stops you from leaving a place?" I didn't look too closely at my logic.

Kitty followed me without a word. I stuck my hand out and slowly wrapped my fingers around the door handle. "If it blows up, it blows up," Kitty whispered.

I yanked the door open. "Aaaaiiiigh!" Kitty and I yelled simultaneously. A woman dressed like a flight attendant in a light blue uniform with a perky floral blouse stood in the archway. I looked right. I looked left. No troops, no guns, no handcuffs. The only thing that came close to being that scary were the thick, flesh-colored stockings the woman wore, which looked like they'd come out of a bin marked CIRCA 1974.

"Mr. Kaysar will see you now," she said, super-friendly.

I tried to act as casual as possible. "We don't have an appointment. We'll come back another time."

"Mr. Kaysar will see you now," the woman repeated.

"I'm so sorry, but we need to go."

The woman blinked rapidly. It was odd. Then I realized: *She's not real.* Did they have robots here?

"Mr. Kaysar will see you now," the woman repeated a third time, now with a noticeable edge in her voice. Her hand swept out before her, indicating the hallway deeper into the heart of the building.

"Um . . ." I looked at Kitty. She shook her head, a frightened, helpless look on her face, of no help at all.

If this woman was a robot of some kind, she'd maybe respond better to a direct order. "Take us to the exit," I said, indicating the opposite direction. "We want to leave this place."

She cocked her head, smiling, probably processing. "Please follow me. Mr. Kaysar is expecting you."

"You said Leonardo Kaysar was a bad man," Kitty hissed. "A bad man, that's what you said."

"Mr. Kaysar will see you now."

Kitty turned on the robot, and I thought she might smack her. I wouldn't have blamed her. However, we had to focus; Leonardo Kaysar knew where we were—*exactly* where we were—and he was reeling us in the way he'd done that very first time in the agency.

In short, if I didn't come up with something, we were totally screwed.

TWENTY-SEVEN

"What are we doing, Roxy?" Kitty was definitely losing it. "We need a plan. Maybe it was okay before, when we didn't have a plan because the plan was to get here, but now we need one." She moistened her lips, eyes like saucers. "We need a plan, Roxanne."

I stared at her for a moment, then turned to the robot. "Take us to the bathroom."

The robot's face brightened. Apparently bathroom trips did not go against her directive. "Right this way," she said, hand waving to the right.

Kitty gave a quiet thumbs-up as we veered away from the direction of "Mr. Kaysar is expecting you."

We reached the restroom, and our robot clasped her hands in front of her. "At your convenience," she said. Which I guess was a polite way to say, "Take as much time as you need, because even if you have the stomach flu, I'll still be here when you come out."

We really needed her to go away. "Uh . . . bring us

coffee," I said, then quickly amended it to the most complicated version of that old standby I could muster. "Make that a half-caff, part half-and-half, part skim, one shot of vanilla syrup, one shot of hazelnut syrup, grande latte. Please let it cool to room temperature."

"And I'll have an iced tea," Kitty said.

I elbowed her.

"I won't have an iced tea. I'll have—"

"An Italian dark roast, one-percent milk, extra foam, shot of . . . almond syrup . . . cappuccino. And please let it cool to room temperature," I interrupted.

"Of course!" the robot said . . . and she left.

"She left," I said.

"She left," Kitty echoed a little curtly, probably annoyed that I hadn't actually let her have an iced tea.

"Let's go." I pushed into the restroom, Kitty right on my heels. We both froze. Inside, a glass wall divided into lateral segments provided an excellent view of the city. Trouble was, I'd forgotten how high up we were. It's not like we could climb out a window and into an alley.

Both of us stood there, looking down, our noses making unsightly splotches on the glass. I pulled away and studied the glass more carefully, noticing a pair of red levers on the bottom of one segment.

Kitty squeaked. I groaned. I immediately thought of vertigo, which probably made vertigo more likely. This was where one of the boys usually came in. This was where Mason should say, "Let me take care of this." Or Leo could say something to the effect of,

"Just follow me, Roxanne." Except the boys weren't here, and I refused to succumb to the goddamn desire to be saved. Basically, all I had was my friend Kitty, who depended on me. And what she said was, "I'm gonna barf. Do something."

"You're not going to barf."

"If you make us go out there, I will."

It looked pretty slick. Even if we popped out through the window, there was nothing to hold on to.

"May I help you?"

I looked over my shoulder. The robot was standing there with a tray, apparently one hell of a barista.

"No, thank you."

"Please enjoy your coffee." She held out the tray. Kitty and I each took a cup. "Please follow me. Mr. Kaysar is expecting you."

I stared at the robot; then I took the cup out of Kitty's hand and dumped both hers and mine in the sink. The robot's expression switched abruptly from happy to concerned. I chose to ignore her displeasure and, instead, wheeled around and unhooked the red levers in the window. I rammed the panel with my shoulder, then bounced back as it easily withstood my assault.

Kitty stood looking between me and the robot. "She's not happy," she reported. I kept shouldering the wall, trying not to look.

Wham! Ouch.

Wham! Ouch.

"She's doing something. She's doing something!"

Wham! Ouch. "What's she doing?"

"I don't know! Contacting her planet or something."

Wham! Wham! "You want to give me a hand here, Kitty?" I said, beginning to get pissy.

"What, like this?" She pulled a third lever on the top that I'd missed.

Wham! This time I nearly went flying outside after the panel. We watched the transparent slice catch the wind, twist horizontally. Of course, once we were standing there in an open escape route, I didn't know what came next.

"What are we going to *do*?" Kitty asked.

"Um."

"What are you staring at?"

"The blue light that's flashing on your face."

We wheeled around, and the robot was gone. So odd, the way the future was silent. No alarms sounded. The robot hadn't yelled. The pedestrians had kept at a murmur. But silence didn't make circumstances any less deadly; it fooled you into thinking there was no urgency.

I wasn't fooled. "We need to get out of here. Now."

The blue light was flashing on Kitty's gaping face. Wind blew her hair, and I knew she had frozen up. That's what I wanted to do, but someone had to talk us through, and Kitty couldn't even talk.

I took her hand and pulled her over to the escape hole and pointed at the ledge that was just beside us. "My friend," I said. "This is going to be really hard. And really fucking scary. But we can do it."

She made a gargling sound. I grabbed her face in my hands and made her focus. "You *have* to."

She blinked back frightened tears and said, "Okay, Roxy."

I took another look outside. To the left, heavy cables linked decorative transparent slats that ran down the length of the building. I stepped onto the ledge, reached out, and grabbed the closest cable, trying not to let Kitty's whimpering psych me out. The metal was cold and prickly. Someone tell me what to do, I thought.

With my hand gripping the wire, the slats moved easily closer. I took the extension cord from my bag, leaned back inside, and rigged a loop around Kitty's waist. "It's a really good knot, Kitty. It's a really good knot. You'll be safe."

She didn't even try. She didn't drop her frozen stare from my eyes. I moved forward along the ledge. Kitty gasped as the cord between us tugged her forward.

She frantically scrabbled her fingers across the glass wall, trying to get a grip, but not yet stepping out. "I can't hold on," she finally said, stricken. She'd figured out what I knew: if she pulled back, if she moved away from the window, she'd take me with her. And it'd be a much trickier negotiation back through the window. I might not make it. And if I plunged, she'd plunge.

"You go, I go," I whispered urgently. "I go, you go. Let's get out of this together." I held out my hand and wriggled my fingers. "Just take my hand, Kitty. Take my hand."

Through the transparent glass I couldn't see any distinct movement, but I wondered how long it would be before Leo called in the troops. He would eventually get tired of waiting for us.

"Take my hand, Kitty."

Her tears finally spilled over. I'd never seen her this undone. She couldn't bring herself to take my hand and step out, and I had to force her. I leaned forward, grabbed her hand, and pulled. She came out, teetered, saw what would happen if she continued to resist, and jumped, landing on the strip. I jumped too. We went sailing off to the side, seesawing back and forth as we held on to the cables for dear life.

When the swaying settled, we started moving from one slat down to the next. They were close enough to reach between, but not easily. We'd made it down only a small distance before my palms were cut from gripping the metal so hard, my knees were killing me from balancing on the slats, and my brain was aching from the amount of psychology required to keep Kitty from just giving up and pitching us over the side.

I looked down. A man wearing a suit was actually on the side of the building, ascending along a maintenance ladder. Looking down below us, I recognized a second figure hanging off the same ladder. He flapped his arms and waved up at me. Mason Merrick.

Leo chasing; Mason below. A redux of that first and fateful day when I walked out to the 7-Eleven. Me in the middle, Leonardo and Mason after me.

It occurred to me again that Mason and Leo had only so much control over the wires of fate, no matter what they were able to do. They had only so much control. I'd always wondered, but probably the only reason that they hadn't killed each other was because their own lives were so intertwined; there was a lot of history between them to unravel. Leo wouldn't dare sacrifice his ability to fix his family legacy.

Kitty wasn't making a sound. Scratch that; she wasn't forming actual words, but there was a kind of a strange humming that came out of her mouth with every exhalation of breath. This *so* wasn't her fight. I looked down at the undulating waves of motoway, roller coaster–like tracks threading through one another above the pedestrian clogged city below, and hooked one arm around the cable. "Hang in there, Kitty," I said, using bent knees to brace myself as I searched Leo's smartie. There was a preset I liked—

ROXY'S APARTMENT-MASON's—along with other variations. Giving a sigh of relief, I pulled the punch from my bag.

"Still hanging on. Literally," Kitty whispered.

"That's good. Keep joking. Whatever you feel you need to do."

"Shut up, Roxanne."

"Okay."

I looked up. I looked down. I looked back; I looked out. "Well. We could continue down this way, try to crash back into the building through one of these other windows, or climb back up. Any of those strike your fancy?" I asked.

"Would this be the wrong time to ask if I can just go home?" Kitty whispered.

I managed a shaky laugh. "I'm working on it."

Crouched on her knees and holding on to her cable

with both hands as we swayed, she said, "I don't think either of us will be in the mood to cook when we get home. I'll order a pizza—an extra large if you think you and . . . whoever is still alive and not stalking you at the end of all of this is going to be back in time."

Hilarious. Would I be back from the future in time for dinner?

"Thanks, Kitty. Thanks for everything."

"You don't need me anymore."

I know. I smiled.

"We hate good-byes," Kitty said.

We stood there swaying high above the city, and, after a moment, I untied the knot linking us together, reached out with the punch and sent her home. It was time.

As she disappeared, everything bled to gray. The world shuddered around me. I blinked once, and everything went black. I turned my head away from the force of the hot wind that slammed into my body, but I couldn't dodge it.

The slat on which I stood went careening sideways, and as it started to arc back toward the building, I saw that I would have an opportunity to get back on solid ground. Well, on solid ladder. I double-checked the strap on the messenger bag and inched to a better position.

As the slat thudded against the building, I reached out and grabbed the rungs of the maintenance ladder. With its momentum stopped short, the slat lurched. I just held on to the metal rail and waited for the wobbling to subside. When it finally did, I told myself not to look down and carefully transferred my weight. Hanging off the side, I started climbing upward. My muscles shook with every step.

The effort took everything I had in me, and when I made it to the roof, I could crawl only halfway to the exit before I had to rest.

But there was no rest for the weary, as they always say. A British accent swore loudly. *Leo.* Followed by, "Son of a bitch!" *Mason.* I couldn't escape.

I didn't move, but neither man came for me. Mason and Leo began beating the living crap out of each other. Again. So déjà vu.

Leo crashed across the pavement, struck by Mason. His gun had come free and skittered next to him. He caught me watching and said, "Give me the flash driver, Roxanne." But then he was up and dealing with Mason again, the two trading blows.

Sweat stung my eyes; I imagined I tasted blood in my mouth, though I couldn't remember being hit. Leo commanded me again. I looked over at his gun. My chest heaving, fingers twitching, I reached out to grasp it, an incongruous image of Kitty's goldfish flashing through my mind. The gun was just out of reach.

Get the fuck up, Roxy, and take control of your fate.

I reached harder, my fingertips brushing the metal stock. I could pick myself up off the ground and stand, not just crawl away on my hands and knees. I could *act.*

I could hear the dull thud of fists against flesh, and I turned and saw Mason was losing. He was holding Leo's leg and each kick he took was as bad as if I were taking it myself.

"Roxanne, don't let him get the gun!" he cried.

I loved Mason and he loved me back; I knew that now. We'd once had a future. He'd even given Kitty and Naveed's daughter back to me, and I had to believe he'd done so while preserving the way things were meant to be. But who knew what I'd done to my own reality, what with the splice I'd engineered by stealing the code back from Leonardo? Who knew what would happen if I gave it to Mason? Would he decide that time was more important than me? Would I respect him if he didn't?

One thing was certain: whatever I did, I would be the one left with the outcome. We were down to the last version of me I would have, and if I trusted Mason I would be stuck with whatever he chose. This was the sweet spot the boys were talking about. This was the sweet spot. This was where it was all going to lock down.

So, what's it gonna be, Roxanne?

I rolled to my side and, instead of curling into myself and waiting for an end, I picked up the gun and got to my feet.

"Stop!"

The men froze, still gripping each other.

"Mason, get up. Leo, stay where you are."

Very slowly the men separated. Mason backed away from Leo, making his way to my side. Both of my hands were wrapped around the pistol. My legs braced wide, I held the gun on Leonardo, completely calm. Then I freed one hand and stuck it in my pocket. My fingers hit metal and I pulled out the flash drive. Both men sucked in a breath.

"Leo, start moving backward."

No one moved. No one spoke. The men registered what I was saying, and a look of pain crossed Leonardo's face. He'd processed my intentions.

"Start moving," I repeated, shaking the gun.

Leonardo started slowly walking backward toward the edge of the rooftop, toward the ladder. I nodded. He continued, stopping short when his heels hit the raised cement ringing the edge.

"I'll bring the wine," he said. Cryptic. He spread his arms, a strange smile on his face.

I felt Mason's hand slip into mine to take the code. Leonardo stepped gracefully backward, teetering on the edge. "Do it," I dared him.

Leonardo's gaze fixed on Mason's hand in mine. I glanced at Mason and gave him a quick nod. His fingers slipped free, dragging the code out of my hand. Leonardo watched.

I thought about shooting him. I thought about the evil things he could set into motion, and the realities he would fabricate for people like me if he was allowed to continue messing with time. But I couldn't be his executioner. There were indeed things about us that were similar, as he'd claimed in an elevator long ago. But I was different than he was.

As Leonardo and I again locked eyes, he simply let himself go. His suit coat fluttered up around him, and he vanished just as I gave the code completely to Mason. The sweet spot locked. I blinked once and the roof beneath me seemed to twist away: a rectangle shape flipping end over end, vanishing from under my feet. Mason and I dropped into empty space, hurtling down between buildings. I lost track of him, falling, falling more, the pavement hurtling up to meet me. This time I didn't flinch or close my eyes or scream or panic. I relaxed.

This is impossible. I don't really exist in this time. Not yet. I'll land. I'll just land. Mason, Leonardo, and I are wired together. If there's even an inch of wire left, I'll land.

TWENTY-EIGHT

I opened my eyes, bracing myself for whatever version of my life I'd brought about. But I wasn't in my life. I was spread-eagled on the ground, staring up at the sky, once more in the silence between rush hours.

From this angle I could see the spire on top of the Kaysar Corporation. I blinked and remembered how close the agency had been to the motoway. About as close as the Market Street agency from my apartment via BART. And if my apartment was behind me . . . then this was the same damn intersection where the 7-Eleven was in the present day, and this was the spot on the ground where I'd lain like a corpse next to Mason's car. I felt like I'd journeyed many miles, but really I'd been moving in circles all along.

The spire disappeared as Mason stepped into view, and I choked up, indescribably happy to see him alive and well.

He tried to look stern, saying, "I have to get this code to headquarters, Rox. It's not over until it's safe." But then he pulled me to my feet, put his arms around me and enfolded me in a tight embrace. "And it's also not over until you're safe at home," he added, his voice edged with emotion.

I closed my eyes and let my body relax into his. "You're not coming with me?"

"I'll be right on your heels," Mason said, "but I've got to lock this all down."

It was hard to accept that we'd be separating just as we'd truly come together. I looked up at him. "Why didn't you just tell me I was your girlfriend all along?"

"Too many reality variables with a Major," he said. "You'd been disappeared, and the protocol on cases like this is very strict. It has to be, if we have any hope of keeping things under control." Then, with a smile: "Besides, when I finally caught up with you that night, you didn't really know me anymore."

I was a different person then.

"And about Louise. I need you to know that she wasn't *ever* my girlfriend, and we definitely weren't sleeping together."

I stared at Mason. "But—"

"She's a coworker. She's how I was able to stay near you."

"My old roommate Louise is a wire crosser? But she was a complete *moron.*"

"A good actress," Mason said. "We just put the music on loud and let you make wild assumptions."

I stared at him in total disbelief.

"And if it makes you feel better, it was absolute torture."

Actually, it did make me feel better.

Mason suddenly bent his head close to mine. "I love you, Rox. I hated that I couldn't say it earlier.

But now we've done it; we're going to end up together, and I'm not going to let anybody take you away from me again. Do you trust me?"

He meant everything to me. Now that I'd taken charge of my life, I knew what and who I was and what I wanted and needed. It was Mason. My feelings had locked in with the sweet spot. And my certainty gave me hope that we could still have life and love in this last version of my reality I would ever have. "I do trust you," I said.

"Then go home, Rox. Go home and I'll be there as soon as I'm done here."

"Is there enough wire for both of us?" I asked.

"You don't need any." He gave me that same crooked grin. "A door is still a door, even when it looks like a line."

I laughed. Before I might have feared he was being selfish, wanting to use the last of the wire on the case against Leo. But I knew him now. I *knew* him.

Mason's hands caressed the sides of my face, and then he leaned in and brushed his lips against mine. He held there for a moment, then kissed me hard, and this time I knew it wasn't good-bye.

Memories, wonderful memories were pouring back—memories of the past and a future yet to come. I'd see him again, exactly when I was supposed to.

"It's so good to have you back," he whispered, tangling his fingers in my hair. I would have liked nothing more than to linger in his arms, but he crushed me in a quick embrace. "Go back to where you came through. You'll know the way back," he said stepping back. Then he suddenly turned and ran, disappearing down the street.

How we all hate good-byes. I stood there, stunned for a moment, then ran as fast as I could toward the playground where I'd first appeared in this time. Panting and gasping, I made the distance to the playground with record speed. How many times had I run this route from the 7-Eleven to home?

A couple of men with oddly formal, slicked-back hair and shiny white jumpsuits were finishing up some maintenance work. I watched them shake out the tube of their painting equipment, the lacquered end of the hose sprinkling blue paint on the dropcloth.

Leaning over with my hands on my knees to catch my breath, I studied the freshly painted outline of the basketball court glistening in the sunlight. I looked back up; the men gazed blankly back at me and continued packing up their equipment.

Mason had said I would know the way home, and I knew he wouldn't steer me wrong, but it was hard to control my panic with no obvious exit in sight. I walked back to the fence, running my hand along the chain link rimming the area. When I turned back, the painters had gone. Just the chemical smell and hurdle-like metal barriers protecting their handiwork remained.

The smell, the blue paint . . . This playground was my condominium complex from another angle, buried under an archeological layer of reality. This line of blue paint was the threshold to my home.

I paused, awed. All these circles I'd run without going anywhere at all. And yet, I'd gone everywhere.

A hot feeling filled me, a feeling like a splice, and I had a sudden flash of fear. The wire hadn't been entirely used. Was I being paranoid? Either Mason or Leonardo could still—

Wait. *I'll bring the wine*, Leonardo had said. I'd let him go, and he'd stepped off that ledge like he knew his time had run out—or that he had one card left to play. *The villain in the story always fights to the end, Roxanne. Run. Run!*

I ran as hard as I could toward the center of the basketball court, ignoring the burn in my muscles. A million thoughts crossed my mind, but all I felt was terror. The seconds counted. They weren't like saved pennies at all, and I needed every single one of them.

My heart nearly pounded out of my chest as I crossed center court and headed for the far end. Just when I thought I couldn't run any farther, I reached the last barrier, took flight and hurdled over the gleaming blue line.

As I felt myself launched back through the layers of reality and time, a faint ringing sounded in my ears. Struggling against the warp and heat in the air around me, I found my voice. "Kitty," I screamed. "Don't open the door!"

TWENTY-NINE

I went flying over the couch.

Kitty's blond hair was swinging as she turned to look at me over her shoulder, her hand on the doorknob. It all seemed to go so slowly. But she opened the door.

It would have made for an hilarious anecdote: me, arms and legs flailing in midair, knocking the vase of flowers off the coffee table. It could have been absolutely hysterically funny, except Leonardo's bullet hit her in the chest.

Kitty went down, bleeding out, just bleeding out all over the apartment floor. I knelt in the blood and held her hand.

"My friend," I said, squeezing her fingers. The kohl around her eyes ran as she turned her face to me, and tears slipped from the corners of her eyes.

"My friend," she whispered.

I heard a beep and I snatched Leo's reader from my bag. The red light next to my name was black. I'd hit the sweet spot; we were out of time. Kitty sucked in a quick breath, squeezed my hand and died. She died. Case closed. The light next to my name on the reader turned green.

"I'm a rather sore loser," a British accent said. I slowly looked up. Leonardo Kaysar stood on the threshold, a gun held at his side. Kitty's hand slipped from mine as I leaned back on my knees.

Leonardo's green eyes glittered, but not with warmth, familiarity, or seductive intent. He raised his gun and I flinched, falling back on my hands. Leo moved in on me, and I scuttled in reverse, awkward in my fear. He pushed me back, back—I moved toward the stairs, hitting the bottom step with my butt. I slowly stood up, each breath a shudder as he took steps toward me.

"I thought nothing more could be done," I whispered.

"Roxanne," he said, shaking his head as if criticizing a small child. "Perhaps there is nothing more to be done as far as *you* go on this case, but there is a new Major out there now."

I started ascending the stairs backwards. "Then you have no more business here with me," I said, raising my chin.

"This isn't business. It's personal." He gestured up the stairs with his gun, and I did as he wanted until I hit the landing. There he gestured me onward toward my bedroom, and I realized what he was doing. He meant to let me go through the motions of escape, but intended me to die alone in my bedroom, shades down, lights off. He'd disappeared me before and wouldn't hesitate to do so again, even if we had briefly shared . . . something. At heart he was all about him.

I could sense him harden with every step as he backed me across the threshold of my room. I tripped on a pile of dirty laundry and fell back on the ground. Landing against the corner of the closet door, I opened it enough to crawl back into the darkness. Leo gave a small laugh. I guess he thought I was still helpless.

I stared up at him. Behind my back, I tipped the lid off the shoebox, praying. I was in luck. It was there. *You've picked up the gun, Roxanne. Now shoot him. It's finally time. No other option.*

I heard Leonardo cock the trigger. "You see, Mason is—"

Mason is mine. I whipped the gun out from behind me and twice blasted that son of a bitch Leonardo Kaysar clean through. He blinked once and toppled backward, revealing a wide-eyed Mason standing in the doorway, his own gun, still unspent, raised high.

Heat roared through the room. I turned my head to the side, my eyes squeezed shut, the enormity of what I'd done already beginning to sink in. The heat faded, and I finally looked back at Mason. My hand started to shake. I dropped my gun and he dropped his.

He saw that I was fixating on the droplets of blood spattered on his white t-shirt. He peeled the shirt off his body. Together we watched it hit the ground, Leonardo's blood vanishing into the folds of the fabric.

Leo's blood vanishing . . . Leo was vanishing, for his body no longer lay on the floor between Mason and me. All that remained was the faint scent of cloves lingering in the air. I'd disappeared him. And when I found the courage to go downstairs, I was almost certain that I'd find Kitty had disappeared too.

Tears filled my eyes as I looked up at Mason. He slowly held out his hand, and I ran to him.

EPILOGUE

Three months later

I come off the treadmill and press my heart rate monitor, nodding in satisfaction at my latest results. I scribble the number down in a folder I keep next to the new fish tank. I drop a little food in the bowl for Kitty's fish and he swims quickly upward to catch the flakes as they drift down through the bubbling water.

"I've been working out really hard," I tell him. "Lots of cardio. So don't you worry. If I can undisappear, so can she. I'll figure out how to get her back. That's what sisters are for. You have the family you make."

I pick up the reader Mason gave me and look. There's a red light by her name. I focus on how I'm going to get things back to how they're supposed to be—getting Kitty back, but without hurting anyone.

The doorbell rings. The sound still makes me flinch, but this time I pocket the reader and smile.

Because this time I know who is behind the door—Mason, as always, carrying a bouquet of flowers.

I flick the light switch and the apartment goes dark. I turn my back on it as I fling open the door and step over the threshold. The thing is, you've always got to open the door, no matter what. Like I always say, it isn't about tomorrow. It's about right fucking now.

My name is L. Roxanne Zaborovksy. I go outside all the time. My body is lean and mean, my mind is as sharp as a knife. I kick ass, I have fun, I love, I trust. I live life.

PROLOGUE

Loudly, proudly, tairen sing,
As they soar on mighty wings
Softly, sadly, mothers cry
To sing a tairen's lullabye.
—The Tairen's Lament, Fey Nursery Rhyme

The tairen were dying.

Rain Tairen Soul, king of the Fey, could no longer deny the truth. Nor, despite all his vast power and centuries of trying, could he figure a way to save either the creatures that were his soul-kin or the people who depended upon him to lead and defend them.

The tairen—those magnificent, magical, winged cats of the Fading Lands—had only one fertile female left in their pride, and she grew weaker by the day as she fed her strength to her six unhatched kitlings. With those tiny, unborn lives rested the last hope of a future for the tairen, and the last hope of a future for Rain's people, the Fey. But today, the painful truth had become clear. The mysterious, deadly wasting disease that had decimated the tairen over the last millennium had sunk its evil, invisible claws into yet another clutch of unhatched kits.

When the tairen died, so too would the Fey. The fates of the two species were forever intertwined, and had been since the misty time before memory.

Rain looked around the wide, empty expanse of the Hall of Tairen. Indeed, he thought grimly, the death of the immortal Fey had begun centuries ago.

Once, in a time he could still remember, the Hall had rung with the sound of hundreds of Fey Lords, warriors, *shei'dalins* and Tairen Souls arguing politics and debating treaties. Those days had long passed. The Hall was silent now, as silent as the long-abandoned cities of the Fey, as silent as Fey nurseries, as silent as the graves of all those Fey who had died in the Mage Wars a thousand years ago.

Now the last hope for both the tairen and the Fey was dying, and Rain sensed a growing darkness in the east, in the land of his ancient enemies, the Mages of Eld. He couldn't help believing the two events were somehow connected.

He turned to face the huge priceless globe of magical Tairen's Eye crystal called the Eye of Truth, which occupied the center of the room. Displayed on the wings of a man-high stand fashioned from three golden tairen, the Eye was an oracle in which a trained seer could search for answers in the past, the present, and the infinite possibilities of the future. The globe was ominously dark and murky now, the future a dim, forbidding shadow. If there was a way to halt the relentless extermination of his peoples, the answer lay there, within the Eye.

The Eye of Truth had been guarding its secrets, showing shadows but no clear visions. It had resisted the probes of even the most talented of the Fey's still living seers, played coy with even their most beguiling of magic weaves. The Eye was, after all, tairen-made. By its very nature, it combined pride with cunning, passion with often-wicked playfulness. Seers approached it with respect, humbly asked it for a viewing, courted its favor with their minds and their magic but never their touch.

The Eye of Truth was never to be touched.

It was a golden rule of childhood, drummed into the head of every Fey from infant to ancient.

The Eye held the concentrated magic of ages, power so pure and undiluted that laying hands upon the Eye would be like laying hands upon the Great Sun.

But the Eye was keeping secrets, and Rain Tairen Soul was a desperate king with no time to waste and no patience for protocol. The Eye of Truth *would* be touched. He was the king, and he would have his answers. He would wrest them from the oracle by force, if necessary.

His hands rose. He summoned power effortlessly and wove it with consummate skill. Silvery white Air formed magical webs that he laid upon the doors, walls, floor, and ceiling. A spidery network of lavender Spirit joined the Air, then Earth to seal all entrances to the Hall. None would enter to disturb him. No scream, no whisper, no mental cry could pass those shields. Come good or ill, he would wrest his answers from the Eye without interruption—and if it demanded a life for his impertinence, it would be unable to claim any but his.

He closed his eyes and cleared his mind of every thought not centered on his current purpose. His breathing became deep and even, going in and out of his lungs in a slow rhythm that kept time with the beat of his heart. His entire being contracted into a single shining blade of determination.

His eyes flashed open, and Rain Tairen Soul reached out both hands to grasp the Eye of Truth.

"Aaahh!" Power—immeasurable, immutable—arced through him. His head was flung back beneath its onslaught, his teeth bared, his throat straining with a scream of agony. Pain drilled his body like a thousand *sel'dor* blades, and despite twelve hundred years of learning to absorb pain, to embrace it and mute it, Rainier writhed in torment.

This pain was unlike any he had ever known.

This pain refused to be contained.

Fire seared his veins and scorched his skin. He felt his soul splinter and his bones melt. The Eye was angry at his daring affront. He had assaulted it with his bare hands and bare power, and such was not to be borne. Its fury screeched along his bones, vibrating down his spine, slashing at every nerve in his body until tears spilled from his eyes and blood dripped from his mouth where he bit his lip to keep from screaming.

"*Nei,*" he gasped. "I am the Tairen Soul, and I will have my answer."

If the Eye wished to cement the extinction of both tairen and Fey, it would claim Rain's life. He was not afraid of death; rather he longed for it.

He surrendered himself to the Eye and forced his tortured body to relax. Power and pain flowed into him, through him, claiming him without resistance. And when the violent rush of power had invaded his every cell, when the pain filled his entire being, a strange calm settled over him. The agony was there, extreme and nearly overwhelming, but without resistance he was able to distance his mind from his body's torture, to disassociate the agony of the physical from the determination of the mental. He forced his lips to move, his voice a hoarse, cracked whisper of sound that spoke ancient words of power to capture the Eye's immense magic in flows of Air, Water, Fire, Earth, and Spirit.

His eyes opened, glowing bright as twin moons in the dark reflection of the Eye, burning like coals in a face bone white with pain.

With voice and mind combined, Rain Tairen Soul asked his question: "How can I save the tairen and the Fey?"

Relentlessly, absorbing the agony of direct contact with the Eye, he searched its raging depths for answers. Millions of possibilities flashed before his eyes, countless variations on possible futures, countless retellings of past events. Millennia passed in an instant, visions so rapid his physical sight could never have hoped to discern them, yet his mind, steadily commanding the threads of magic, absorbed the images and processed them with brutal clarity. He stood witness to the deaths of billions, the rise and fall of entire civilizations. Angry, unfettered magic grew wild in the world and Mages worked their evil deeds. Tairen shrieked in pain, immolating the world in their agony. Fey women wept oceans of tears, and Fey warriors fell helpless to their knees, as weak as infants. Rain's mind screamed to reject the visions, yet still his hands gripped the Eye of Truth, and still he voiced his question, demanding an answer.

"How can I save the tairen and the Fey?"

He saw himself in tairen form, raining death indiscriminately upon unarmed masses, his own tairen claws impaling Fey warriors.

"How can I save the tairen and the Fey?"

Sariel lay bloody and broken at his feet, pierced by hundreds of knives, half her face scorched black by Mage fire. She reached out to him, her burned and bloodied mouth forming his name. He watched in helpless paralysis as the flashing arc of an Elden Mage's black *sel'dor* blade sliced down across her neck. Bright red blood fountained. . . .

The unutterable pain of Sariel's death—tempered by centuries of life without her—surged back to life with soul-shredding rawness. Rage and bloodlust exploded within him, mindless, visceral, unstoppable. It was the Fey Wilding rage, fueled by a tairen's primal fury, unfettered emotions backed by lethal fangs, incinerating fire, and access to unimaginable power.

They would die! They had slain his mate, and they would all die for their crime! His shrieking soul grasped eagerly for the madness, the power to kill without remorse, to scorch the earth and leave nothing but smoldering ruins and death.

"Nei!" Rain yanked his hands from the Eye and flung up his arms to cover his face. His breath came in harsh pants as he battled to control his fury. Once before, in a moment

of madness and unendurable pain, he had unleashed the beast in his soul and rained death upon the world. He had slain thousands in mere moments, laid waste to half a continent within a few bells. It had taken the combined will of every still-living tairen and Fey to cage his madness.

"*Nei!* Please," he begged, clawing for self-possession. He released the weaves connecting him to the Eye in a frantic hope that shearing the tie would stop the rage fighting to claim him.

Instead, it was as if he had called Fire in an oil vault.

The world was suddenly bathed in blood as his vision turned red. The tairen in him shrieked for release. To his horror, he felt his body begin to dissolve, saw the black fur form, the lethal curve of tairen claws spear the air.

For the first time in twelve hundred years of life, Rainier vel'En Daris knew absolute terror.

The magic he'd woven throughout the Hall would never hold a Tairen Soul caught up in a Fey Wilding rage. All would die. The world would die.

The Tairen-Change moved over him in horrible slow motion, creeping up his limbs, taunting him with his inability to stop it. The small sane part of his mind watched like a stunned, helpless spectator, seeing his own death hurtling towards him and realizing with detached horror that he was going to die and there was nothing he could do to prevent it.

He had overestimated his own power and utterly underestimated that of the Eye of Truth.

"Stop," he shouted. "I beg you. Stop! Don't do this." Without pride or shame, he fell to his knees before the ancient oracle.

The rage left him as suddenly as it had come.

In a flash of light, his tairen-form disappeared. Flesh, sinew, and bone reformed into the lean, muscular lines of his Fey body. He collapsed face down on the floor, gasping for breath, the sweat of terror streaming from his pores, his muscles shaking uncontrollably.

Faint laughter whispered across the stone floor and danced on the intricately carved columns that lined either side of the Hall of Tairen.

The Eye mocked him for his arrogance.

"*Aiyah,*" he whispered, his eyes closed. "I deserve it. But I am desperate. Our people—mine and yours both—face extinction. And now dark magic is rising again in Eld. Would you not also have dared any wrath to save our people?"

The laughter faded, and silence fell over the Hall, broken only by the wordless noises coming from Rain himself, the sobbing gasp of his breath, the quiet groans of pain he didn't have the strength to hold back. In the silence, power gathered. The fine hairs on his arms and the back of his neck stood on end. He became aware of light, a kaleidoscope of color bathing the Hall, flickering through the thin veil of his eyelids.

His eyes opened—then went wide with wonder.

There, from its perch atop the wings of three golden tairen, the Eye of Truth shone with resplendent clarity, a crystalline globe blazing with light. Prisms of radiant color beamed out in undulating waves.

Stunned, he struggled to his knees and reached out instinctively towards the Eye. It wasn't until his fingers were close enough to draw tiny stinging arcs of power from the stone that he came to his senses and snatched his hands back without touching the oracle's polished surface.

There had been something in the Eye's radiant depths—an image of what looked like a woman's face—but all he could make out were fading sparkles of lush green surrounded by orange flame. A fine mist formed in the center of the Eye, then slowly cleared as another vision formed. This image he saw clearly as it came into focus, and he recognized it instantly. It was a city he knew well, a city he despised. The second image faded and the Eye dimmed, but it was enough. Rain Tairen Soul had his answer. He knew his path.

With a groan, he rose slowly to his feet. His knees trembled, and he staggered back against the throne to collapse on the cushioned seat.

Rain gazed at the Eye of Truth with newfound respect. He was the Tairen Soul, the most powerful Fey alive, and yet the Eye had reduced him to a weeping infant in mere moments. If it had not decided to release him, it could have used him to destroy the world. Instead, once it had beaten the arrogance out of him, it had given up at least one of the secrets it was hiding.

He reached out to the Eye with a lightly woven stream of Air, Fire and Water and whisked away the faint smudges left behind by the fingers he had dared to place upon it.

«Sieks'ta. Thank you.» He filled his mental tone with genuine respect and was rewarded by the instant muting of his body's pain. With a bow to the Eye of Truth, he strode towards the massive carved wooden doors at the end of the Hall of Tairen and tore down his weaves.

«Marissya.» He sent the call to the Fey's strongest living *shei'dalin* even as he reached out with Air to swing open the Hall's heavy doors before him. The Fey warriors guarding the door to the Hall of Tairen nodded in response to the orders he issued with swift, flashing motions of his hands as he strode by, and the flurry of movement behind him assured him his orders were being carried out.

«Rain?» Marissya's mental voice was as soothing as her physical one, her curiosity mild and patient.

«A change of plans. I'm for Celieria in the morning and I'm doubling your guard. Let your kindred know the Feyreisen is coming with you.»

Even across the city, he could feel her shocked surprise, and it almost made him smile.

Half a continent away, in the mortal city of Celieria, Ellysetta Baristani huddled in the corner of her tiny bedroom room, tears running freely down her face, her body trembling uncontrollably.

The nightmare had been so real, the agony so intense.

Dozens of angry, stinging welts scored her skin . . . self-inflicted claw marks that might have been worse had her fingernails been longer. But worse than the pain of the nightmare had been the helpless rage and the soul-shredding sense of loss, the raw animal fury of a mortally wounded heart. Her own soul had cried out in empathetic sorrow, feeling the tortured emotions as if they had been her own.

And then she'd sensed something else. Something dark and eager and evil. A crouching malevolent presence that had ripped her out of sleep, bringing her bolt upright in her bed, a smothered cry of familiar terror on her lips.

She covered her eyes with shaking hands. *Please, gods, not again.*

CATHY McDAVID

Every twenty-five years the cycle begins anew—a legendary creature reawakens and preys upon the innocent. When she was seven, Gillian watched in horror as it killed her mother. Now the beast is back…for her.

As the chosen Hunter, Nick is the only one who can destroy the creature. Yet a gorgeous psychology professor keeps pushing her way into his investigation—and into his most intimate fantasies. For her protection, Nick's determined to stay by Gillian's side, every day and each delicious night. And meanwhile, the monster bides its time….

ISBN 10: 0-505-52722-7
ISBN 13: 978-0-505-52722-6 $6.99 US/$8.99 CAN

From the extravagant vampire world above, to the gritty defiance of the werewolves below, the specter of darkness lives around every corner, the hope of paradise in every heart. The city knows a tentative peace, but to live in Crimson City is to balance on the edge of a knife. One woman knows better than most. She's about to be tested, to taste true thirst. Fleur Dumont is about to meet the one man who may understand her: a tormented protector who's lost all he loved. Theirs is one tale of many. This is…

Crimson City

Where desire meets danger and
more than just the stars come out at night.